UNTERS

Kosloff

"You're the head of Dirty Tricks of the State department . . . what do you want me to do?"
"Stop a revolution."
"Whose?"
"A certain El Hassan . . ."

Ryan

"I have a job for you."
"I've retired."
"It involves the payment to you of three hundred ounces of gold . . ."
"For doing what?"
"Liquidate a group of 10 persons—one of particular importance."
"Who?"
"El Hassan!"

Hidetada

The prince said, "We are withdrawing you from the assignment, for one of more importance . . . you will leave immediately for North Africa and find El Hassan."

Everybody wants

EL HASSAN

THE BEST YE BREED

by

Mack Reynolds

ace books

A Division of Charter Communications Inc.
A GROSSET & DUNLAP COMPANY
1120 Avenue of the Americas
New York, New York 10036

THE BEST YE BREED

Copyright © 1978 by Mack Reynolds

An ACE Book

First Ace printing: March 1978

Published simultaneously in Canada

Printed in U.S.A.

CONTENTS

I

PAUL KOSLOFF

HAPPILY, IT WAS a grim night. It was cloudy and there was a fine drizzle. Paul Kosloff didn't know whether or not the grounds of the mansion were patrolled, either by men or by dogs, but, if they were, either man or beast was going to be shelter-conscious.

Most likely, the grounds were so patrolled. His target was known to be security-conscious almost to the point of phobia.

The iron picket fence surrounding the estate was his first hurdle. There were no trees near it and it was too high to climb easily. Besides, undoubtedly it was gimmick-wired at the top in such manner as to tip off the guards—either that or electrocute him. He was going to have to go through it.

The main gate was out of the question. He had seen the two men stationed there, one to each side in armored booths and undoubtedly armed to the molars. He continued to stroll along, on the other side of the street, following the fence. And, yes, behind the house was a smaller gate which was unattended.

Paul Kosloff crossed over to it. It had a heavy lock. He brought a scrambler from his pocket and activated it, then an electronic lock pick which he had gotten from the boys in the Rube Goldberg department. Its magnets sucked up to the lock, over the keyhole, and he slowly rotated it. When the lock reluctantly gave up its secrets, he pushed the gate open and slipped through. He relocked it, then deactivated the scrambler.

Thus far things were going better than he had hoped. Bending almost double, he scurried toward the rear of the mansion.

Luckily, this part of the estate was mostly gardens, complete with trees, complete with shrubs. He had a good chance of going undetected, certainly until he got reasonably near the house.

The dog, running hard, a brown streak with distended, slavering jaws, was upon him almost before he spotted it. A Doberman pinscher, recognizable even in this light by its long forelegs and wide hindquarters.

Paul Kosloff had worked out with war dogs while taking commando training long years before. He had just time to fling himself into position before the dog jumped. He spun sideward to the left and his right hand shot out and grabbed the right paw of the large smooth-coated terrier. He continued to swing mightily. The dog had time for only one loud yelp of confusion, before he smashed it into the trunk of a tree.

It fell to the ground, momentarily, at least, stunned. Paul Kosloff, to make sure, kicked it twice in the side of the head, immediately behind the clipped ears.

He wiped the back of his left hand over his forehead, finding a beading of cold sweat there. He shook his head and continued on his way toward the house.

A chink of light began to manifest itself, and a door was opening. He dodged behind the bole of a large tree, and flattened himself against it.

A voice called, "Roger! Is that you, boy?"

Paul Kosloff held his breath.

"Roger! What have you got, boy?"

A few moments later, there was a curse and Paul Kosloff could hear someone approaching.

The voice was closer this time. "Here boy, here boy. Damn it, what were you yelping about?"

As the footsteps came closer, Paul Kosloff slithered around the tree trunk, keeping it between himself and the other.

Completely on the other side, he bent double once again and headed for the house and the open door. It was all in the laps of the gods now. Was there anyone else inside? Behind him, he could still hear the guard, still calling the Doberman. The fat was going to be in the fire if he discovered the unconscious watchdog.

Paul Kosloff hurried into the interior of the large house and found himself in a small guardroom, furnished only with a single table and two chairs. On the walls were flac rifles, shotguns and laser beam pistols.

There was another door at the far side of the room. He got through it in a hurry and closed it behind him before speeding down the dimly lit hall beyond. Given luck, he wouldn't run into any servants. Not at this time of the night. It was past two o'clock.

He came to a small elevator and looked at it for a moment, but then shook his head. The man he was seeking was noted as a nut on burglar alarms and related devices. He might even have something like an elevator rigged.

He found a flight of narrow circling stairs slightly beyond. A servant stairway by the looks of it. He started up. His destination was on the third floor. He wondered if there were any more guards.

At the third floor, he peered cautiously down the ornate hallway. And, yes, there was a guard before the door that was his goal.

The other's back was turned. Paul Kosloff took a desperate chance and sped across the heavily carpeted hall to the room opposite. The chance paid off. The door was unlocked. He entered the room beyond quickly, closed the door behind him.

He fumbled at the wall for a light switch and found it. The plans of the mansion he had studied had been correct. It was a billiards room, the table in the exact center. He strode over to it, took up the eight ball and then returned to the door and flicked off the light.

He had to gamble now that the guard's back was still turned. If it wasn't, he'd had it. He opened the door a narrow crack and rolled the ball toward the circular staircase. It began to bounce down the stairs, at first slowly, then faster. It didn't sound much like footsteps to him, but it would have to do.

He kept the door open, the slightest crack, and

watched as the guard came hurrying up and hesitated, looking down the stairwell. The ball was well along by now and going faster. At this distance, it sounded more like a person descending as fast as possible.

The guard suddenly flicked his hand inside his coat to emerge with a laser pistol, and began hurrying down.

Paul Kosloff gave him a few moments, then left his hiding place and hustled along the hall. He gently tried the doorknob of the room that was his destination. It wasn't locked. He pulled a comb from his pocket, drew it through his hair a couple of times and returned it. He straightened his suit, moistened dry lips, then opened the door and walked through, nonchalantly.

The man reclining on the bed, reading, looked up at him.

"Paul Kosloff?" he said.

"Well, I'm not the ghost of Spiro Agnew," Paul Kosloff said, closing the door behind him. "What in the hell is this all about?"

"How did you get in without detection?"

"I didn't completely. You've either got a dead dog or one with a whale of a headache out in your garden. Again, what's this all about?" Kosloff pulled up a chair without invitation and sat down.

"A double motive," the man in the bed said. "First, I wanted to find out whether you're as good as you're supposed to be as an espionage-counter-espionage agent. And, second, I wanted to give you an assignment without anyone, anyone at all, even knowing we've ever met. Do you know who I am?"

"You're the head of what some of us field men call the Commission of Dirty Tricks of the State Department, often working hand in glove with the CIA."

The other looked at him. "Very few people know of me. In my section, we need publicity like a broken leg."

Paul Kosloff said evenly, "Yes, I know. I was just a child when the Bay of Pigs took place, but there have been other farces since. Publicity doesn't help."

The man in the bed was obviously not pleased at that. He said, "Kosloff, do you consider yourself a patriotic American?"

The cloak-and-dagger operative said reasonably, "How could I be? When a special bill was brought before Congress to grant me citizenship, it was decided my odor was too high and it was turned down. Let's face reality. I'm persona non grata everywhere, including the country of my birth—Russia—where they took a dim view of my 'defecting' even though I was a child in arms at the time and all the rest of my family had been liquidated in the purges. Relatives smuggled me out over the Finnish border and finally got me here to America."

The commissioner said, "What I should have said was, 'Are you basically pro-American or anti-Communist?'"

The international troubleshooter took him in. "I thought they meant the same thing."

"Not necessarily."

Paul Kosloff was getting tired of this routine. He said, "All right. I've been ordered to contact you secretly. What do you want me to do?"

"Stop a revolution."

"That's my specialty. That's what you people have been having me do for . . . as long as I can remember. Why the buildup? Do I have to assassinate some present-day Trotsky or Mao, or what?"

"The revolution is to take place, or is taking place, in North Africa, all of North Africa, but we are particularly concerned with Algeria, Tunisia and Libya."

Paul Kosloff stared at him before saying, "They've already got Marxist governments there. Perhaps not totally commie, but awfully close to it."

"That's what I've been building up to. The revolution we're talking about is against the socialist-communist-anarchist, call them what you will, governments in North Africa. It would also involve the Sudan, which considers itself socialist, and Mauretania, also supposedly left wing. A certain El Hassan and his followers wish to overthrow them all, not to speak of the right-wing military dictatorships to the south."

"Why not let him?" Paul Kosloff growled.

"His ultimate aim is to unite all of Africa north of the Congo."

The troubleshooter pursed his lips in a silent whistle. "It'd be a neat trick to pull off but I still say, why not let him? If those first countries you named aren't commie today, they will be tomorrow."

"Because if we do, it's one more nail in the coffin of our economy."

Paul Kosloff waited in silence.

The other said impatiently, "I assume that you haven't read a book published way back in the 1950s by Vance Packard, a muckraker of the time, entitled *The Waste Makers*. In it, he points out that although the population of America was but a small fraction of the world's, the United States economy was using up some fifty percent of the Earth's resources. He also pointed out that ten years before the United States had been the largest exporter of copper in the world, but was now the largest importer. His book was ignored and all efforts were continued to raise the gross national product year after year. One by one we lost self-sufficiency in almost every raw material we needed for our industry."

"What's all this got to do with it?" Kosloff said.

"We need North Africa's oil, her nickel, copper, iron, chromium, phosphates. We need them badly. The area is comparatively untouched, so far as raw materials are concerned. Practically nothing save oil has been exploited to date. We have reached accomodation with the present regimes in these leftist nations and purchase almost everything they produce and have either sent in, or have made arrangements to send in, further development teams to begin the exploitation of still more of their resources."

"Well, why couldn't you do the same with this El Hassan?"

The other nodded, but said impatiently, "Because that's one of the strongest planks in his revolutionary platform. He contends that the non-developed countries with raw materials, especially North Africa, are being robbed by the industrialized countries such as the United States of the Americas, Common Europe and Japan. He wishes to shove prices for raw materials sky high.''

''Can he do it?''

''If he wins his revolt, he probably can, and, if he does, so will the other nondeveloped countries. The Arab oil cartel was an early example of what can be done in that field. Eventually, it could mean collapse of the economies of the developed nations.''

''I see. Who is this mysterious El Hassan? I don't believe I've ever heard of him.''

''You haven't!'' The other was surprised. ''Where have you been these past few weeks? He's come on the scene like a whirling dervish in a revolving door.''

Paul Kosloff took him in. ''I've been back in the boondocks in South America, trying to track down a present-day Ché Guevara. It turned out that he was a myth and didn't exist. There weren't any papers in the area. But even if I'd been in one of the larger cities, I doubt if I would have heard about this El Hassan. Censorship is all but universal and one of the great taboos in running stories telling about revolutionary movements abroad. They don't want to let the people know that revolutions are possible—anywhere.''

His superior leaned back. ''Very well, El Hassan isn't as mysterious as all that. We have a very complete dossier on him. In actuality, he's an American.''

''An American!''

''That is correct. His name is Homer Crawford

and he took his doctorate in sociology at the University of Michigan. He's an American black who was given a position with the Sahara Division of the African Development Project of the Reunited Nations. He and his team, also largely American blacks, had the job of speeding up the modernization of North Africa. In *their* case, largely in the Western Sahara. Their task was to break down bottlenecks. Break down tribal lines. Talk the desert peoples into going to the new schools, taking jobs with the new irrigation projects, building the new dams, drilling the new oil wells, opening up the new mines, getting out from under their traditional religious taboos.''

"And . . . .''

"His team, thinking things weren't going fast enough, got together with other organizations that were attempting to accomplish much the same thing. The Africa for Africans Association, a private, nonprofit outfit working out of New York; Great Britain's African Department, though they largely work further south; the French Community's African Affairs sector; and various others. All of these groups consist of members with African racial backgrounds, blacks who were born and educated abroad but have returned to the continent of their racial heritage to goose it forward into the modern world.''

Paul Kosloff said unhappily, "Sounds pretty damned praiseworthy to me.''

"Ummm,'' the other looked down at a paper he had on the bed. "Unfortunately, Crawford and his close intimates evidently came to the conclusion that those people weren't going to be goosed unless stronger measures were taken. Most of them are tribesmen with a ritual-taboo social system. At that stage of development, Crawford seemed to think, they needed a hero to follow, a charismic hero to lead them into the promised land and to ruthlessly break down all barriers that stood in the way. He modestly volunteered for the job."

"And? . . ."

"His forces are sweeping North Africa. It would seem that the area was rotten-ripe for such a development. The old tribes and clans were going under with the coming of the new roads, the airlines, the new industries. What does a tribe of, say, Tuaghi—that's plural of Tuareg—that formerly conducted caravans of camels across the Sahara, do when roads are pushed through their areas and trucks by the thousands start speeding over them? What do bands of former brigands do, in the face of the new weapons of the white man? What do clans of Tedas, who formerly herded goats, do, when the officials of the Sahara Afforestation Project buy up their animals and shoot them? Goats are the most destructive animals in the desert, so far as trees are concerned. They prefer the bark of young trees to grass. What do former Heratin serf farmers do, familiar only with their primitive agricultural methods, when the new solar-powered water wells go in and the oases are expanded a hundred fold, so that modern mechanized methods can be utilized?"

"So El Hassan is succeeding?"

"Fantastically. He was, the other day, recognized the head of state of all North Africa, by India. Who'll follow her example, God only knows."

"India? *Why*?"

"Because she's smart enough to jump on the bandwagon. North Africa is poor in textiles. United, the market would consist of tens of millions. India is desperate to export her cotton textiles."

Paul Kosloff took in a deep breath.

He said, "So it looks as though El Hassan might make it. Where do I come in?"

His superior looked him straight in the eye. "You've been called the Cold War's Lawrence of Arabia. You're our most dependable field man in these cloak-and-dagger affairs. We want El Hassan stopped by fair means or foul."

Paul Kosloff looked at him cynically. "So who are you going to send in to try the fair means?"

II

SEAN RYAN

SEAN EUGENE RYAN awoke from no deep dream of peace. His mouth tasted as though rats had chosen it for a latrine.

He took a long moment to orientate himself, groaned a hungover groan, and stared up at the peeling ceiling. The room he inhabited was the smallest, the cruddiest, the most poorly furnished, in the third-rate hotel he called home. There were other things he called it as well. Sean Ryan had arrived at the end of the line.

He swung his legs over the side of the bed and discovered that he had removed jacket and shoes but otherwise had slept in his clothes. He came to his feet and managed to make his way over to the cracked mirror above the washstand. He didn't look any better than he felt. He hadn't shaved the day before. He looked down and realized that he had just about enough soap for one more shave. He took up the water pitcher, went down the hall-way to the bathroom, filled it and returned to his room. He drank about a pint of the lukewarm water and then steeled himself to take the risk of shaving.

He tucked the collar of his shirt in, noticing, without bothering to notice in particular, that the collar was dirty. He had worn the shirt for four days and should have known better than to sleep in it the night before. It had been his last clean shirt. Not that that had made a great deal of difference. It was frayed at collar and cuff.

He soaped up with the lukewarm water, carefully applying the lather. He took the blade out of the safety razor and stropped it in the palm of his hand. He couldn't remember how long he'd used the blade but it was far from sharp.

He cut himself two or three times, a result of poor blade and shaking hand, washed the remnants of soap from his face and stood back and looked again. The view wasn't reassuring. He remembered the night, years ago, when he had once spent over a hundred British pounds on vintage champagne—and snorted.

He didn't know what time it was. Long since he had pawned his watch. Pawned? Both he and the pawnbroker knew full well that he had sold it. There would be no redeeming.

He'd have to get down to the dining room and see if he was still in time for breakfast. If he wasn't, he suspected that it was going to be a hungry day. In an Irish hotel, at this level, one paid for bed-and-breakfast. A far cry from the Continental breakfast of coffee, croissants and marmalade, an Irish breakfast could tide you over for the better part of the day. You got two fried eggs, two or three rashers of bacon, largely fat, little lean, fried to-matoes, fried potatoes, several slices of thick, heavy toast and butter, along with your tea. Yes, if necessary, it would tide you over for the balance of the day. Perhaps you could invest in a couple of sweet rolls and another cup of tea, or even coffee, in the late afternoon, but you could live on the number of calories in an Irish breakfast. In his day, he had gone for a week or more, hell, a month or more, on less.

But for a moment he regarded himself in the mirror, after he had taken on his jacket and folded his collar out over the jacket top. He had two or three ties but they were so woebegone that he looked worse wearing one than without.

The jacket had once been excellent, a product of a period when he had money to blow. It was Donegal tweed and tailored to him perfectly—when he had weighed possibly a stone and a half more than he did now. But that was some years ago and now it was the only jacket he owned, so that he wore it daily—including such occasions as when he was in the drunk tank, or sleeping it off in an alleyway. He had patched it at elbow and at cuff with soft leather. And this he had done personally—no tailor for him. Sean Ryan, in his day, in the field, had learned to do his own sewing and did a quite respectable job.

For a moment, he dreamed. If he could only get a few pounds. If he could only get himself a new outfit, a suit, a snowwhite clean shirt, a decent tie, new boots. Why, then he could go out and look for a reasonable job. After all, he had been to college, he was a gentleman, a retired officer. He had more decorations than he could off-hand remember. He snorted at that one. He even had one decoration that took up an eighth of his chest, if worn. It involved a golden dragon. Had it come from the Nationalist Chinese or from Thailand?

But then he faced reality. How could he get his hands on a few pounds? Long since, he had borrowed from every friend, every relative, near or far, every remote acquaintance who was generous enough, foolish enough, or, face it, pitying enough, to help him. There was no one else left. But even if there had been, and he could have refitted himself, what credentials could he offer a potential employer?

What was your last post of employment?

I was the bodyguard of the Emir Alhaji Mohammadu, Kudo of Kano, Nigeria. Which was a polite way of putting it. He and two other whites, one an Italian, one a Greek, were the hatchetmen of the Emir, used on delicate occasions when the three hundred and some odd pound Emir did not wish to commit his fellow countrymen, though the Emir was far from a delicate man when it came to—ah—subversion.

And what was your position before that? Sean had to think twice. Yes, probably that romp in— what did they call the country now?—he forgot. Borneo, in the old days. It had been a bloody mess. Not exactly a job to reveal to a prospective employer in Dublin.

He had held off the moment long enough. He reached for his wallet and examined its contents. There were no contents, insofar as paper money was concerned. He fished into his trouser pockets

16

and came forth with several coins, a few shillings, a few pence. Less than a pound in all. So he had suspected. He couldn't have gotten as blotto as he had obviously been without blowing all on hand. It came back to him now. He had started buying himself Jameson's, the best of the Irish whiskeys, so far as he was concerned, instead of sticking to the more plebian Guiness stout. He could afford whiskey about as much as he could champagne.

Sean Ryan had luck in the dining room. He was the last of the hotel's guests to appear on the scene and Molly, the sole waitress, who also doubled as a chambermaid, was in the process of cleaning up. But for some reason, Molly had a soft spot for Sean Ryan. She brought him his breakfast.

Only the fact that he was still hungry from the day before made it possible for him to get it all down, over the rebellion of his hangover. But get it down he did, to the last crust of the heavy Irish bread.

On the way out, he put the proprietor off with his story of a check coming at the end of the week. Actually, it was the dole, though these days they called it unemployment insurance. Just enough to keep from starving, if managed, but hardly enough for a drinking man.

The hotel was located within sight of the Guiness brewery, the second largest in the world. The first largest was in England and also a Guiness establishment. Sean Ryan passed it and went up to Usher's Quay, and turned right, paralleling the River Liffey which wound through Dublin as the Seine did through Paris. He headed in the direction of O'Connell Street and the center of town. He made his way to the Pearl bar on Fleet street and entered. The Pearl bar, which boasted in one back corner possibly the smallest urinal Sean Ryan had ever seen. It had once occured to Ryan that every playwright and poet in over a hundred years of Irish literature had relieved himself in that urinal, from Oscar Wilde to Brendan Behan, by the way of Sean O'Casey, Synge, and all the rest. It was a writer's bar in the oldest Dublin tradition. No women allowed, of course. There was a tiny room off to one side where a man could leave his wife, if she wasn't too particular about the drabs she associated with, and she could sit at a table and have half a pint, while he stood at the bar in the saloon proper.

Sean Ryan went to the bar, immediately in front of the row of old style spigots, climbed shakily up onto a stool and said, ''A pint.'' The bartender had already begun to draw it before the words were out.

An Irish pint is a full twenty ounces, almost as much as an American fifth. The Pearl served foreign export, the double charged Guiness stout. The bartender held his hand on the glass until Sean Ryan had put forth his money. He recognized his man.

With an initial sigh, Ryan got half of the strong brew down before he took his lips away and put the glass down for a moment. He knew that he had to nurse it. Even stout wasn't as cheap as it once was.

An uncutuous voice beside him said, ''Major Ryan?''

Sean Ryan turned his head slowly. He had never seen the other before. A roly-poly fat man with a greasy-dark complexion and bland face. He wore clothes that were not quite in place, here in Dublin, nor would they have been in England. Nor, in actuality, in Europe, at least not in the Western countries of Common Europe. The black material was good, the tailoring was fair, but the suit wasn't of the West.

Sean Ryan said, ''All right, one of us knows the name of the other. Shall we go on?''

The greasy one made a slight bow and said, ''Saul Saidi, at your service, sir.''

Sean Ryan shifted his eyes and considered the accent. The man looked like a Moslem, but wasn't. Sean could tell a follower of the Prophet, somewhat in the same manner as an Orthodox Catholic can tell an Orthodox Jew, and vice versa. You can't exactly put your finger on it, but there is something.

Sean said, ''And how is Beirut these days?''

The fat little man looked at him, blinking, but rose to the occasion. ''It is beginning to recover considerably. The tourists are beginning to flood in once more, especially from the Arab countries.''

So Ryan had guessed right. The other was a Lebanese. Contrary to popular belief, the Christians in the country immediately north of Israel, are as numerous as the Moslems. Saidi, if that was his real name, was undoubtedly of Christian background, though originally Semitic racially.

Sean Ryan said, ''And what would you be wanting?''

The other bowed slightly again. ''The honor of buying you a drink.''

Ryan finished his pint of stout in one long swallow and got down from his stool. "You've got a customer, man dear," he said. "Lead on, Mac-Duff and damned be he that first calls, hold enough."

The Lebanese looked at him blankly but led the way to one of the wooden booths that lined the wall parallel to the long bar.

They sat across from each other and the fat man summoned the Pearl's sole waiter, a bit imperiously. The waiter, a semi-clean apron about his waist, rubbed the table a double meaningless lick with a soiled rag, before saying, "Sure and wot'll it be, bhoys?"

The Lebanese looked at him reproachfully at the address but turned to his guest.

Ryan said, "I'll be having a double Jameson."

Saul Saidi said, "A ginger beer. A chilled ginger beer, if you please."

While the waiter was away, the Lebanese took in the other across from him. His small, dark eyes were of the type that would miss little. He saw a man of perhaps fifty, who had obviously seen life the hard way. Ryan's skin, which should have had the lightness of complexion of the Irishman, had a yellowish tinge. Perhaps too much atabrine in his time—or too much quinine? There were two small scars on his face, one on his chin, and fairly deep, one on his forehead, disappearing into an eyebrow. His front teeth were obviously dentures, though the others seemed excellent. His eyes were faded blue, traditionally the killer's eyes. He even had some pockmarks on his face. Sometimes in the back-areas of the world when they give you a smallpox injection, it can result in your acquiring a slight case of the pox, particularly if the serum is handled in the inadequate manner it often is in the boondocks. It was not a reassuring face, but, then, Saul Saidi had not come here to be reassured.

When the drinks arrived, Sean Ryan steeled himself to hide the trembling of his hand—the strong stout had helped, already—and knocked back half of the Irish whiskey. The Lebanese sipped a few drops of ginger beer politely.

"All right," Ryan said. "You know my name. Why?"

"I have come a long way to interview you, Major."

"That doesn't answer the question."

"I have a job for you."

Ryan eyed him for a long moment, before saying cynically, "I've retired."

"So we understand. However, we thought to induce you to come out of retirement for one last assignment."

"Who is we?"

"I am afraid that I cannot tell you that."

"Then, thanks for the drink." Sean Ryan finished it and began to rise.

The other held up a hand. "It involves the payment to you of three hundred ounces of gold, payable in Hong Kong."

Sean Ryan sank back into his seat and stared at the other. He didn't know what gold was going for by the ounce in the international banking houses specializing in exchange, these days, but he knew damned well that he had never seen that much money in his life.

"For doing what?" he said.

"For leading a commando group on a single operation."

"What commando group?"

"A group of twenty-four mercenaries. It hasn't been recruited as yet. That will be part of your task."

Ryan had finished his whiskey. He snapped his fingers at the waiter and held up one finger to indicate the need for a refill.

Saul Saidi said, "Major Ryan, what is the highest rank you have ever held in the military?"

Ryan twisted his mouth wryly and said, "General."

The other blinked at him. "And what is the highest rank you have held in an, ah, orthodox army?"

"Major."

"In what army, sir?"

"British."

"You saw action with the British? Where?"

"Among other places, in North Ireland, as a boy, during the troubles in Belfast—and elsewhere."

The fat man nodded. "That coincides with our research."

The fresh whiskey came and Ryan knocked a third of it back. He was feeling better by the minute. He said, "What's this commando assignment?"

"Briefly, you will recruit two experienced junior officers to be your seconds in command, and one sergeant. Your men will consist of twenty, all of them the most highly experienced mercenaries. If your mission is successful, your officers will receive two hundred ounces of gold apiece, the sergeant one hundred and fifty; each man, one hundred. All deposited to your accounts in Hong Kong, and hence tax free.''

Sean said, ''Beggin' your pardon, but what happens if the mission is successful but one or more of the boys take a hit?''

''The gold will be paid over to whatever heirs they designate. If there are no heirs, the sum will be divided amongst the rest of you, evenly.''

''Suppose the mission isn't a success?''

''You will be paid all expenses, from the moment you sign up. Food, clothing, hotels, travel. If you fail in your mission, your expenses will continue until you arrive back at the point at which you were recruited. In your case, here in Dublin. And there will be a small symbolic payment in cash. Say, one hundred pounds.''

Ryan took back more of the drink. He said, ''You still haven't told me the assignment.''

The Lebanese nodded. ''It is necessary to liquidate a group of possibly ten persons, possibly a few more might be involved. One of these is of particular importance. In fact, our group would be inclined to feel the mission accomplished if but the one most important of this number was, as I say, liquidated. Do you speak Arabic, Major?''

''No. French is my only language other than English. Oh, I have a few words and phrases of various other languages, including Arabic, but I don't pretend to speak them.''

''Then it would be best if some of your commando group know Arabic, and, if at all possible, some of the lingua franca of North Africa.''

"Such as Swahili?" Ryan said, his eyes narrowed questioningly.

"No," the Lebanese told him. "I doubt if you will be operating in mideastern Africa."

Ryan finished the second whiskey before saying, "And who are these people you want hit?"

"El Hassan and his closest adherents, but particularly El Hassan."

Sean Ryan ogled him. "El Hassan!"

"You know of him?"

"What little there is to know. I read the newspapers. Where's he currently located?"

"We're not sure. The last we know, in Tamanrasset, in the Ahaggar Sahara."

"Tamanrasset! A commando operation! Man dear, are you daft? I've never operated in that area but it must be a thousand miles south of Tunis. And you're not even sure that he's there. A commando action involves coming up on a coast in ships, making a quick raid ashore and then beating your way back before the enemy can organize a defense and counterattack."

"We have it all worked out."

Ryan laughed at him.

The fat man who called himself Saidi said patiently, "The better part of a million American dollars is eventually involved, Major. Obviously, we have no intention of throwing it away. We have your cover all arranged, all has been thought out in detail."

"What cover?"

"You go in from Algiers, in Algeria, in a Land Rover hover jeep and two desert lorries. Your story is that you're looking for El Hassan to volunteer your services."

"We'd be white men. He's attempting to take over all North Africa for the blacks and the other wogs."

The Lebanese was smooth in his oily way. "That would be part of your cover. Obviously, a handful of white mercenaries would be an ideal bodyguard for our El Hassan. You couldn't possibly put over a *coup d'état*."

"He's not stupid, or he wouldn't have gotten this far. He'd turn us down."

"Most likely. But by that time, you'd be in his vicinity and improvise your opportunity to, ah, hit him I believe was the expression you used."

"Great. And then how would we be getting away? A thousand miles from the nearest city of any size, and the country swarming with El Hassan's people."

"You will carry a two-way tight beam radio, complete with scrambler. Upon completion of your mission, you will call and an aircraft will swoop in to your rescue. You will have to hole up only for a couple of hours at most."

Ryan looked at him skeptically. "Surrounded by a few thousand bloody mad nomads including Tuaghi and the Holy Mother only knows who else?"

"You will be armed with extraordinary weapons."

"Such as what?"

"Such as long range grenade launchers for your rifles."

Ryan laughed bitterly, and signalled for another whiskey. He might as well get as many free drinks as he could out of this before turning the other down cold.

Saul Saidi said softly, "The grenades they project carry mini-fission charges."

This time, Sean Ryan really boggled him. "Mini-fission charges? Do I look daft? Man dear, there is no such thing as a fission charge small enough to be launched in a grenade from a rifle."

"You are mistaken, Major. This is the age of miniaturization. For decades, the Yankees, in particular, have had nuclear fission shells small enough to be fired from field cannon. These more recent mini-fission charges are a well-kept secret, and I will not even disclose what country developed them. Each, to use the Americanism, packs a wallop approximately that of a blockbuster bomb of the Second World War."

Ryan whistled almost inaudibly between his teeth. Another suspicion came to him. "What if the rescue plane doesn't show up after we've done El Hassan the dirty? It'd be to your advantage to let us rot there. Then you wouldn't have to pay up."

The Lebanese made a gesture with his two hands. "My dear Major, we are not thieves. The pilot and co-pilot of the aircraft will be handpicked by you, yourself. Friends of yours. The plane will be based at In Salah, not too far north, or, if by that time El Hassan's adherents have overrun that town, to Adrar still further north, but within easy range. It will be to you within an hour or so and take you to a safe refuge where I will meet you and together we'll go to Hong Kong and complete the transaction. My signature will be necessary before the gold is released to you.''

Ryan finished his third double and thought about it for long moments.

Finally, he said, ''What if something happens to you before you can make this signature in Hong Kong?''

The Lebanese said smoothly, ''Then that would be unfortunate, would it not, Major Ryan?''

Sean Ryan looked at him coldly and said, ''Man dear, I suggest you begin thinking of an alternative to that situation.''

III

TOKUGAWA HIDETADA

COLONEL TOKUGAWA HIDETADA'S train, that running between Canton and Kowloon, stopped at the border town of Lo Wu. His things went through a minimum of inspection, and, followed by two coolies carrying his luggage, he crossed the bridge and entered a compartment of the train which would take him to Hong Kong proper. This area was the so-called New Territories, on lease to the British colony supposedly until 1997, from the People's Republic of China. Actually, nobody seemed to know how matters stood. If Hong Kong gave up the New Territories, she could not possibly survive, certainly not with her full population of over three million. The colony including the New Territories measured only 381 square miles in area, but the island of Hong Kong alone was but 32 square miles in area. One does not crowd three million people into such limited quarters.

However, the People's Republic was making no noises, up to this point, on terminating the lease.

And Tokugawa Hidetada thought he knew why. It was more profitable for the communists to have Hong Kong remain an appendage of the West. Hundreds of millions of dollars worth of trade annually flooded through the free port. Hong Kong was the People's Republic's window to the West. In her own right, she was a most profitable source of hard money from abroad, since the colony was far from self supporting in food and in the raw materials she utilized in her highly modernized industry. These she must needs buy from the mainland. No, it would not be profitable for the People's Republic to close down the British colony of Hong Kong. Had she wanted to, she could have accomplished it easily enough long decades before. Hong Kong itself had no source of water, save rain. Water had to be piped in from the mainland. Cut off from that water supply, and the People's Republic had every right to cut it, had she wished, Hong Kong could not have lasted a week.

Colonel Tokugawa Hidetada was a small man, in the Japanese tradition. Had he been walking along the street in the Ginza of Tokyo he might well have been thought of as the most average man in sight. He even wore very thick lensed glasses, and had the slightly bucked teeth beloved of American cartoonists depicting a son of Nippon. He did not look like a colonel. Most certainly, he didn't look like the ace Japanese espionage-counter-espionage operative, working out of the Japanese department which was the equivalent of the American CIA, the Soviet KGB.

He took the train to the Kowloon station next to the Star Ferry terminus and then, carrying his own bags now, the ferry to Victoria, the city of Hong Kong island. The crossing took five minutes and since he had made the trip more times than he could possibly remember, he ignored the exotic sights and sounds of the teeming harbor, the large number of foreign ships, the *wallah-wallah* launches, the junks and sampans.

On the Victoria side, he took a hovercar to the Japanese consulate.

One of the two plainclothesmen there politely murmured greetings to him and took his bags from the cab and led the way into the interior.

The pretty Japanese girl at the reception desk was attired in a shibui kimona. At the colonel's approach she came to her feet and bowed thrice deeply, before resuming her seat.

He told her that he had an appointment with Prince Genji Shikibu.

Her desk equipment was all but identical to any that might have been found in Common Europe or the United States of the Americas. She utilized it.

Within moments, a European clad consular aide appeared from a rear door and exchanged polite bows with the colonel and led the way for him, although Tokugawa Hidetada had been over the route a few score times.

The aide knocked discreetly at a beautifully engraved door of black wood and opened it. The colonel entered.

The room beyond was a combination of half Japanese, half western. Aside from the inevitable portrait of the Mikado, the room's sole decoration was a statuette carved of white and green jade, set into an alcove. It was exquisite. The last time the colonel had been here, the alcove contained an antique ivory piece. The prince periodically changed his displayed art objects, but there was never more than one in any room of his quarters. The Japanese do not believe in art in quantity, preferring to be subjected to but one piece at a time. There is no such thing as an art museum in the land of the rising sun. The art conscious people do not wish to be beaten over the head with a surfeit of beauty.

The furniture of the room, including desk, a center table and the chairs, were of the West.

The prince arose at the colonel's entry. He was a man in his early sixties and wore a black silk formal man's kimona and a *happi*, hip length loose jacket of heavy dark blue cotton. On the kimona were discreet *mon*, family crests of the prince which added to its elegance.

The colonel, hands stiff at his sides, bowed deeply several times and the prince nodded and gestured to the table. They sat and almost immediately a girl entered. She wore a heavily embroidered, brilliantly dyed kimona and was heavily made up and coiffed almost in the style of a geisha. She bore a tea tray and bobbed her bows half a dozen times before serving the men, who paid her no attention. She was, undoubtedly, the colonel thought, one of the prince's concubines.

When she had gone, they sipped their tea and the colonel commented upon its excellence.

The prince finally stroked his wisp of white beard and said, "And your mission in Canton, Colonel?"

"I am embarassed to reveal that I have had

insufficient time to bring it to a successful conclusion. Although I speak the Cantonese dialect and hence am able to merge quite easily into the streets, the authorities are quite efficient in their security measures and one must proceed with great care."

The prince nodded understanding and said, "It is of no matter. We are withdrawing you from the assignment, for one of more importance."

Tokugawa Hidetada bobbed his head in acceptance of that and looked into the other's face politely, awaiting his new instructions.

"We are aware, Colonel, that your duties kept you in the Near East for nearly five years. How is your Arabic?"

"Not quite perfect, Your Higness, but almost so. I have a slight accent. However, that is not the handicap in Moslem nations that it might be elsewhere. The Arabic of Saudi Arabia differs somewhat from that of even nearby Egypt and that of Egypt from, say, Algeria. Thus a Moroccan, speaking with me, might well think I was from Jordan or Syria, and a Syrian might come to the conclusion that I was from Algeria."

"Very well. That is not of major importance. Your dossier tells me that you are also conversant with Esperanto."

The colonel bobbed his head in admission. "It has been a hobby since my youth."

"Excellent. It is one of the reasons that you have been chosen for this assignment."

The colonel held his peace politely.

Prince Genji Shikibu said, "I doubt that you have heard of El Hassan."

"No, Your Highness. Your servant is shamefully ignorant."

"It would be unlikely that news of his astounding appearance onto the world scene would be released by the Cantonese press. It will probably be some time before the Chairman and the Central Committee of the Chinese Communist Party have decided upon a stand to take on El Hassan."

He poured more of the green tea, before going on.

He said, "Northern Africa, Colonel, has erupted. News filtering out is fragmentary. However, this much we know. Within months, actually not much more than weeks, a new figure has manifested itself in the Sahara and, indeed, throughout the area north of the Congo. His movements are sweeping through the desert and its borders like wildfires. Areas far and beyond the size of all Japan have been taken over by his followers."

The colonel indicated his surprise by sucking in air, politely.

The prince took a new tack. "As you are aware, Colonel, Japan is for all practical purposes without natural resources. We must import practically all, for our industries. For instance, we are the third greatest producer of finished steel in the world, but both our iron ore and coal must come from abroad. It becomes an increasing problem. Indeed, our economy is confronted with disaster. The first blow came with the Arab oil cartel and we were hard put to avoid complete collapse."

The colonel nodded politely to accept the truth of that. All Japan was acquainted with the fact.

The prince went on. "Africa, and particularly

North Africa, is one of the few remaining all but completely undeveloped areas of the world. If El Hassan is successful in realizing his ambitions he will be in control of a wealth of raw materials in one nation unrivaled, save possibly, only possibly, in the Soviet Complex. There are few raw materials necessary to modern industry that are not to be found in profusion in Northern Africa. Colonel, I must be blunt. We must gain access to these raw materials, or Japan dies."

The colonel's face went blank.

The prince took a deep breath and then continued. "In Mauretania alone—and El Hassan's followers are already said to be in control there—are deposits of copper far greater than those of Chili or Katanga, iron deposits richer than those of Labrador or Venezuela. In Algeria and Libya oil gushes from the sands, far beyond the needs of our country."

The colonel bobbed his head in acceptance. "And my assignment, Your Highness?"

The other hesitated. "We actually do not know. El Hassan is a mystery. Is he a religious fanatic, a new Mohammed come out of the desert? Is he a communist, strongly opposed to us capitalist nations? Is he a racist, strongly against all but blacks? Is he an anarchist, decrying modern industry, modern socioeconomic systems? This we must know. We must know whether our path leads to supporting this mysterious El Hassan and coming to agreements with him to secure his raw materials in return for our manufactured products, or if we must vigorously combat him and continue to deal with the present governments of the states he is attempting to overwhelm.''

The colonel nodded.

The prince hesitated before adding, ''The rumors about El Hassan are endless. Some indicate that he has reservations about trading North Africa's raw materials to the developed countries, except at exorbitant prices. However, other rumors indicate that some of his closest colleagues are less extreme and desire the aid of such countries as Japan to speed the modernization of Africa. One in particular, Field Marshal Bey-ag-Akhamouk, seems particularly to have strong opinions of his own. Perhaps you will find it suitable for us to back him, if he is at odds with this El Hassan.''

The prince came to his feet.

He said, ''You will leave immediately for North Africa and find the answers to the questions we ask about El Hassan and his follower Bey-ag-Akhamouk and their effect upon our future. You will report directly to me and take no overt action, no matter what the provocation, until we have passed upon it.''

The colonel also stood and bowed his acceptance. ''Your Highness,'' he said.

IV

SERGE SVERDLOV

COLONEL SERGE SVERDLOV was retracing a route he had covered so often that he didn't bother to watch the passing scene as his automated hover limousine took him past St. Basil's Cathedral, on one side of Red Square, to cross the Moscow River by the Moskvoretski Bridge and into the traffic of Pyatnikskaya. The car turned west at Dobryninskaya Square to Gorgi Park. It ran along that on Kaluga until it pulled up before the aged Czarist baroque palace, once belonging to the Yusopov family, the scion of which had assassinated the mad monk Rasputin, but which now housed Sverdlov's branch of the ministry.

He had sometimes wondered why the organization of which he was a part had never moved to more spacious and certainly more modern quarters. It was, from his viewpoint, by far the most important, most powerful, and most feared ministry of the Soviet Complex.

It had a lengthy history. In its beginnings under

Lenin, it had been known as the Cheka, which took its name from *Chrezvychainaya Kossmissiya*; its full title being Extraordinary Commission for Combating Counter-Revolution, Sabotage and Speculation. It had been abolished in 1922 to make way for an organization still more famous, the GPU, standing for *Gosudarstvennoye Politicheskoye Upravleniye*, or State Political Administration. Stalin decided ten years later in 1934 to do away with the OGPU and reorganized it under the name of NKVD or People's Commissariat of Internal Affairs. Twelve years later, it was replaced by the MVD, the Ministry of Internal Affairs. Still later, the organization split into internal and foreign branches and the KGB, Sverdlov's organization, the Committee of State Security, became the *secret* police, particularly involved in counter-espionage, espionage and security. It fulfilled much the same functions as the Central Intelligence Agency of the United States in gathering and evaluating information but also had police powers similar to those of the FBI.

Yes, it was to this branch of the Soviet Complex's government that Serge Sverdlov devoted his services. He was a mediumly built man but more than ordinarily lithe; the slight slant of eyes, the darkness of complexion, give suspicion of his Cossack heritage. His teeth were white, perfectly so, and his smile good—when he smiled. But there was something about his eyes. The story was in international espionage circles that he had killed more men than cholera. He had worked abroad on enough assignments that he had picked up taste in clothing and was attired more nearly as a London clubman than a Moscow gumshoe.

He left the hover limousine and strode toward the elaborate entrada of the Yusopov palace. There were no flags above it, no signs nor anything else to indicate that the present nature of the pre-revolutionary building was what it was, save the two uniformed guards in front. They snapped to the salute upon his approach but since he was in mufti he ignored them and passed on into the building.

There were two more guards there, but Colonel Sverdlov was well known and he ignored them and went on.

He was thoroughly familiar with the building and, as he had often before, wondered that anyone, even a Czarist prince, would choose to live in such sterile surroundings. He strode along marble halls. All about were a profusion of alleged art objects which went back to the old days, paintings, statuary, furniture. No one, down through the decades since the revolution, had ever bothered to move them. The tastes of the Czarist aristocracy had been abominable.

The colonel reached the heavy doors of the office to which he was bound and the lieutenant at the desk there looked up, at first impatiently, but that expression was immediately wiped from his face.

"Yes, Comrade Colonel," he said snappily.

Sverdlov said, "I believe that the Minister is expecting me."

"Yes, Comrade Colonel. His orders are that you be admitted immediately."

The colonel opened the door and passed through.

The office beyond was large but not ostentatious. The Minister was of the old school and had actually first joined the organization as a youth when Beria was still in his final days and Stalin in full power. He affected simplicity, despite his rank. The fact that he still held his position was testimony to his ability to roll with the blows.

Minister Kliment Blagonravov was already looking at the door at Colonel Sverdlov's entry. He was a heavy man, heavy of face and heavy-set. His head was shaven, though that old style of the Party's military men and upper-echelons of police officials had all but disappeared. His simple jacket of the type once de rigueur in the times of Lenin and the Old Bolsheviks, now an affectation, was hung over the back of a chair and his collar had been unbuttoned, but he was still sweating. Not for Kliment Blagonravov the effeminacy of air-conditioning.

He projected a camaraderie with his more trusted agents, and said now, in supposed heartiness, "Serge! We see too little of you these days!"

The KGB agent was fully aware of the iron beneath the lard of his ultimate superior. He said ruefully, "I see too little of Moscow, Comrade Blagonravov. No matter how dedicated, one misses home."

"Yes, yes, of course. It is a shame that Party duties keep you abroad so much, Serge. You are too confounded efficient. Sit down, sit down." The bureaucrat swung in his chair so that he could reach the bar set into the wall behind him. As the colonel found a chair, he opened the door of the refrigerator compartment and came forth with a bottle, slightly yellowish in color of contents. He plucked two three-ounce glasses from the bar's top and swiveled back to his desk.

"As I recall, Serge, your favorite is Zubrovka vodka. A sprig of that particular Polish grass to flavor it. Personally, I prefer Stolitschnaja but I shall join you." He poured the glasses full and pushed one of them over to his subordinate.

Sverdlov nodded his thanks, even as he took up the glass. It was proverbial that no matter what the hour, one did not get through Blagonravov's office without emerging with at least a slight glow on. Woe betide the teetotaler summoned into the Minister's presence.

"It's been a long time," the colonel said, holding the glass up in toast. "The drink in Indonesia is atrocious, particularly what they are pleased to call vodka. It comes from Japan, so I understand, and is probably made from rice."

"The world revolution!" the minister said, holding his own chilled spirits up.

"The revolution," the colonel said, repeating the standard formula.

They knocked back the vodka in stiff-wristed motion.

"And how go things in Indonesia?" Blagonravov rumbled.

His operative shrugged. "It is unbelievably corrupt, Comrade. At all levels. The worker in the street would become a communist for one cigarette. For two, he would become a Christian, and for three he would slit your throat."

The other growled, "I understsnd that the corruption applies even to ranking members of the local party."

Sverdlov cleared his throat. "Yes," he said. "Even petty graft. No one seems free of it."

The minister sighed his disgust. "How can one sponsor revolution with such elements? But enough of Indonesia." He refilled the glasses.

The colonel looked at him to go on, attentively.

His superior finished his drink first and said, "What do you know of El Hassan?"

Sverdlov said, "Very little. It would seem he makes considerable effort to remain a mystery man. From what came through in Djakarta, he attempts to unite the whole of North Africa. To maintain his air of mystery, he has adopted the artificial language Esperanto, which supposedly all of his followers and all delegations from foreign countries must speak in his presence."

"Do you have Esperanto?"

"No. Arabic, yes. As you will recall, I was stationed in Algeria during the most recent revolution."

Blagonravov nodded. "You can begin your studies of Esperanto immediately. I understand that it is possibly the easiest language in the world to acquire."

Serge Sverdlov inwardly winced. He was no student.

The minister went on. "We have already lost two top agents in this matter and have had a third, not so important, defect to El Hassan."

The KGB operative stared at him. "Already?

But he has been on the scene but a few weeks."

"Comrade Abraham Baker, the black comrade who did so much work in America, was one of his original team of the Sahara Division of the African Development project of the Reunited Nations. When matters came to a head—we do not know the details—evidently El Hassan, whose real name is Homer Crawford, an American professor of sociology, seemingly liquidated him. Shortly after, we sent in Anton . . ."

"Anton!"

"Yes. To infiltrate the El Hassan movement and attempt to rise high in its ranks, with the far future in mind. What happened to this outstanding comrade is confused. It would seem that he resigned, or pretended to, from the Party on the same night, just recently, that El Hassan's tribesmen destroyed the Arab Union forces in Tamanrasset who were attempting to annex the Sahara. Anton died in the fighting."

"And who was the third agent who was eliminated?"

"Not exactly eliminated. This former comrade, Isobel Cunningham, had been recruited by Abe Baker while they were still both students in New York. When the crisis came, she evidently defected to El Hassan and now is one of his intimate clique."

The minister poured still a third vodka.

"And what is my assignment?" Colonel Sverdlov said.

His superior looked at him, all but apologetically. "Frankly, I would rather have sent Ilya Simonov, but he is busy on an assignment in

Prague, Czechoslavakia, seeking out the sources of the dry rot which seem to surface so often in the Soviet Complex these days, the elements who are dissatisfied with our society in spite of the fact that we have now attained to the affluence we have so long promised.''

He knocked back the stiff vodka. "Your task is to promote the program of El Hassan.''

Serge Sverdlov gaped at him. "*Promote* it! You say that he is attempting to take over all North Africa. This would include Algeria, Libya, Mauretania, Tunisia—not to speak of some of the smaller nations to the south. All are Marxist, or, at least, to some degree socialist.''

Kliment Blagonravov sighed a fat sigh. "Serge, Serge,'' he said. "It is astounding how few, even among those who deal in the field of political economy and dialectics, have studied the basics. It is the same in the West, as it is in the Soviet Complex. Half a century ago, an American president, a wealthy capitalist and aristocrat himself, Franklin D. Roosevelt, realized that if he was to promote the continuation of the American social system that a good many reforms were necessary. Otherwise, there would have been a revolution during their great depression. He inaugurated them. Immediately his fellow capitalists began to scream that he was a socialist, a communist, a Marxist, or even an anarchist. Obviously, they hadn't the vaguest idea of what any of these movements actually were.''

Serge Sverdlov was frowning. He hadn't any idea of what the other was getting to.

The Minister wagged a lardy finger at him.

"Serge, when Karl Marx and Friedrich Engels originally called for the proletarian revolution, they envisioned it as first taking place in the most advanced nations in the capitalist world. England, Germany, the United States and so forth. Socialism, or communism—they used the terms interchangably and meant the same thing by them—was the next step *beyond* capitalism, and could not be attained until there was a highly developed economy. Backward, primitive societies, could not realize true socialism, or communism, since they did not as yet have the foundations for it. Capitalism was a necessary step in the evolution of society. Without it, following feudalism and chattle slavery, in their turn, socialism was impossible."

The colonel stirred in his chair. Of course, all this had been taught in his classes in Marxism while he was still in secondary school. However, no one interrupted the minister when he was on one of his lengthy harangues.

Blagonravov went on, pontifically, "It was bad enough, in Russia and later in China, when, as a result of the confusion following World Wars One and Two, that the Party was able to come to power."

The colonel blinked at a statement such as that from a ranking Party bureaucrat, but held his peace.

The other went on. "The communists were in power, but did not have the base upon which to build true communism. Under Stalin in our country and Mao in China, the most ruthless measures were taken in order to lift them by their bootstraps, as the Yankees put it. Nothing counted but quick industrialization. Five year plans in Russia, Great Leaps Forward in China. Anything, anything, to industrialize. Until, at long last, industrialization was achieved and now the Soviet Complex is as powerful as any of the imperialist powers, even the United States of the Americas. For instance, as far back as 1974 we passed them in the production of steel, the most important basic of an industrialized society.''

A question came to the colonel's mind, which he wouldn't have dreamed of asking. If the Soviet Complex had at long last achieved full industrialization, then why was not the dictatorship ended and true communism, or socialism, established? Why did not the State wither away, as once called for by Marx?

The minister poured another drink and pushed Sverdlov's over to him. Hadn't they both been Russians, both would have been smashed by this time. Even as it was, the colonel could feel the alcohol. Happily, he had known what was coming and had eaten a huge breakfast. He wondered if his superior went through this routine with everyone whom he interviewed during the process of a long day.

Blagonravov continued with his explanation. ''Of recent years, a good many movements throughout the world have sprung up proclaiming themselves socialist. Usually, not always, they are actually military dictatorships. They use the term socialism because it is often popular with the people, few of whom actually know what it truly means. They usually nationalize a few basic industries such as the railroads, communications, the airlines, if any, and expropriate foreign holdings such as mines and oil fields, and anything else of value, and proclaim this to be socialism, or Marxism. Allende was a good example, down in Chile, some decades ago. Algeria, Libya, Tunisia and Mauretania are other good examples. In actuality, capitalism in such countries has not been done away with. The State has simply taken the place of individual capitalists; workers continue to work for wages, farmers continue to sell their products on the market, banks continue to operate the old monetary system and foreign trade is pushed in order to make profits—for the State. The term for such a socioeconomic system should be State-Capitalism, rather than socialism or Marxism.''

"I believe that I have assimilated all this, Comrade Blagonravov,'' Sverdlov said.

"Very well. Then the point remains that North Africa is not as yet ready for the communist movement. It does not as yet have the foundations. Even those comparatively advanced countries such as Algeria. They have far, far to go. Indeed, in some parts of the interior, feudalism and even elements of slavery still exist.''

"So what are we to do, at this stage?''

Blagonravov nodded before finishing off his latest vodka. He said, "It is the belief of the Central Committee and Number one, that this El Hassan, evidently a charismic character beyond the ordinary, can bring advance to North Africa more quickly than the largely corrupt and opportunistic military elements now in control. Our present line, then, is to support him. Let him come to power.

Let him utilize whatever forces he can bring to bear, including the cooperation of the Reunited Nations, to bring North Africa into the 21st Century. When he has done so, then North Africa is ready for our propaganda.''

"I see," the colonel said.

"That was the task of Comrades Baker and Anton before you. They gave their lives for the world revolution. You are to take their places."

Serge Sverdlov frowned. "Nothing more?"

"Yes, something more. You are to insinuate yourself into their inner circles as Anton did. Work your way as close to El Hassan himself as is possible. When you are well established, then we will infilter other Party members and you will make every effort to make them prominent in the government of El Hassan as well. This will continue, indefinitely, and until the day arrives when we will be ready for our *coup d'état* and take over."

The other stared at him. "But Comrade, I am a white man. El Hassan proclaims the black, the Hamitic, the dark skinned Arabs and Berbers. The Caucasians are an anathema."

Blagonravov laughed his humorless, heavy laugh.

"My dear Serge, you are unacquainted with the latest in cosmetic surgery and related sciences. We have drugs today which can change the pigmentation of your skin—it is reversible, of course, and you can change back later. We will not make you as black as a Senegal or Bantu, but you will be as dark as the average member of El Hassan's immediate clique. Seemingly, ah, touched with the tar brush, as the American Southeners say. Your somewhat too light hair will be cut short and dyed black. You will have a supply of dye to renew the treatment as often as necessary.''

The minister laughed with heavy joviality. ''My dear Serge, you are about to become a nigger.''

V

BEY-AG-AKHAMOUK

THEY HAD CORNERED the remnants of the forces of Colonel Midran Ibrahim, of the Arab Union, in a wadi, not far north of Tazerouk which boasted one of the few wells of potable water which the colonel's forces had still held at the time Fort Laperrine and Tamanrasset had been taken by storm by the Taughi and other rampaging tribesmen of El Hassan.

The more proper name of a wadi is *oued* since it implies a fissure in the earth which channels off water when there is any and that is seldom in the Ahaggar, the land of the Tairog Tuareg and possibly the most desolate area on earth save Antarctica. When the occasional deluges of rain precipitate—and there can be years between when not a single drop is seen—the wadi becomes a rushing river, sweeping everything before it and woebetide he so foolish as to have placed his encampment at its bottom. Otherwise, it is dry, baked hard by the sun, and for this reason often used as a road through the erg, the shifting sand dunes of the Sahara, or the reg, the areas of the desert covered by gravel. The wadis split up the land into deep, and sometimes wide, cracks and fissures and are somewhat the equivalent of the arroyos of the American Southwest and of Mexico.

Bey-ag-Akhamouk and Kenny Ballalou, both of El Hassan's immediate staff, with a force of local Tuaghi and Teda tribesmen from the south were having little in the way of difficulty. The Egyptian colonel, obviously shaken by his defeat and trying desperately to escape north, had entered the wadi to obtain greater speed. He had a half dozen desert lorries, two hover jeeps and two light armored cars. Bey and Kenny were not sure of the exact number of infantrymen, but it probably numbered several hundred. Certainly, no more.

They were whip-lashing the Arab Union force, up and down the wadi for a distance of approximately a kilometer. Bey-ag-Akhamouk, with a flac rifle and two heavy machine guns and perhaps a score of riflemen, were dug in beyond a bend in the wadi, to the south. Behind another bend to the north was Kenny Ballalou with another flac rifle, another machine gun and another score or so of tribesmen.

The flac rifle was probably the most universal hand portable firearm ever devised. It combined the virtues, if virtues they could be called, of the recoilless light cannon, the bazooka, the heavy machine gun, and a light anti-tank gun. The clip held twenty rounds, which were armor piercing and explosive. Short of a heavy tank, they would take any motorized military vehicle. And the ergs of the Sahara do not lend themselves to even medium tanks, not to speak of heavy ones.

In short, the flac rifles were competent to hold anything that Colonel Midran Ibrahim had at his command.

Almost from the moment the ambush was sprung, the Arab Union forces dissolved into hysteria. They had already been fleeing for long hours from the debacle they had left behind them, in terror of being flushed by the hordes of Tuaghi camelmen. The Tuareg! The Forgotten of Allah! The Apaches of the Sahara! The Sons of Shaitan! And El Hassan's most devoted followers—to a man. The Arab Union trucks were insufficient to carry more than their water and supplies and a few wounded officers. Their tanks, their artillery, the gun carriers, the Soviet Complex equipment that had been their pride as the crack regiment of the Arab Union, had all been abandoned at Fort Laperrine and Tamanrasset. They were fugitives in an area that has been named the end of the world and their refuge was the better part of a thousand miles to the northeast.

For the first hour or two, Bey and Kenny had whip-sawed them back and forth, up and down the wadi. Spurred on by officers and non-coms almost as terrified as they were themselves, the Arab Union soldiers would charge up the wadi, only to be met by a curtain of fire they could not resist. Back they would head in the opposite direction, only to be met at the next bend by another sheet of flame.

Individuals and sometimes small groups would

attempt to scale the wadi banks but to do so they could carry with them naught but holstered handguns, or rifles or submachine guns slung over their shoulders, their hands needed to climb. At the top they would be knocked off as soon as they appeared by Bey-ag-Akhamouk's snipers, settled comfortably behind rocks or thorny bush. The tribesmen were at a pinnacle of glee. Now *this* was the manner in which to fight the Arab Union and the Arabs who for long centuries had come south to conduct their *razzias,* to round up the men to be herded north for the slave markets, to violate the women and steal the goats and camels. Yes, this was the way to fight them, rather than to dash wildly into the fire of their automatic weapons, their tanks, or to submit to the bombings of their aircraft. *Wallahi*! But El Hassan and his viziers would sweep the Sahara of the troops of the Arab Union and bring the Peace of Allah to all.

Bey groaned inwardly. Like the veteran combat man he was, he did not like indiscriminate, useless slaughter. Victory was necessary but to the extent possible the fewer casualties inflicted the better. But he knew why the crazed enemy failed to surrender, though confronted with an impossible situation. They were more terrified of falling into the hands of the Tuaghi alive than they were of death. They, when they were successfully advancing across the Sahara, in their strength, with the support of their armor and motorized artillery, had not conducted themselves exactly as benevolent liberators.

And now it came to a head. In a final desperate

frenzy, they were charging again, and this time, one of the armored cars gingerly edged its snoot around the bend in the wadi. Bey, who was himself manning the flac rifle, winged a couple of shots at it, deliberately aimed to bounce off the side. He didn't want to destroy the vehicle. The forces of El Hassan could utilize it to advantage, later. It took the message and hurriedly backed up around the wadi bend.

This time, the full force of the remaining infantrymen were charging, wild-eyed. A last desperate attempt to break out, and, for a moment, Bey wondered at his ability to hold them. A flac rifle, no matter how universal, held but a twenty-round clip, and wasn't meant to be utilized against individual foes. It was meant for tanks, armored cars, machine gun nests, pillboxes, foes intrenched in buildings, even aircraft under certain conditions, but not hundreds of frantic charging infantrymen. The two machine guns flanking him, mowed down the attackers, but they continued to advance, on the run.

One of his machine guns fell silent. The gunner had obviously been hit by one of the random shots being fired by the advancing elements. It soon started up again, as one of the others took over, but less accurately now.

The frantically charging enemy had nearly reached Bey's emplacements when from behind came the pounding of hundreds of the pads of *hejin* racing camels, the sound of the ululating war cry of the desert, *Ul-Ul-Ul-Allah Akbar*!

He swung his eyes about from the Arab Union

soldiers who had only yards to go to reach his gun's nest.

Behind him, up the wadi, at full tilt, swarmed the Camel Corps of Guémama, war chief of the Kel Rela clan of the Tuaghi. Some shook modern rifles at the skies, some ancient long barreled muzzle-loaders, some brandished the Tuareg, Crusader-like broadswords, with their two edges, their round points and their flat, rectangular cross members. Some were armed only with long bladed spears, though all had strapped to their left arms the traditional razor sharp arm daggers of the Tuareg.

"Sweet Jesus," Bey groaned at the sight.

Some of the Arab Union troopers were near enough that Bey could make out their bugging eyes. It was the end. They dropped rifles and sub-machine guns, turned, yelling their fear, and ran, some of them with arms held high.

Bey jumped to his feet and to the middle of the wadi and held up his arms, in desperation. He had little real hope of preventing the massacre. In fact, he was in considerable danger of being trampled to death.

Guémama himself, a submachine gun held high in one hand, led the charge. His face was a mask of excitement but at least he wasn't frothing at the mouth as were some of those behind him.

To Bey's relief and actual surprise, the young chieftain came to a halt, only a few yards before him and held up an arm to restrain his rampaging followers.

"Why do you halt us, O Bey-ag-Akhamouk! *Insh'Allah,* we shall slay all these Arab Union *giaours,* may they burn in *Gehennum!*"

The others were shrilling their war cries behind him, shaking their weapons, firing their rifles into the air, in anticipation.

Bey said, keeping his voice impossibly even, "I have heard from El Hassan on the Roumi device which allows one to talk at great distance. He desires that all the remaining dogs be spared, until he can put them to the question and learn greatly of what goes on to the north."

The Tuareg scowled but the orders were from El Hassan himself and they made considerable sense. Besides, what could be more pleasurable than to herd the pigs of the Arab Union back to Tamanrasset to be put to the torture at leisure?

He held up an arm again and shouted to his men in Tamaheg, the Berber language of the Tuaghi.

Bey, disguising inward relief said, "Let your men go forth then, and relieve the remaining dogs of any weapons they may still retain, though seemingly they, in their great cowardice, have thrown them away. Round them up and put them under guard." He laughed contemptuously, as was expected by the tribesmen and said, "Few guards will be necessary. Women could guard them. Put the rest of your men to gathering up their weapons and put them in the lorries which they have abandoned. Do not kill the wounded you find, especially the officers. El Hassan wishes to question them all. Put those among the dogs who understand how to drive the Roumi vehicles to the task and escort them back to Tamanrasset with the loot."

"*Bilhana!* with joy," Guémama blurted and

though obviously disappointed at not being able to conduct the slaughter which he'd had in mind, turned and shouted orders to his men.

He struck his *hejin* camel with his *mish'ab* camel stick and barked in command, "*Adar-ya-yan*," to bring it to its knees. The camel went through its awkward, rocking motion and subsided to the sands.

The young warrior jumped to the sands, his face in great glee. He was dressed in standard Tuareg garb; baggy trousers of dark indigo-blue cotton cloth, a loose, nightgown-like white cotton shirt and over this a gandoura outer garment. On his feet were red leather fil fil boots and over his head and face the teguelmoust, the lightweight cotton combination veil and turban. It was indigo blue and some ten feet long and a Tuareg man was never seen without it, for the Tuareg, unlike the other tribesmen of the desert, go veiled, while the women are veilless. Traditionally, it is to protect their complexions from the sun, since the Tuareg considers himself a white man, though as a whole they are as dark as the Belas whom they enslave.

"*Wallahi!* O Bey-ag-Akhamouk," Guémama chortled. "*Bismillah!* Thus it should be! These are the last of the Arab Union dogs to be rounded up." Next to El Hassan himself, whom the Tuaghi chieftain worshipped, Bey-ag-Akamouk was his favorite among the new leaders of the tribesmen of North Africa.

Bey-ag-Akhamouk clapped him on the shoulders, with both hands in an American gesture, usually not acceptable to a Surgu noble, but now, in the full glow of victory, received with a triumphant laugh.

Kenny Ballalou came up, dragging a .10 caliber Tommy-Noiseless by its sling and followed by a Teda tribesman with his flac rifle. He looked, and was, exhausted. He still wore bandages from the wounds he had taken at Fort Laperrine.

He said, in English, "What the hell happened?"

And Bey said, in Tamaheg, for the benefit of Guémama, "They attempted a final desperate charge in effort to break out. Guémama with his valiant warriors arrived at the last moment, and the cowardly Arab Union dogs broke and ran." Kenny had just passed through the portion of the wadi that had been cordoned off, so Bey added, "How many of them are left?"

"About two hundred unwounded and walking wounded," Kenny cleared his throat and looked at Bey. "The boys seem to be polishing off those hit so badly that they can't stand."

Bey turned to the Tuareg and said, "It was the wish of El Hassan to return to Tamanrasset with all the captured. See what you can do, O Mokkadam of men."

Without further words, Guémama was back onto his camel and off up the wadi.

Approaching them, his face wan and his once beautifully tailored uniform torn and disheveled, was Colonel Midran Ibrahim, his hands tied behind his back and escorted by two of the veiled camel corps men. Neither of the two Americans had ever seen the Egyptian officer before, but they recognized him through his insignia.

Without words, Bey went behind the other, reached out and drew the arm dagger from the sheath of one of the Tuaregs. The tribesman made no motion to resist the taking of his weapon, assuming that his commander was about to use it to the best advantage on the colonel.

However, Bey cut the rope binding the other and returned the knife to its owner.

He said gently, in Arabic "I was astonished, Colonel, not to see you in the advance of your men in the various attempts to break out of our ambuscade."

The colonel rubbed his wrists to restore circulation, and said contemptuously, "We are taught at the military institute that a commanding officer must not risk himself. His guidance of his men is more important than heroics. Would Napoleon or Wellington have exposed themselves at Waterloo?"

"It's been done," Kenny said mildly. "Our Stonewall Jackson died at Chancellorsville. Even Big Mouth Custer, didn't get back from the Little Big Horn."

Bey said, "We'll return to Tamanrasset immediately. Your wounded will be placed in the lorries and in and on the armored cars. Do you have any medics with you?"

The colonel was evidently taken aback. Like the tribesmen who had brought him up, he had expected immediate execution. He said, "We have one doctor, slightly wounded, and two of his nurse-assistants."

"Good," Bey said. "Dr. Smythe, of our Medical Corps, will be able to use their aid.'' He looked at Kenny Ballalou. ''How about rounding up the fastest of their trucks? We'll get going soonest. They ought to be faster than our hovercraft.''

''Right,'' Kenny said, and went on up the wadi.

Colonel Ibrahim said, not attempting to disguise his suprise, ''You do not mean to kill us?''

Bey laughed sourly. ''It will give us good marks in world opinion if we refrain from butchering our prisoners—in the manner that has been the wont of the Arab Union.''

The colonel, at least, had the decency to flush. He said, stiffly, ''In which vehicle will I ride?''

''You won't,'' Bey told him. ''You'll walk, with your men. The vehicles are needed to carry the wounded.''

Bey made a motion to a couple of the riflemen who had backed his flac rifle and the machine guns and instructed them to return the colonel to the column which was to take up the return march to Tamanrasset and Fort Laperrine.

Kenny came up in a hover jeep. Bey-ag-Akhamouk recognized it cynically as one of the Skoda models from Czechoslovakia in the Soviet Complex. In spite of supposed world detente, the great powers continued to supply the smaller with the tools to slaughter each other.

Kenny came to a halt next to him and said, ''This was as fast as anything they had and it leaves more room for the wounded than if we'd taken a truck. Those trucks are going to have to go slowly, or they'll bounce anybody inside with a bad hit to death.''

Bey could see the flac rifle the other had tucked into the back of the jeep. He lugged his own over and put it in too and then the remaining cannisters of clips.

Kenny Ballalou said, "Should we take Guémama along with us?"

And Bey said, "Hell, no. If we did, not a single Arab Union trooper would make it back to Tamanrasset. As it is, he wouldn't disobey an order of El Hassan under torture."

They started up, heading back down the wadi in the direction from which the Tuaghi camelmen had come only a short time ago.

Kenny said, "That's the most gruesome sight I've ever seen. There's more dead than alive in that wadi and more wounded than whole. How many did Guémama's men knock off when they came up?"

"So far as I know, none."

Kenny looked over at him from the side of his eyes, even as he wrestled the vehicle down the winding way. "Then why'd you give him all the credit, Bey?"

The other grunted and said, "Because he's the nephew of Melchizedek, the chief of the Kel Rela clan of the Kel Rela tribe. But that's not all. The Ahaggar Taureg consist of three tribes each headed by a warrior clan which gives its name to the tribe as a whole; the Kel Rela, the Tégéhé and the Taitog. The chief of the Kel Rela clan is also chief of the Kel Rela tribe and automatically paramount chief, or Amenokal, of the whole confederation. That's Melchizedek, and though he's supposedly fighting chief, he's too old to take the field. Guémama, who's the apple of his eye, is also his nephew and the son of his favorite sister. Descent among the Tuaghi is in the matriarchal line. Guémama will become Amenokal when the old boy dies. And *that's* not all, either. The kid's the most popular character going among the young Tuaghi. They'd follow him to hell and gone.—And he'd follow Homer the same way.''

Kenny Ballalou looked over at his companion. ''How in the hell do you know all this?''

Bey grunted in self-deprecation. ''I thought that you knew I was born a Tuareg. A missionary took me to the States when I was only three years old. However, I am a member of the Taitog tribe, which makes me a subject of the Amenokal, in spite of the fact that I hold a doctorate in Political Science from the University of Minnesota.''

Kenny took him in from the side of his eyes again. Bey-ag-Akhamouk was a handsome physical specimen in the Tuareg tradition. It was debated among anthropologists whether the Tuaghi were of Berber or Hamitic descent. In fact, the more far-out contended that they were descendents of Crusaders who had never made it home from the Holy Land. Be that as it may, he was tall, as the desert men went, wiry and strong, and his well featured face lighter in complexion than was usually found, even among the Tuaghi. Kenny wondered about that missionary. Was Bey his natural son?

VI

EL HASSAN

THEY HAD ONLY BEEN gone a few days in their pursuit of the retreating Arab Union forces and Bey-ag-Akhamouk and Kenny Ballalou were astonished at the changes that had taken place in so short a time. They had left at night, with all the debris of furious battle littering the area, in particular, between Tamanrasset proper and Fort Laperrine. El Hassan's Tuaghi and other tribesmen had attacked in force, while most of Colonel Ibrahim's armor and other mechanized equipment was plunging out into the erg and reg in an effort to seize the waterholes upon which El Hassan's people were dependent. The deciding factor was when the *heratin* sedentary workers and serfs, stirred up by infiltrated El Hassan propagandists, had erupted from the *souks* of Tamanrasset, armed largely with hoes, scythes, sickles, axes and other agricultural implements and stormed the fort. They had been cut down in swaths by the few machine guns the colonel had left to defend the area, but nothing could hold them.

The forces of El Hassan, those disciplined enough to take orders, were the only element that prevented a complete destruction of the overwhelmed Arab Union Legionaires.

But now, seemingly overnight, all bodies had been removed, and most signs of the recent combat were already erased, though large squads of native workers were everywhere, still patching, still rebuilding. Most of the material damage had been done on the outskirts of Tamanrasset, rather than on Fort Laperrine. The elements of the Arab Union left behind to hold the almost abandoned fort, had possessed a few motorized recoilless guns and had shelled the town, until overwhelmed. But even this damage was rapidly being repaired. The workers seemed in a holiday mood, despite the arduous labor to which they were subjecting themselves.

Kenny looked over at Bey, as they approached. He said, "Homer's pulled another rabbit out of the hat. How'n the hell did he ever get these people to work so hard? Traditionally, they're experts at goofing off."

"Search me," Bey said, looking around. "Possibly it's because it's the first time they've ever done something that would profit themselves. I don't see the tents. Where are Homer and the rest?"

A Tuareg warrior was passing. Bey called out to him in Tanaheq, asking the whereabouts of El Hassan and his viziers. The other answered and Bey looked back at Kenny. "They're inside the fort," he said.

They pulled through the main gate, which was in

the process of being repaired, and headed for the parade ground. Once Foreign Legionaires, Chasseurs d'Afrique, Spahis, and Tirailleurs d'Afrique had paraded here. Now it was as warm with Tuaghi, Teda, Ouled Tidrarin, Sudanese, Songhoi and even occasional Rifs from the far north, not to speak of representatives of various tribes that neither Kenny nor Bey recognized. All were armed, and armed with modern weapons of Soviet Complex design. On the face of it, El Hassan had taken little time to confiscate the captured modern equipment of the Arab Union and distribute it among his followers.

Bey asked questions again and they drove over to the former administration building of the fort and parked the hover jeep. There were quite a few other vehicles in the vicinity, ranging from additional jeeps, to heavy trucks and even several medium tanks. El Hassan had supplied his forces adequately with his military loot. Well, they both decided, inwardly, they'd need it.

They found Homer, Isobel and Cliff Jackson in the former officer's mess, all three looking as though they hadn't slept for as long as they could remember.

Homer Crawford and Cliff Jackson were dressed in military khakis, obviously liberated from the foe. Isobel wore a man's shirt of the same material and had evidently taken two pair of khaki shorts, ripped them up and reconstructed them into a culotte, a divided skirt. On her figure, it looked fine. She was a pretty wisp of a girl, somewhere in her mid-twenties and seemingly couldn't have been more out of place than in this Saharan background.

The three were seated at a long, heavy table, strewn with papers and dispatches and a battered typewriter which sat before Isobel. They looked up at the entrance of Bey and Kenny.

Homer ran a black hand back over his short wiry hair, in a gesture of weariness, and said, "I thought you two were pursuing that bastard Ibrahim." But he looked relieved to see them, as did the other two.

"Consider him pursued, man," Kenny said, slumping down onto a bench, and putting his Tommy-Noiseless on the table before him.

Bey said, "Guémama is escorting the survivors back."

"Guémama!" Cliff Jackson blurted. "With those fanatic camelmen of his? If any of the prisoners get back here, they'll be lucky." The big Californian former UCLA athlete was the least sophisticated of the El Hassan crew and had a tendency to gush.

Bey sighed and said, "I told them that El Hassan had sent word that he wanted to put the prisoners to the question and find out everything he could about what the Arab Union was up to. They can't wait to get back to watch the torture going on."

"Oh, great," Homer growled. "Now I'll have to talk them out of that little pleasure. How many prisoners are there?"

"Possibly two hundred, including the wounded," Kenny said.

Isobel winced. "No more than that?"

Bey looked over at her. "When they started from here, quite a few were wounded. There was insufficient room in their vehicles—those that they still had—for wounded, other than officers. They were carrying too much equipment. The others had to keep up as best they could. There was insufficient water, and in this part of the world, the sun we shall always have with us. We hung on their flanks and knocked off the stragglers, and sniped at the main column. Short of the Khyber Pass, this is possibly the best area in the world for guerrilla fighting. From time to time, they'd flip their lids and send the armored cars— they had two of them—or their jeeps to flush us out. The only casualties we took were probably tribesmen who laughed themselves to death. Finally, they gave those tactics up and put the armored cars to each flank and the jeeps to the front and rear to cover those on foot. Damn little good it did them. We continued to pick them off, one by one, or to overrun stragglers, two or three or so at a time."

Bey took a deep breath. "It was pretty bad. The tribesmen had the time of their lives. It got a little sickening to Kenny and me."

Homer said, understanding in his voice, "What finally happened, Bey?"

"Their officers seemingly went completely around the bend. They took to one of the larger wadis, probably figuring that they could make better time. We ambushed them. At first they wouldn't surrender, probably figuring on being butchered. When Guémama and his boys came up, slavering at the mouth, they panicked completely and it was all over."

Homer Crawford said, "How did Guémama work out?"

"Fine. He controls his men like a top sergeant."

Kenny said, "What in the hell are you three doing in Western dress? What're the Tuaghi going to say when they see you without a teguelmoust? With your faces, ah, obscenely revealed?"

Both Bey and Kenny still wore the complete Tuaghi attire, as had all of them, even Isobel, up until the present.

Homer shook his head and said, "This camp now represents a score of different tribes, some of which I've never even heard of. Some of them are blood-foes of the Tuaghi, or have been until the advent of El Hassan's unifying movement. We can't afford to present ourselves as favoring one element. From now on, *all* of El Hassan's immediate staff will wear desert khakis and so will all of our armed forces, Tuaghi and otherwise. If any potential trooper doesn't like the idea, he won't be accepted into our service. We've got to break down these age-old traditions. Some of them are crazy. Wearing black wool burnouses, for instance, in this climate. Or Moroccan babouche slippers. They have no back to them. You walk by kind of shuffling forward. If you try to walk backward, the slippers fall off your feet. Or can you imagine trying to run at any speed in them? Or take the *haik* as worn in Morocco and Algeria. It so covers the woman's head that she can't hear well and only one eye is exposed. Can you imagine walking through modern traffic in a city in this outfit? They get hit like ten pins.''

Homer Crawford was bitterly definite. "No, the traditional clothes of the North African have to go!"

"Where'd you get your outfits?" Kenny said, unimpressed by this harangue.

"We liberated them from the Arab Union soldiers," Cliff told him. "Except for those *kaffiyeh* headdresses of theirs, they wear the same clothes the British did when they were fighting Rommel or, for that matter, the same as the Israelis wear."

"Well, you're not going to outfit all of our armed forces with what you swiped from Colonel Ibrahim's men."

Homer laughed. "We've placed a sizeable order in Dakar by radio, along with other immediate necessities."

He picked up a small brass bell from before him and rang it. A tribesman, garbed self-consciously in desert khakis, the same as those of Homer and Cliff, entered and came to attention, rather sloppily, but at least he made the attempt.

Homer said, "Locate my viziers, James ben Peters and Doctor Smythe and the *juju* man, Dolo Anah, and request their presence."

The guard left.

Both Bey and Kenny were ogling Homer. "What in the hell do you mean, you ordered them from Dakar?" Kenny demanded. "With *what?* We haven't enough money between us to play a slot machine."

Homer laughed and said, "Ask our Vizier of the Treasury," and looked over at Cliff Jackson.

Jackson was a big man, even larger than Homer Crawford. Blacker than most American Negroes, he bore himself with the lithe grace of a giant cat. Under Homer's orders, the Californian, whenever occasion allowed, stripped himself to the waist and wandered around the encampment bare-chested. The Tuareg, beautiful physical specimens in their own right, admired masculine strength. Their eyes followed this companion of El Hassan everywhere.

Cliff shook his head and said, "It's the damnedest thing you ever saw. Since you two left, pounding after old Ibrahim, a dozen or more delegations have come from Common Europe, India, the United States of the Americas, and, for Christ's sake, even South Africa. Half a dozen of them are trying to lay money onto us."

Bey and Kenny were bug-eyeing him. "Money? What in the hell for?" Bey said.

"Well, for instance, the Swedes. They're the only ones I've accepted anything from, so far. They laid ten million gold Kronen on us in advance payment for bauxite. They don't have any bauxite of their own and they've got a king-size aluminum industry. They want in on the ground floor."

"*What* ground floor?" Kenny demanded, unbelievingly.

"Well, it seems that Rio de Oro is ass-deep in bauxite, probably the biggest undeveloped fields in the world."

"Where in the devil's Rio de Oro?" Bey said.

Jimmy Peters had just entered. Originally from Trinidad, he was smaller than the American men and chunky of build. He wore old-fashioned spectacles and had an air of education and cultivation. Until he had joined El Hassan he had been with the African Department of the British Commonwealth. On his face could still be seen the lines brought on by the death of his brother, Jack, who had been as close to him as a twin. He was dressed in the new khaki uniform of the El Hassan forces.

Jimmy Peters was known for his all but photographic memory and said now, "The former Spanish Sahara was divided into two provinces, Rio de Oro, about 70,000 square miles, and Sekia el-Hamra, some 32,000 square miles. Population has been estimated everywhere from 27,000 nomads to 45,000, though I'll be damned if I know how anybody could ever have counted them. The country's fantastically rich in phosphates and particularly bauxite, possibly the richest deposits known. Morocco to the north, Algeria to the east, and Mauretania to the south, have all claimed the country since the Spanish pulled out. They never have made a permanent settlement, the area's up for grabs."

Isobel said, "What would we need with an encyclopedia, with Jimmy around?"

Had Jimmy Peters been lighter in complexion, he would have flushed, but he grinned his shy grin at her. They were all in love with Isobel Cunningham.

"But what of it?" Bey demanded. "We haven't taken this Rio de Oro, at least as yet. So far as I know, we have no elements of our people in that area at all. Mauretania, yes, but not the former Spanish Sahara."

Cliff said with a short laugh and a shake of the head, "Evidently, the Swedes are willing to wait. They want that bauxite so bad they can taste it."

Homer said, "We're being picky and choosey about whom we make deals with. We're not out for the quick buck, we're looking forward to the development of North Africa, for the benefit of the North Africans, not a bunch of multinational corporations."

Rex Donaldson and Doctor Warren Harding Smythe entered. The heavy-set, gray haired doctor, whose feisty energy belied his weight, was, as usual, sputtering. "What . . . What!" he demanded. "Why am I torn away from my patients? I have enough work on my hands for a dozen doctors, a double score of nurses and . . ."

Bey said, "An Arab Union doctor should be here by tomorrow, Doctor Smythe, and two trained medicos with him."

And Isobel said, "And we have also picked up radio signals that several of the other American Medical Relief teams are coming in, to ask questions about their continued operations in the areas where El Hassan's followers have taken over. Surely, they'll pitch in locally, while the emergency continues."

Rex Donaldson, formerly of Nassau in the British Bahamas, formerly of the College of Anthropology, Oxford, formerly field man for the African Department of the British Commonwealth, was a small, bent man who usually operated in the Dogon country to the south, breaking down tribal barriers, prejudices against the new schools, and the ritual-taboos traditions of the area in general, was now on El Hassan's immediate staff.

He looked at Bey and Kenny and said, "Hello, chaps. How did you make out with our chum, the colonel?"

"A bit bloodily," Kenny said. "But he and the remains of his forces are coming in."

Homer said, "Will everybody be seated about this table here? The cabinet of El Hassan is in session, or should we call it a *djemaa el kebar,* in the Arabic fashion?"

The others all moved up to places at the table, save the doctor, who stood glaring.

"*Mr.* Crawford," he sputtered. "By no stretch of imagination can I be considered one of your cabinet. I have informed you, long since, that I am opposed to what you are trying to do. You are attempting to force these people into the 21st Century, overnight. They are not capable of assimilating such changes. I fear for their mental health under the pressures of what has been called Future Shock. I and the other teams of the American Medical Relief are here to fight disease, to build clinics and hospitals, and, above all, medical schools—not to change institutions that are not ready for change."

Homer Crawford looked at him in exasperation and said, "Doctor, you contradict yourself. You wish to build medical schools, but who will be your students in them? Bedouins who cannot read or write? You speak of clinics. Very well, your American Medical Relief teams—and we admire their work—number a score or two in an area

72

bigger than the United States. Your funds are far from unlimited and I understand that large elements in the American Congress, calling for financial retrenchments, wish to cut your appropriation down to a point that would make it meaningless. Then who will maintain these clinics and hospitals? Who will buy the medicines necessary to treat everything from endemic syphilis to ophthalmia, the eye disease almost universal among nomad children?"

Doctor Smythe stared at him in frustration.

Homer said, "I propose to name you Vizier of Health. Immediately, a university will be begun here in Tamanrasset. There will be a College of African Medicine. The instructors will be largely American blacks but we will also draw upon medically educated blacks from the former British and French colonies."

"And who will finance this mad dream?"

Homer Crawford nodded in acceptance of the validity of that question and said, "We have recently received word that the Africa for Africans Association, to which Miss Cunningham and Mr. Jackson belonged, has been swung over to our support in New York, through the efforts of our Foreign Minister, Jake Armstrong. A million dollars has already been raised. Jake is placing ads in American Negro magazines and other publications, for American black doctors to come to Africa both as teachers and practitioners in the field. No matter what your feelings, Doctor, and we respect them, the cause of better health in North Africa will be better served if you take your position not as a simple general practitioner, but as the head of all medicine in the rapidly expanding domains of El Hassan.''

As he was speaking, a power reached out from the former sociologist, a psychic power, which he was unaware he wielded, but which was well known to all his immediate colleagues. His personality had suddenly dominated the room.

Such must have been the power once held by Joshua of Nazareth, by Mohammed, and, for the sake of evil, Hitler. Such must have been the power of personality of the young Alexander when he stood, surrounded by Parmenion, Ptolemy, Antepater and the others of the Companions, with the thirty thousand spearmen of the phalanx arrayed behind them, on the west bank of the Hellespont and looked over at the far shore of Asia Minor with Persia and India beyond. What must he have said in Greek? The equivalent of, "All right, boys. Forward. We'll give them a bit of a show.''

Shaken by the raw psychic power, Doctor Warren Harding Smythe sank to the bench directly across from Homer Crawford. He got out, still attempting to maintain his rejection, "And from where would the resources come to sponsor all this?''

Homer said, "Doctor, North Africa is possibly the richest area in the world so far as undeveloped raw materials are concerned, including oil. We intend to exploit them. And for the sake of North Africa, not the so-called developed nations.''

The doctor, in a last resistance, said, trying to surface a sneer, "And how do I know that you will not use the proceeds of this abundance of raw materials for your own sakes?''

The others about the table laughed bitterly, or smiled sour smiles.

Homer said, "Doctor Smythe, the true revolutionist is an idealist, not an opportunist. Can you imagine a Jefferson, a Tom Paine, a James Madison, a Washington, being seduced by bribes or feathering their own nests through their eventual positions of power? Or Robespierre, Danton and Marat? They had greater things in mind than wealth. Or even Lenin and Trotsky. Those who came after, in Russia, yes. Those who hadn't spent the long years in exile or prison as a result of their fight for the revolution which later came a cropper. But you couldn't have bought Lenin with all the gold in Fort Knox."

Homer Crawford shook his head. "No, Doctor. Do not look at the immediate staff of El Hassan if you are seeking out opportunists."

It was getting a little heavy for Cliff Jackson. He said, "Hey, speak for yourself, Homer. If somebody offered *me* all the gold in Fort Knox . . ."

"Shut up," Kenny growled at him.

Jimmy Peters pushed his glasses back on his nose and said, "That reminds me of something. Bribes. These American types, in particular, seem to be all intrigued with bribes. And the Italians too, for that matter. At any rate, I've been offered bribes three times."

Homer scowled at him. "For what, in particular?"

The other shrugged in puzzlement. "I never quite figured it out. I came to the conclusion that they were just lining me up for future reference."

Kenny said, "Take 'em."

All eyes went to him.

He said, as though nothing was more reasonable, "Take all bribes offered. Except for Homer, of course; he can't do it. Otherwise we take 'em and throw them in the kitty. We can use the money."

Isobel was amused but she said, "What happens when the time comes that they expect you to deliver—whatever it might be they want?"

"The hell with them," Kenny said, reasonably still. "Let 'em go whistle. Nobody asked them to bribe El Hassan's closest colleagues."

VII

EL HASSAN

HOMER LOOKED AROUND at them and said, "Very well, here we are. El Hassan's Cabinet." He looked at Smythe. "You're our Vizier of Health."

The doctor closed his eyes momentarily, but didn't protest.

Homer looked at Bey. "Field Marshal Bey-ag-Akhamouk, you're our Vizier of Defense."

Bey nodded.

Homer Crawford looked at Cliff Jackson. "And you're already our Vizier of the Treasury, who promises not to sell out for anything short of the contents of Fort Knox. Which reminds me. Does it still have any contents?"

Nobody bothered to answer.

He said, "Old Jake Armstrong, over in New York, is our Foreign Minister, and Vizier of State." He thought about it a moment and mused, "I wonder if they've let him in the front door of the Reunited Nations building as yet."

He looked at Jimmy Peters, who blinked back owlishly at him. "What are you?"

Jimmy said, "Well, I used to be a teacher when I first got out of college." He cleared his throat and added, "3rd Grade, grammar school."

Homer said, "Right. Vizier of Education. It's going to be an important post under El Hassan." He turned his eyes to Kenny Ballalou.

Kenny said, pretending an air of wistfulness, "When I was a kid, I always wanted to be an FBI man."

Homer said, "Okay. you're our Vizier of Security, combination of FBI, CIA and neighborhood cop on the beat."

It was Isobel's turn. Homer looked at her thoughtfully. "Didn't you used to work on a newspaper?"

"I was editor of the college paper at Columbia."

"All right, you're our Vizier of Information. Since Dave Moroka was killed in storming the fort, we need somebody to handle the press releases. And in view of the fact that you're our best typist, you're also my personal secretary."

"To hear is to obey, O El Hassan," she said, wrinkling her nose at him

Homer's eyes went to Rex Donaldson, who promptly looked defiance. "You chaps can go to hell," he said. "It's donkey's years since I've sat behind a desk and I'm out of the habit. You make me a Minister Without Portfolio or something, in charge of coordination, or something."

Homer thought about it. He said, "I think you're right. We'll need a man continually in the field, going around to developing trouble spots. With a minister's rank, you'd have clout. Besides, it wouldn't do for we more necessary types, here at home base, to get shot in the ass."

"Gentlemen, gentlemen, if such you are," Isobel protested. "Your language. My blessed old mother once wanted me to take Holy Orders and become a nun."

Doctor Smythe could stand it no longer. He sputtered, "Do you mean to tell me that this is the manner in which governments are formed?"

Most of the men around the table looked embarassed in varying degrees. Homer had just given the doctor a rather elevated pep talk a few minutes before.

But Isobel said, "How did you think they were formed, Doctor? By elections? In the United States some ninety-five percent of the people who work in government are appointive, from the Supreme Court, and the President's Cabinet and aides, right on down to the stenographer who types out your application for unemployment insurance."

Doctor Smythe, irritated, came to his feet and said, "I doubt if my presence is needed and I am desperately in demand at the improvised hospital. I shall consult with you further as to my duties . . . El Hassan."

"Thank you, Doctor," Homer bowed his head respectfully.

When the older man was gone, Homer Crawford looked around at them again. "Okay, first item on the agenda. What's the name of our new country?"

Everybody scowled.

Kenny said, "Well, what about the North African Confederation, or, maybe, the Union of North Africa?"

"That last one sounds too much like the Union of *South* Africa, heaven forbid," Rex Donaldson said.

Jimmy Peters said, "Ifriqiyah."

They all looked at him.

He was embarassed, adjusted his glasses on his nose and said, "It's the name the Romans used for North Africa. Later the Arabs borrowed it."

"Great," Homer said. "Let's put it to the vote."

All were in favor.

Homer Crawford turned to Isobel. "Put it on all of our stationery."

"What stationery?"

"We've got to have stationery," he said reasonably. "Isn't there a printing shop in Tamanrasset, left over from when the French were here? The town's big enough to support one."

Isobel sighed in resignation. "I'll look into it."

Homer looked around and said, "What's next?"

Bey, the practical, when it came to matters military, said, "How many prisoners do we have on hand?"

Homer said, "Counting the two hundred you've captured, about a thousand."

Bey stared at him. "A thousand! Out of the whole regiment and all the auxiliaries Ibriham brought down with him? That's all that's left?"

Homer shook his head. "The rest have defected to El Hassan."

And Bey said indignantly, "Well, let 'em defect back again. Who in the hell wants a few thousand Arab Union legionaires behind their back? What would we do with them?"

But El Hassan was still shaking his head. "It's

one of the best propaganda bits that have dropped into our laps. How will it look in the world press when the word goes out that thousands of Arab Union troopers have gone over to us? We'll do the same with them as the Romans used to do. If a bunch of German mercenaries came over to them, they shipped them down as garrison troops in Egypt. If a few thousand Syrians offerd their services, they sent them to Spain, and so on. That's what we'll do. We'll send elements of these Arab Union soldiers down south, to Chad, Senegal, Nigeria, or wherever, under Ifriqiyah officers, of course, and garrison them down there.''

Bey said, ''How about the other thousand who didn't defect? We haven't the food and water for them to keep them indefinitely in a prison camp. For that matter, we haven't enough food and water for our own men. We're up to our eyebrows in warriors from all over half North Africa, I mean Ifriqiyah.''

Homer said, ''I'd say, subject to vote, of course, to send them back on foot to the Arab Union accompanied by enough trucks and ambulances to carry supplies, water, and their wounded. We'll accompany them as far as, say, Ghadames, and let the Arab Union take over from there.''

Kenny grumbled, ''And give them the chance to come back and fight us again, some day?''

It was the wiry Rex Donaldson who laughed at that. ''Those poor blokes, after the fight they've had and after trekking half a thousand miles across the ergs on foot, couldn't be talked into coming down here again by the silver-tongued Demosthenes.''

Isobel said slowly, thoughtfully, "Besides, they'll spread around to their villages, their towns and cities and the word will go out that far from being massacred by El Hassan, as they deserved, they were treated for their wounds, and sent home with ample food and water. Someday, sooner or later, we're going to have to take *all* of North Africa, including those areas now in control of the Arab Union. It won't hurt for the people to know that they have nothing to fear from El Hassan, that he comes to liberate, not suppress."

That decision passed. They sat back and thought some more.

Homer said finally, "We're going to have to issue an Ifriqiyah Monroe Doctrine. No North African borders are to be altered through foreign intervention. No foreign military units are to be allowed in North Africa."

Cliff took him in skepticaly and said, "But we're the ones who are changing the borders. Hell, we're assimilating whole former countries. Chad just came over, lock stock and barrel."

Bey was surprised. "When?"

"Just this morning. The military dictatorship in the capital N'Djamena, they used to call it Fort Lamey, was overthrown bloodlessly." Cliff shrugged his huge shoulders. "And the mobs opted for El Hassan."

Kenny said, "That's going to be a problem. Half the nomads down there are starving to death. As soon as we can, we're going to have to spend some of this mineral wealth money we're being begged to accept, on trucking in massive relief to the area."

"That'll come," Homer agreed. "This Ifriqiyah Monroe Doctrine thing. It'll apply to *foreign* non-North African, powers. Not to us. It was the same with the American Monroe Doctrine. It didn't apply to the United States. It sent its troops in whenever it wanted. When Napoleon the Third sent French forces into Mexico to support the French puppet Emperor Maximilian, the Americans were embroiled in the Civil War. But as soon as it was over, the United States turned a baleful eye on old Napoleon and he got out in a hurry, leaving Maximilian in a lurch. But we Americans invaded Mexico and interfered with her internal affairs so often you'd think there was a revolving door on the border. We took the best territories they had, including Texas and California. The same with Cuba. We kept our troops there until everything on the island worth owning belonged to American corporations and the following governments, even after the troops left, were kept under our thumb, until Castro, that big villain, came along. Or look at Panama. It used to be part of Colombia, but when Colombia balked at some of the arrangements for a canal, the first Roosevelt backed a revolution in Panama and the Colombians were forced to cede the area. Then there were countries such as Nicaragua, Haiti, Guatemala, the Dominican Republic. Joining the American Marines was like getting a conducted tour of Latin America."

"All right, all right," Cliff said. "I'm in favor. An Ifriqiyah Monroe Doctrine. We take umbrage at any foreign troops in North Africa and any attempts to change any borders—except when we do it.''

The motion was carried.

They hadn't worked out a constitution, as yet, but automatically they had fallen into a system where all votes were of equal value, including that of El Hassan himself.

Bey said then, ''We've still got the problem of all these followers of El Hassan. We haven't the resources to keep them in arms. Besides, they're needed at home to take care of the flocks and to farm the oases, keep their embryo industries going, and, above all, to work in the new mines, on the irrigation projects, the dams and all the rest of the new developments. Besides that, with so many of them away, who knows what kind of banditry is going on back on their home territories?''

Homer considered it.

He turned finally to Isobel and said, ''Take some notes on instructions to Guémama upon his return. He is to carefully select one thousand of the best warriors of all now gathered, who will serve as El Hassan's elite corps. They must be of the type who are cool in combat and don't froth at the mouth. They are to be of the type who can take orders and obey their officers. Preferably they are to be veterans who have possibly served in the past under the French, British or Spanish and hence know the workings of modern weapons. Especially to be located are those who can drive and repair vehicles. He is to seek these out and, with the assistance of those among them who were formerly non-coms in the foreign armies, begin their training, until the return of El Hassan and Bey-ag-

Akhamouk, his Vizier of Defense.''

Isobel shot a quick look at him, but continued with her notes.

Homer went on, ''Also he is to recruit *goums,* camel patrols, of twenty men each. And each of these are to be led by a responsible *mokkadam,* undivided in his allegiance to El Hassan and Ifriqiyah. These small harkas will be mounted upon *hejin* racing camels and will be the equivalent of the former *Méharistes,* the Desert Camel Corps of the Roumi. They shall patrol all the domains of El Hassan and protect the land from those who would raid, especially those who would attack the new irrigation works, the afforestation projects and so forth which El Hassan sponsors.''

He thought for a moment, then added, ''Most likely, these *goums* will consist largely of the Tuaghi, since they know best the Sahara, but other capable warriors will not be excluded.'' He paused again, before finishing up. ''All others, after these have been selected, will return to their homes, until summoned again by El Hassan and they will carry the message of El Hassan wherever they go, to their own people, and all others.''

Bey scowled and said, ''What the hell's all this about?''

Homer turned his eyes to his military head. ''Isn't it obvious? We need an elite corps here in Tamanrasset for major developments, but we also need a desert camel corps to protect outlying installations. The *goums* won't be able to defend against major attacks but their very presence will be a warning. They are representatives of El Hassan. They will be issued ample funds and any who loot, or molest women, will answer first to his *mokkadam,* his headman, second he will answer to Guémama, and finally to El Hassan himself. Frankly, Bey, I'm worried about such projects as that of Ralph Sandel's Sahara afforestation deal at Bidon Cing, there on the Tanezrouft crossing of the desert. Our enemies are going to want to knock out every Reunited Nations project underway. Such destruction will undermine El Hassan, possibly even be blamed on him. We've got to protect every effort now being made by American and other educated blacks to develop the country.''

Isobel was looking at him strangely. She said, ''You mentioned back there, that Guémama was to take over the initial training of our new forces, until the return of you and Bey. Where do you expect to be, Homer?''

He sucked in air before reaching down into a briefcase which leaned up against the chair in which he sat. He came up with a small box, opened it and brought forth something wrapped in tissue paper. He unwrapped the paper and stared down at the gruesome contents, as did the others. Isobel turned her head in feminine rejection. It was a severed finger and on it a gold college class ring, which most of those present recognized.

Homer said emptily. ''When we first decided to attempt to take Tamanrasset, Bey was sent down into Teda country to raise a column; Kenny was sent into Nemadi, since he was the only one of us who spoke the dialect of Hassania. Elmer was sent up into Chaambra country for the same purpose, though there El Hassan has thus far met the strongest opposition. Isobel, Cliff and I took on the recruiting of the Tuaghi.''

He pointed at the severed finger. ''I received that the same night that we completed the storming of the fort. It came from Abd-el-Kader, an old foe, and leader of the Ouled Touameur clan of the prestigious Ouled Allouch tribe of the Berazga division of the Chaambra nomad confederation. Obviously, Elmer Allen has been captured. Whether or not he is still alive, we can't know. However, it's most likely that he still is. He is of more value to Abd-el-Kader alive than dead. Being able to display as a prisoner, probably in chains, one of the closest followers of El Hassan is an emblem in his turban. Since then, there have been new developments.'' He turned to his Vizier of Education. ''Jimmy, give us the word on the Mahdi.''

Jimmy Peters thought for a moment, then began slowly, ''It's a Moslem religious tradition something like that of the coming of the Messiah in the Jewish faith. Supposedly, Mohammed declared that one of his descendants would come and fill the earth with equity and justice and would bear the name of al-mahdi. Some Moslems claim that he has already appeared, in the same manner that the Christians claim that Jesus was the Hebrew messiah, while the Jews deny it. Over the centuries, various leaders have appeared on the Islam scene and claimed to be the mahdi. The most recent, Mohammed Ahmes, a Sudanese, in a period of less than two years, conquered an empire larger than Texas, Alaska and New Mexico combined. It was his forces who defeated the British-Egyptian army of 'Chinese' Gordon and captured Khartoum. It was several years after his death that the British finally defeated his followers."

Kenny said impatiently, "What the hell's all this got to do with it? What's it got to do with the pickle Elmer's in?"

Homer Crawford looked over at him. "Abd-el-Kader has proclaimed himself the mahdi and calls for a *jedah*, holy war, against El Hassan. If he's allowed to continue, half the marabouts in the Moslem countries bordering the Mediterranean will rally to him. They know goddamned well that El Hassan's movement will ultimately be their kiss of death. They live in the Middle Ages. Everything that needs to be known is in the Q'ran, no other books are needed."

Bey had been thinking about it. He said musingly, "We've got to strike fast, before this spreads. He's got to be squashed before he rallies too many followers. We already know his message. He's in favor of returning to the good old days. The days of the *razzia*, the days of looting the sedentary centers, the oases. The days when the Chaambra nomads controlled most of northwest Africa."

Homer said, "What did you have in mind, Bey?"

"Strike fast. We'll send a flying column up into Chaambra country. A thousand of our best men. We'll hit him before he can get organized."

Homer grunted sour humor of rejection. "Some field marshal you turned out to be. Where's your sense of logistics, Bey? We'll push a thousand men, with their equipment across the desert? *How?* We haven't got enough motorized transport, to begin with, and even if we had, there is no direct route from Tamanrasset to northwestern Algeria and Chaambra country.''

Bey scowled, almost sulkily. His opinions were almost invariably taken when it came to matters military.

Homer went on. ''Suppose the Arab Union supports Abd-el-Kader and sends out a couple of bombers, surreptitiously, and they spot us on the reg, on the roads where our motorized transport, those that aren't hover vehicles, must travel. One small fission bomb would finish off the whole so-called flying column. And they could debate in the Reunited Nations forever, and who could prove who dropped an illegal fission bomb in the wastes of the Sahara?''

Bey said grudgingly, ''I suppose you're right, Homer. But what *can* we do?''

Homer said, ''This is a personal thing. Two old foes, Homer Crawford and Abd-el-Kader. Crawford and his team will go alone, in the same hovercraft they formerly utilized when operating for the Reunited Nations African Development Project. It's built to cross the ergs. We can go directly and comparatively speedily, to the rescue of our colleague. It'll be dramatic and there's nothing that appeals to the nomad more. In one blow, we'll end the mahdi movement and recruit thousands in the doing.''

Kenny Ballalou closed his eyes in pain. ''Man, you've *really* gone round the bend.'' He added, as an afterthought. ''Who all will go along?''

Homer said, ''This is a volunteer thing. I'd like to see you, Bey, you Kenny, and Cliff. Cliff wasn't a member of the original team, but . . . ''

Cliff groaned and said, "I spent a hitch in the army. The one thing the old timers drilled into us was . . ."

"We know, we know," Kenny said. "Never volunteer for anything."

Bey came to his feet and said, "I'll start equipping the hovercraft. Anything special, Homer?"

Homer said, "Power packs sufficient to fuel us all the way to Chaambra country. We'll head from here to In Salah, and from there to Adrar and then up to Beni-Abbes. But we'll circle them all. We won't stop for provisions, power packs or anything else. We don't want any news of our coming to get through."

Kenny got up and stretched and said, "I'll have to make my farewells to a lttle ol' chick from the Tégéhe Mellet tribe. She's crazy for me."

"Ha," Cliff said, standing as well. "She must be crazy. I'll get my gear. But I don't see how this government is going to go on without a Vizier of Finance around."

When the three had left, Homer said, "That reminds me. Jimmy, Isobel, while I'm gone you two are going to be in charge. The story is that El Hassan and his viziers are in seclusion, meditating, working out the problems facing Ifriqiyah. Give the same story to the various delegations that are turning up from the so-called civilized world, and the journalists."

Jimmy Peters winced. "Suppose somebody invades us, or something?"

"Repulse them," Homer said, grinning.

Jimmy threw up his hands in disgust and said, "I'm going to see about the damned stationery. I have a sneaking suspicion that the El Hassan government, without El Hassan, is going to be doing a lot of paperwork."

He went on out and Isobel and Homer were alone. They had both come to their feet as the others left.

Isobel came up to him and put both of her hands on his shoulders and looked full into his eyes. She raised herself on tiptoes and put her mouth to his.

Afterwards, she said, "Homer. Come back, darling."

He smiled at her ruefully. There had been no time in their relationship for the potential romance between them, though both were aware of its existence.

He said, "After that, how could I do otherwise?" He kissed her again. "I'll be back, Isobel."

VIII

SEAN RYAN

SEAN RYAN, MEGAN MCDAID and Bryan O'Casey were killing time sightseeing in Algiers. Sean Ryan had stopped in the Algerian capital for a couple of hours once, on his way to Port Said and a Middle-East job, but had spent the time in a harbor bar. Megan had never been in Africa before at all. But Bryan O'Casey knew the town fairly well.

O'Casey said, "Let's see what I know about Algiers. Not much. The Arabs used to call it Al-Djezaor, a description of all those little islands that cluster in the harbor. It was the Turks that linked them to the mainland with a long dyke, which they later fortified. When the French took over, they couldn't pronounce it so they changed it to Algiers. Damned if I know how old the town is. Probably Hannibal, in his day, trudged up the staired streets to Charthaginian *boites de nuit*. By the looks of some of the dogs still plying their trade in them, they might have been the same ones that took him on."

"Why, Bryan," Meg said. "How would *you* know what the local prostitutes look like?"

He made with an exaggerated leer.

Sean Ryan looked at his watch, as they began to ascend into the Kasbah. "We've got about an hour or so."

They were passing a tourist restaurant, overly done in its efforts to project a native atmosphere, without driving away squeamish foreigners nervous about sanitation.

Meg said, "I do wish that we had the time to have lunch. I've already read so much about *couscous* and *meshwe*."

They were all dressed tourist-wise, complete to the two men having cameras slung around their necks. Meg wore a tweed walking skirt and very sensible, thick-soled shoes.

Bryan O'Casey said grimly, "We can get European food back at the hotel, French at that. You'll have all the couscous you'll want and more down in the interior. Complete with well-aged mutton, complete with rancid camel butter. And don't ask me why it has to be rancid. They like it that way. They place it between the camel and the saddle and pack it along until it gets good and rancid."

He made a sweeping gesture with his hand as they ascended the stepped wide street, the only wide street in the Kasbah area, as they were to find. He said, "This is the famous Kasbah. Every old North African city has a Kasbah, but this is the famous one. The Berbers and the Arabs after them used to build their towns on hills like this for defensive purposes. Now it's the slums of the city, populated with Moors, Arabs, Turks, bastard

Koolooies, blacks, people from all the races of Africa, the Middle East and the Mediterranean. Just smell it. Once in awhile you'll get a whiff of the scent of myrtle and jasmine from some rich man's garden, just enough to keep you from passing out. Talk about pollution.''

Sean Ryan said, ''This looks like tourist row, with all these souvenir stands. Let's get off onto some of these narrow side-streets.''

Narrow was the word for it. Often as narrow as corridors, they were shadowy with houses tottering toward each other, often supported by struts. Periodically, they'd have a quick glimpse, when somebody was passing through a door, of narrow-columned patios and of gardens and even fountains, the homes of the wealthier Moslems who chose to live here with their fellow followers of the Prophet, rather than in the modern European section. Grated windows of these establishments permitted outward vision from the interior but limited seeing into the houses from the street. The pedestrians teemed. Women, veiled in white, usually looking enormous, yet light-footed in their balloonlike trousers, men in jeballahs or bournouses, beggars as filthy as only beggars in a North African town can be, multitudes of playing, screaming children, also instantly convertible into beggars. Small girls with henna-reddened fingernails and in pigtails ran about. The open air meat and other food shops, their goods covered with plenty of flies, threw out unpleasant odors.

Bryan said to Meg McDaid, ''Are you sure you'd like to eat in one of the native restaurants?''

''No.''

The two men chuckled.

As they passed what was obviously a bar, Bryan said, "Like a drink? They've got a native *raki*—I think they make it from dates—which tastes worse than Irish poteen."

Sean laughed glumly and said, "Beggin' your pardon, but nothing tastes worse than poteen, man dear. Besides, I'm on nothing stronger than beer, until this job is over."

As they sauntered along, Bryan said, "As I recall, they've got a beer here called Stork. They sell it all over North Africa. There must be a half dozen breweries in different countries."

Sean said, disinterestedly, "What does it taste like?"

The other laughed. "Beggin' Meg's pardon, it tastes like piss."

And Meg said mocking, "Why Bryan, how would you know?"

That was the second time she had pulled that one, so Bryan looked at her and said, "Once when I was operating down in Somalia, the small detachment I was with was overrun by the Ethiopians. We went on the run, with them after us. One doesn't surrender to the Ethiopians. In fact, off hand, I can't think of any natives, here in Africa, you surrender to. And damned few white men, unless they're fellow mercenaries, in which case you'll probably run into some old chums—and might even switch sides, if your adherence to the mercenary's code is a bit shaky. At any rate, they were after us. The Sahara is as bad in Somalia as it is to the south of here. In three days we were completely out of water. Most of our camels had died, but we had three left.''

Sean knew what was coming and inwardly he was amused but he said nothing.

Meg was staring in fascination at her lover.

He went on. ''Possibly, it's a fact known not even to the average M.D., Meg, mavourneen, but if you put sugar in urine, either animal or human, it will support life for a time, prevent dehydration.''

Meg closed her eyes in distaste and feminine rejection.

Bryan said with mock cheerfulness, ''So I say that Stork beer tastes like piss, and I stand by my statement.''

Sean said, looking at his watch again, ''I think we'd better get back for this talk with Saidi, without any alcohol at all, either on our breaths . . . or minds.''

Bryan shot a quizzical look at him. ''You don't trust this Levantine friend of yours?''

Sean growled, ''Have you ever met anybody who was after trustin' a Levantine?''

The narrow winding streets had become a maze, equal to that of the famed labyrinth of the palace of Minos of antiquity.

Meg said, ''Bryan, and how in the name of the Holy Mother are we ever going to find our way out of here?''

Bryan laughed. ''You can't get lost in the Kasbah. All you have to do is head down hill. Every time you come to a turning, or a corner, you take the down route. You wind up at the bottom in the so-called European section of town—now largely taken over by the better-off Algerians who got their fingers in the expropriation pie when the French pulled out.''

They passed ten or fifteen donkeys laden down with fire wood. Not even a jeep could have gotten through these streets.

Meg said, "Has it changed any since you were here last, Bryan?"

He snorted and in a take-off of the Irish brogue said, ''Shure, Colleen, and it's been twenty years since oiv been here. But it hasn't changed a mite. And I'm after suspectin' that it hasn't changed in the past thousand.''

Meg nodded, dodging a prehistoric beggar who looked as though he had, at least, leprosy. She said, "I saw one of those movie film revivals the other day. It was about the Kasbah. Charles Boyer played Pepe Le Moko, or whatever his name was, and Hedy LaMarr was the girl. And, you know, it looked exactly the way it does now.''

They wound their way down hill and, as Bryan had prophesied, emerged into a modern section of the North African city.

It was too far to walk, so they took a hovercab to the heights of Mustapha Supérieure and to the once deluxe St. Georges hotel, at 24 Avenue Foureau Lamy. These days, there were better hotels in town, but Saul Saidi had suggested this one for the officers of his expedition, his 'commando' raid.

Sean, Bryan and Meg had gotten together only a short time before.

The same day Saul Saidi had met him at the

Pearl Bar in Dublin, Sean had taken the train south to Cork. His wallet was heavy with more money, advanced toward expenses, than he had seen in years. There was no doubting the reality of the mission.

At Cork, which was only a few hours on the Express, he took the bus to Blarney, five miles out, and transferred to the bus to the little village of Coachford to the southwest.

From the village of some twenty cottages and one inn, he took the narrow dirt road which led to Bryan O'Casey's thatch roof farmstead cottage.

He hadn't been here for some six months—the last time, he had come to borrow from his former comrade-in-arms—and he paused for a moment outside the waist-high rock wall, and his eyes took in the fact that, if anything, it was more run-down than ever. Meg's ancient Austin wasn't in sight, and he wondered worriedly if the two had given up and left.

He went through the gate and found the cottage door open and yelled through it, as he approached, "And is anybody at home?"

Bryan came up, grinning, as Sean passed over the threshhold.

They went through the usual hand grinding and pounding and joyfully calling of each other's names and then both stood back and took the other in.

Bryan said, "You've lost weight and you look like you've got a hangover going back through the months."

And Sean grunted deprecation and said, "And it's a fact that any weight I've lost, you've put on.

And where would Meg be?''

Bryan led the way into the kitchen. He had an ancient portable typewriter on the table, surrounded with disordered papers. The floor was littered with further crumpled sheets.

Bryan pushed a chair back for his visitor and said, "Believe it or not, Sean, she's out making a house call."

Bryan O'Casey was as Irish-looking an Irishman as was likely to be found. About forty, an inch or two over six, and born to be lanky, though now carrying a few more pounds than called for, he was blue of eye, sandy of hair, and smiling of mouth. He didn't appear the fish-cold-blooded soldier of fortune Sean had known him to be for a decade and more.

Sean sat and when his host had seated himself behind the typewriter, said, frowning lack of understanding, "Why, believe it or not? She's still in practice, isn't she?"

Bryan scowled, picked up a semi-burnt out Peterson shell briar and loaded it from the leather pouch that had been sitting next to the typewriter.

He said, disgust in his words, "Can you imagine any Irishman in the whole country who would allow a woman doctor to come near enough to examine him beyond the point of advocating a few shots of Vitamin B for his shakes? Not even the women, even her relatives, will come to her as patients. They want a man doctor, not a handsome young woman."

Sean could imagine that. Meg McDaid was the only woman Irish M.D. he had ever met. And he suspected that the fact that she and Bryan were living out of wedlock didn't help any in this hundred percent Catholic community.

He dropped it and said, "And how's the book going?"

Bryan tried to smile and look enthusiastic but dropped that and shrugged unhappily as he lit the pipe. The shag he was smoking smelled a horror. It must have been the cheapest on the market. He said, around the pipe stem, "With all I've been through, with all I've seen myself and heard of from such as yourself, sure and I thought the writing of my memoirs, *Soldier of Misfortune,* would be a cinch. It isn't."

"What chapter are you on?"

"Number Two, but every time I reread Chapter One, I realize that it's got to be rewritten."

Sean stared at him. "What've you done with all your time since I saw you last?"

His friend looked embarrassed. "About six months ago I decided that writing longhand was what was holding me up. Maybe it was all right for Shakespeare, but it gave me writer's cramp. So I bought this antique and taught myself to type." He said, lowly, "Sean, I hope that you're not still on your uppers." He was unhappy. "If you've come for a little loan . . ."

Sean grinned and shook his head and brought his wallet from his hip pocket and displayed the sheaf of banknotes. He said, "I'll be paying up what I owe you, man dear. And how would you like a job?"

The other knew immediately what he was talking about and scowled. "I thought we were both retired, Sean. I thought we both retired while we were still breathing. Neither of us are exactly boys any more."

"It's three hundred ounces in gold for me Bryan, two hundred for you. Banked in Hong Kong, if we bring it off. All expenses, whether or not we do."

Bryan stared at him.

Sean was still giving him the full story when they heard Meg's car come up. And shortly after, Megan McDaid entered, black doctor's medical kit in hand and discouragement in her face.

However, she brushed her difficulties aside on seeing Sean, who had come to his feet. She came into his arms and kissed him heartily. Actually, they were not too well acquainted, but she knew him to be her lover's best friend and liked him, herself, thoroughly.

When greetings were through and the men in their chairs again, she said, "Bryan, you haven't offered Sean a drink. We've got a few bottles of stout." She looked at him suspiciously. "Unless you've been into them."

Sean said, "I'll not be having any, Meg dear. I've got to straighten up. This is a business call."

Meg sank into a chair herself and frowned puzzlement.

Bryan told her the story. Then leaned back and relit his pipe, his face expressionless.

She said, "But you're not going, Bryan? Who is this El Hassan? What government is it that . . ."

Bryan interrupted her, saying, "Mavoureen, do you know how much an ounce of gold brings in Irish pounds these days? We would have enough to migrate to Canada or the United States. We'd have enough for you to establish a practice and for me to take all the time in the world for my book . . . and other books after.''

Meg McDaid was of the beauty that only the Black Irish produce. The hair, which she wore long, was jet, the eyes green, the nose, chin and ears near perfection. She was past her girlish years but still the most handsome woman, in face and figure, that Sean Ryan could ever remember having seen.

She looked full into the face of the man she loved and said, ''If you go, I go too.''

Saul Saidi was already awaiting them on the terrace with another, when they came up.

The Levantine scowled in puzzlement at Megan McDaid and then looked questioningly at Sean Ryan. Both of the men had come to their feet from the table up against the terrace railing, upon the approach of the three.

Sean made introductions. He said, ''Doctor Megan McDaid, Captain Bryan O'Casey, Mr. Saul Saidi and . . . '' He looked at the tall, narrow faced, blue eyed, blondish haired, stranger.

The stranger bowed gently and took Meg's hand and kissed it, murmuring, *''Enchanté*, Madam Docteur.'' He looked down at the hand, which was ringless. ''Or should I say, Mademoiselle?''

''You could even say Ms. in the American fashion,'' Meg said. ''But I'm not married.''

''How delightful,'' he murmured again, and raised his eyebrows in an over-exaggerated expression of ecstasy.

''Come off it, Raul,'' Bryan O'Casey growled. ''She's all mine.''

The Frenchman grinned and turned to the two men. "A pleasure, gentlemen." He shook hands with Bryan. "Though, of course, I am already well acquainted with this old Irish clod." He shook with Sean and said, "My name is Captain Raul Bazaine." He flicked a thumbnail over his thin blonde mustache in most French fashion.

Sean said, "I'm Major Sean Ryan, commanding this detail, if all goes as Mr. Saidi has outlined."

The pudgy Levantine was sputtering, "But . . . but this lady . . ."

Sean said easily, with an ease he didn't entirely feel, "Shall we then be seated and I'll explain?"

Meg and the four men took chairs at the table which gave them a splendid view of the city.

Saul Saidi attempted to rise to the occasion. "Would anyone wish an apertif?" He raised a commanding finger to a waiter.

Meg had a Cinzano, Captain Bazaine a *pastis,* the Levantine an orange squash, Bryan a Scotch whiskey, since Irish was unknown in Algiers.

Sean said, "I'll not be having anything."

The Levantine raised eyebrows at that but said nothing.

When the waiter was gone, Saidi said, an ominous quality in his usually smooth, oily voice, "And this Mademoiselle?"

Sean Ryan took over. "Is Captain O'Casey's . . . fiancée. And not Mademoiselle . . . but Doctor. Mr. Saidi, please realize that we are white men going into the interior of the Sahara, an area with which at least most of us are unacquainted." He looked at the Frenchman. "Though I understand Captain Bazaine is. However, I doubt if his medical qualifications go beyond those of the usual mercenary in the field.''

Bazaine stroked his mustache again and smiled acceptance, but held his peace. He was still eyeing Meg appreciatively.

Sean went on. ''We shall be subjected to the usual, and, so I understand, quite endless, African diseases from dysentery to fevers that are not even in the lexicon of western medicine. Beyond this, as combat men, we are exposed to being hit, to taking wounds. What makes more sense than that our group would include a medico?''

Saidi said testily, ''Your cover is that you are a group of more or less ragtail mercenaries, out of employment and seeking jobs as the bodyguard of this upstart El Hassan. One would not expect such a contingent to be able to afford a qualified doctor.''

Bryan said mildly, ''She needn't go in as a doctor. We can call her a nurse. The fact that she is my fiancée and, let us not mince words, my mistress, makes it even more likely that she might be along. I'm in favor of her being one of our number. So is Major Ryan.'' He looked at the Frenchman, ''Captain Bazaine?''

Bazaine bowed to Meg McDaid. ''She would be a most practical—and most charming—addition to our company, *n'est-ce pas*?''

The Levantine thought about it. Finally he shrugged hugely and said, ''She is expecting recompense?''

Meg chopped out a less than feminine laugh and said, ''Of course.''

Sean said, ''Equal to that of the sergeant.''

Saidi said, "How do I know that you are a qualified doctor?"

Meg smiled and said, "I have credentials."

But Bryan was looking at the lardy Levantine.

Saidi cleared his throat unhappily and said, "Very well, Doctor McDaid will be one of your number. I assume that she will be able to assemble her medical kit here in Algiers."

Meg said, "I have brought it with me, Mr. Saidi. I researched the requirements before leaving Dublin. The medical school library there is quite adequate, even for desert diseases."

"Very well. Let us get down to practical matters." The heavy-set man looked at Sean Ryan. "You were successful in recruiting your troop?"

Sean nodded. "Yes, I first contacted my old comrade in arms, Captain O'Casey, here. With the need in mind of men acquainted with the desert and North Africa in particular, he in turn made contact with Captain Bazaine, with whom I have not had the pleasure of serving before. Then, between the three of us, we sent out the word to former comrades. Sometimes, they in turn suggested still others. It was difficult to find our twenty dependable combat veterans on such short notice, but not too much so."

"And the sergeant?"

"Is an American, possibly one of the most experienced mercenaries in our ranks."

"And where are these men quartered now?"

"At the Oasis Hotel, on the rue de Laurier."

"Very well. At the conclusion of our planning here, we shall go see them and make final provisions for your pay and such matters."

He brought a red jacketed packet from an inner pocket and unfolded it to reveal a map, saying, "This is the Michelin 152 Map of the portion of the Sahara in which we are primarily interested." He spread the chart out on the table and the others bent over it.

The waiter came up with their drinks and they held their silence until they had been served and he left. Sean Ryan eyed Bryan's drink, but shook his head infinitesimally and returned to the map.

Saul Saidi took a pencil from his breast pocket and used it for a pointer. He said, "We have had to make some alterations in original plans. We had first thought to base your rescue craft in In Salah, only 683 kilometers north of Tamanrasset, where El Hassan was last reported. However, the El Hassan disease is spreading like an epidemic and we cannot be sure that In Salah will not be subjected to it—if it has not already fallen. Hence Adrar has been substituted." He pointed it out on the map. "It is, unfortunately, another 351 kilometers further northwest. Happily, we have excellent cover there for both your aircraft and the pilots who will rescue you after you have disposed of El Hassan and his immediate followers."

"There is something that hasn't been completely clear to me," Bazaine said. "This plane that comes to our rescue. Suppose, after we've pulled the job, we go to ground somewhere out in the hammada, the rocky uplands between the mountains in that area. How is it going to land to pick us up, *hein*?"

The Levantine beamed greasily at him. "The craft, which we already have on hand at Adrar, is a helio-jet. It can land anywhere, and has sufficient capacity for all of you. Have you located the pilots you wish to utilize?"

"Yes," Sean said. "In fact, they're waiting in Tunis to get the message on where they are to go."

"Excellent," the Levantine said. "We'll phone them tonight and they can proceed down to Adrar. Of what nationality are they?"

"Both French, both acquainted with the Sahara, and the helio-jet will be no problem. They can fly anything," Captain Bazaine said. "I contacted them, on Bryan's suggestion, when he got in touch with me. In fact, Bryan is well acquainted with one of them. They served together in the guerrilla fighting in Indonesia."

Sean said, his voice flat, "I want to see those two pilots *and* the helio-jet before we go in after El Hassan."

The Levantine nodded as though his words were absolutely to be expected. "And that calls for a change in route. You will all fly to Columb-Béchar, which is not too far from the Moroccan border in northeastern Algeria, and is the startoff point for the Tanezrouft route across the Sahara. Your equipment will be there, a hoverjeep and two desert lorries. Also your weapons and uniforms. There are rumors that already small elements of El Hassan adherents have appeared in Timimoun, 564 kilometers to the south of Columb-Béchar, but they have not completely taken over. Frankly, I cannot understand the Algerian government. They seem powerless to raise defenses against this madman."

Captain Bazaine said dryly, "I understand that

on some of the occasions they've sent troops to deter the growth of his following, they have defected to El Hassan, and the authorities dare not send more.''

Saul Saidi sniffed but said, "At any rate, you will make your contact with your rescue craft and the two pilots in Adrar, then push on over to In Salah to the east and then head down to Tamanrasset, always making inquiries as to where El Hassan might be. It is quite possible that he has already left the vicinity of Tamanrasset.''

Meg said, "I can just see us trekking all over the desert seeking this elusive El Hassan. He might be in Timbuktu, by this time, for all we know."

"Or, Kano,'' Captain Bazaine said unhappily. "I read in one newspaper account that they're going over to him wholesale in upper Nigeria. In which case, we'd have one devilish wait for our rescue craft to get through to us.''

"Just who in the hell is this El Hassan, anyway?'' Bryan O'Casey growled. "The more I hear about him, the less I know.''

Saul Saidi tried to smile but it came off inadequately. "It truly doesn't matter a great deal, from our viewpoint. He has been named everything from a deserter from the former French Tirailleurs d'Afrique, to a Moroccan marabout, to the second coming of the Christian messiah, to an American professor of sociology.''

Meg laughed at that last one.

Sean said, "As we travel around the desert looking for our mysterious El Hassan, what is our cover when we run into his adherents?''

"That's no difficulty. Simply tell them you are in

search of El Hassan to offer your services. You won't be alone. Delegations from the countries of the developed world are zeroing-in upon him for a multitude of reasons, usually opportunistic. And individuals and groups are trying to find him to offer themselves as technicians, teachers, doctors and what-not. He has evidently issued orders to his followers not to molest such groups at the risk of their heads. And now, should we join the enlisted men and make final arrangements about pay and related subjects? I myself would like to check them out before you leave on your mission.''

In its day, the Hotel Oasis, on rue de Laurier, had been one of the better hostelries in Algiers. This was no longer its day; still, it boasted a small banquet room and it was here that the full strength of the so-called commando expedition met in force for the first time.

The men, twenty of them, had lined up three rows of chairs, and were sprawled in them.

Saul Saidi, his three officers, Meg and the sergeant were seated behind a longish table facing them. The sergeant was an American black and the oldest man present save, perhaps, the Levantine.

The men were as unreassuring looking a group as could easily be imagined. They all bore the air of those who have been there—and back. And more than once. It was difficult to put one's finger upon just what it was that amalgamated them. Some were moderately handsome, some vicious of face, some scarred to the point of ugliness. Some were moderately well dressed and seemingly semi-prosperous. Others were in the unkempt clothes and shoes typical of a sailor long on the beach.

They were of at least half a dozen nationalities, French and German predominating.

From the side of his eyes, Bryan O'Casey could see that Meg had her lower lip in her teeth, in dismay. Inwardly, he was sourly amused. What had she expected, swashbuckling types such as the Errol Flynn she loved to watch in the old film revivals?

When all were settled down, Sean Ryan stood and looked out over the men. It was a new Sean to Meg McDaid. He projected a cold air of command.

He said, "You've all been briefed on this assignment. If anybody wants to back down, now is the time. If he does, and talks, he will, of course, later be subjected to the code of the mercenary. No matter to what part of the world he goes, sooner or later one of us will run into him. Our lives depend on the true nature of our expedition not becoming known to El Hassan and his people."

They stirred a bit, but no one answered.

Sean said, "I've served with several of you before. The others, I don't know. I'll introduce the other officers, our non-com and doctor. Later on, we'll get to know all of your names. It's not important now."

He turned and indicated Bryan. "This is Captain Bryan O'Casey. Some of you have served with him. Those who haven't probably know his reputation." He indicated the Frenchman, who was sprawled lazily, one arm on the table, looking quizzically at Meg, as though wondering how she was taking meeting this riff-raff. "And this is Captain Raul Bazaine. Once again, some of you have served with him, others will know his reputation."

He turned to Meg. "This is Doctor Megan McDaid, a licensed doctor. We're going into unhealthy territory with an unhealthy assignment. We're lucky to have a medico along."

The men were staring at her in open appraisal. Some, too open.

Bryan said mildly, "In case there is any question, Doctor McDaid is my fiancée." He brought his ancient briar from a side pocket, his tobacco pouch from another and began to load up.

Meg bobbed her head at them, nervously. One in the rear gave a small wolf whistle. Bryan glared, but was unable to fix its origin.

Sean turned to the black who sat at the table with them. "And this is our sergeant, Lonzo Charles. Lon's an old hand."

The American black nodded, out over the group. He was typical of thousands you might have run into in any large northern city of the United States. About five-eight, stocky of build, he was obviously at least a quarter white, since his features were largely Caucasian, though his lips were thick, his skin a dark brown. He had a look of tiredness and disillusionment, but that wasn't out of place in this gathering.

Somebody in the second row, one of the Germans, said in poor English, the language all were using, "I don't believe I haff ever heard of the sergeant. Most of us haff been sergeants in our time. Some of us haff held higher rank."

Sean looked at Lon Charles. He had never heard of the other either. Raul had recommended him.

Lon said, "I done most of my fighting out in the

Orient, like. I started off with the Green Berets."

Someone else blurted, "Green Berets! You mean the Vietnam thing? You must be as old as the hills. Why, I was only a child when that took place."

Lon Charles said mildly, "So was I. I was seventeen when I went into Nam. Off and on, I been fighting ever since."

A Frenchman in the first row smiled nastily and said, "I've never served under a wog non-com."

Lon sighed and came to his feet and rounded the table and approached the other. He said, still mildly. "They don't say wog where I come from. They say nigger, but it means the same thing. Stand up, soldier."

The Frenchman, who was approximately the same size as the sergeant not only came to his feet but suddenly turned partly sideways and kicked high with his right foot, as gracefully as a ballet dancer.

The black moved viper-fast. He stepped slightly back, reached out with his left hand, grasped the foot and lifted it higher still. The Frenchman went over backward and crashed his head to the wooden floor, dazing himself.

Lon Charles looked down at him and then out of the rest of the mercenaries who were regarding him without expression. He said, "I seen this *savate* type of fighting before. But you got to remember it was us Americans who invented stomping. If you want to see what fighting with the feet can come to, I'll give you a lesson in stomping some time. A man gets stomped once and maybe he gets by; maybe even twice. But no man ever gets stomped three times and goes around normal. His kidneys and his gall and his balls and the rest of his guts and his ribs is all busted up.''

He turned and headed back for his chair.

Meg, her face white, began to rise to hurry to the fallen man, but Bryan put a restraining hand on her. ''Easy,'' he said.

Sean took a breathful and said, ''That's the last fighting between ourselves we're going to have until this assignment is successfully terminated. Anyone who disobeys this order will be turned out of the group.'' He looked at them emptily and added, ''I suppose you all realize what it means to be turned out alone into the Sahara without transportation and only the amount of food and water you can carry on your back.''

He turned and looked at the Levantine, who had remained expressionless of face and silent, thus far.

Sean said, ''And this is Mr. Saul Saidi, the representative of the government which has employed us. He will speak to you and answer any questions pertaining to our pay, or whatever.''

Sean sat down and Saidi took his feet. He said, ''Your gold can be deposited to the bank of your choice in Victoria, Hong Kong. Most of the largest of world banks have branches there. I recommend, in particular, First National City Bank of New York, Barclay's of London, or the Suisse Bank of Geneva.''

IX

SERGE SVERDLOV

COLONEL SERGE SVERDLOV was retracing almost identically the route a colleague and close friend—if it is possible to have a close friend in the colonel's trade—had taken only short months before.

His complexion, all over his body, was that of a light skinned negro and the cosmetic surgeons in Moscow had also made a few tucks about his lips to give him a heavier mouth. To his disgust, they had also circumcised him, since his cover indicated him to be a Moslem. His darkened skin was reversible, but hardly the circumcision.

He bore a Libyan passport and had flown in to Gibraltar on an Arab Union roco-jet. He had no difficulty whatsoever in passing through immigration and customs and took a taxi the short distance into town. He inquired in a store owned by supposed fellow Arabs, though it turned out they were from Tunisia, rather than Libya, and was told that the Mons Capa ferry to Tangier wouldn't leave for an hour. He left his two bags at the store and spent the time wandering up and down Main Street which he found to be aptly named, since it was the only main street in town. It was a tourist way par excellence; save for a couple of bars and two or three hotels, all was devoted to tax-free shops, largely in the hands of Indians. With the exception of cameras and other optical and electronic equipment from Germany and especially Japan, the products offered were of second or third rate quality, obviously aimed at sailors and tourists.

He went up a side street, found a bar, and went in to find they stocked only British brews. He had long since arrived at the conclusion that British bitter was the worst beer in the world, but he had no time to spend seeking out another bar. He ordered and drank a pint of bitter.

The ferry running to Tangier took approximately two hours and he spent the time on deck, watching the rock of Gibraltar drop behind. The straits of Hercules were moderately choppy and Tangier, once the Tingis of the Phoenicians and hence one of the oldest continually occupied cities in the world, was at the far end of them, across from Trafalgar where Admiral Nelson triumphed . . . and died. The city was built on the end of a peninsula with a crescent bay before it and a perfect beach that must have stretched for at least three miles. It was an impressive setting. The town ran up the mountainside and, from a distance, with its mosques, its aged palaces, its white, pink and blue typically Moslem houses, presented an appearance suitable for a time traveler. Tangier must have looked thus when the Moorish hordes swept across the straits to bring the blessings of Allah to Spain.

When he landed, he made the same mistake as had his earlier arriving colleague. He assumed that Arabic would be the prevailing language. It wasn't. Rif, a Berber tongue, was that largely spoken. Serge Sverdlov resorted to French, both at customs, where again he had no difficulties, and in ordering a Chico mini-hovercab. Peculiar to Tangier, it was the smallest cab he had ever been in with room hardly for himself and his bags.

He directed the driver to the El Minza hotel, which was immediately off the Plaza de France, the main square of the European section, and on Pasteur Boulevard, once, he had read, a financial center rivaling those of Switzerland and New York, when the International Zone had prevailed and Tangier had been a free city.

At the door, there were two natives, jet-black as bantus, rather than Rifs or other Moroccans. They were dressed in red jackets, yellow barbusha slippers, voluminous yellow pants and on their heads wore the red fez of Northern Africa. He had changed money in Gibraltar and hence had the dirhams to pay the cab and later to tip the boys, who took his bags and hustled him to the reservation desk. He had cabled ahead for a room.

It was necessary to leave his passport overnight for the routine of police redtape. He didn't bother to check out the room but sent the boys up with his luggage and immediately left for his contact.

Had he known, he was duplicating the movements of his colleague almost exactly. But then, they had both received their instructions from the same source.

He strolled, as any tourist might stroll, up the Boulevard Pasteur and turned right at the king-size sidewalk cafe there, across from the imposing French Embassy, and began descending the Rue de Liberté toward the medina, the native section of town. And now those in European dress thinned out and their place was taken by swarms of costumed Rifs, Arabs, blacks, and even an occasional Blue Man up from the desert. The name, he had heard, came from the fact that their cotton robes were dyed in an inadequate indigo that came off on their skins, giving them the eerie blue look.

At least half of the men wore the brown, camel hair burnoose, that universal garment with its hood, which tripled as coat, rain coat and blanket. The women wore either the white tent-like haik and veil, or the more attractive tailored jellabah of the upper classes.

The section he had just come from could have been part of the French Riviera, but now he was descending into the world of Medieval Islam, into the Baghdad of Harun-al-Rashid.

He passed through the teeming Grand Zocco street market, with its hundreds of stands, and multi-hundred merchants squatted down on the ground before rugs upon which sat their products, ranging from fruits and vegetables, through herbs and magic potions, to openly displayed kif—marijuana, as it is called in the Americas—and the Cantharides beetles, commonly known in the West as Spanish fly and utilized in North Africa as an ingredient of El Mojoun, along with kif, in the making of hashish fudge.

Across from the market he passed through the ancient, horse-shoe shaped gates of the old city and took the Rue Singhalese, which was the only street in the medina wide enough to allow even a small car. He descended this as far as the Zocco Chico, once considered the most notorious square in the world.

He was playing the stranger, the tourist, and from time to time stopped to look into windows. As in Gibraltar, most of the shops seemed Indian-owned. At last, he peered into one, as though in indecision. The window featured ebony figurines from the interior, carved ivory from the Orient, Japanese cameras, chessmen of water jade, odds and ends of supposed art objects from all over the world.

A fat Hindu materialized in the doorway, smiled greasily and made motions of washing his hands in a gesture so stereotyped as to be ludicrous. He said in English, "Sir, would you like to enter my shop? I have amazing bargains." And he repeated the same in French.

Serge Sverdlov assumed that the shop owner could repeat the message in Arabic, Spanish and a dozen other languages, but before the other could do so, seemed to come to a decision and entered. The seemingly innocent invitation had been the first of a routine of passwords.

The Russian looked about the overstocked shop and was satisfied to find it empty of customers. He said to the Indian in French, "I was looking for an ivory elephant from the East.''

The other's round face went empty but he said, ''A white elephant, sir?''

''A red elephant,'' the colonel told him.

The Hindu's face was still bland, but he bowed slightly and said, ''In here,'' and led the way to the rear where he brushed aside a curtain. Behind it was a heavy door which he opened. The rooms beyond were more spacious than the shop front had been and more comfortable. They passed through a livingroom cum study to an office beyond. The door was fully open and the Indian merely gestured for the colonel to enter, and then left.

Kirill Menzhinsky, agent superior of the KGB for North Africa, looked up from his desk, smiled a greeting and came to his feet and held out his hand to be shaken. The two were passingly acquainted.

''Colonel Sverdlov,'' he said. ''I have been expecting you.''

Serge Sverdlov nodded acceptance of that. Obviously, the minister would have called ahead on the scrambled tightbeam. The other motioned to a chair before the desk and the colonel took it and crossed his legs. ''It's been quite a time, Comrade Menzhinsky,'' he said.

His superior smiled at him. ''Yes. I believe the last time was in Moscow when Number One himself decorated you with the Hero's Award.''

Sverdlov said nothing to that. The other Russian came to his feet and went over to a small bar in a corner.

He looked over his shoulder and said, ''A drink,

Comrade? As I recall, you were never one to refuse a drink. In Tangier, one can get anything, even the best of vodka.''

''Vodka would be excellent. I suspect that it is the last opportunity I will have to enjoy it for a time.''

The other chuckled as he poured. ''Or anything else, for that matter. In the Sahara, one, especially if he is passing as a Moslem, does not drink. The Prophet forbids.'' He brought the glasses back. ''But then, of course, you know all this, since your record shows you spent considerable time in Algeria during the troubles there.'' He made a humorous mouth. ''In fact, I understand you *caused* quite a few of the troubles.'' He handed one of the glasses to the colonel.

The KGB official took his chair behind the desk and held up his glass. ''To the world revolution, Comrade.''

Sverdlov gave the standard response. ''The revolution.''

They knocked back the high proof spirits.

Kirill Menzhinsky put down his glass and said, ''And now, I suppose that Comrade Blagonravov has briefed you on this El Hassan and his immediate clique.''

The colonel nodded and said, ''Brief, is the only word. Precious little seems to be known about the man, other than that he is an American, which is astonishing.''

The other nodded in his turn and picked up a paper, saying, ''Slowly, we are accumulating more information on our mysterious Dr. Homer Crawford. I shall give you the same information I did Comrade Anton before we sent him in." He read, "Homer Crawford, born in Detroit of working-class parents. In his late teens, interrupted his education to come to Africa and join local revolutionists in Morocco and Algeria. Evidently was wounded and invalided back to the States where he resumed his schooling. When he came of military age he joined the Marine Corps. Following one hitch, as they call it, he resumed his education again, finally taking a doctor's degree in sociology. He taught for a time until the Reunited Nations began its African program. He accepted a position and soon distinguished himself."

He took up another paper and went on. "According to both Comrades Baker and Anton, who preceded you and are now dead, Crawford is an outstanding personality, dominating others. Comrade Baker, in particular, reported a somewhat mystical quality in him. An ability in times of emotional crisis to break down men's mental barriers against him." He twisted his mouth ruefully at the other's surprise at his words. "Evidently, throughout history there have been similar examples. Our own Lenin was one, Ghandi of India was another. So have been various religious leaders in the past."

"And his closest followers?" Sverdlov said, avoiding the unscientific connotations of what his superior had said.

Menzhinsky took up another paper. "Elmer Allen. Born of small farmer background on the Caribbean island of Jamaica. Managed to work his way through the University of Kingston where he took a master's degree in sociology. At one time he was thought to be Party material and was active in pacifist groups and so forth. However, he was never induced to join the Party. Upon graduation, he immediately took employment with the Reunited Nations and was assigned to Crawford's team. He was evidently in full accord with Crawford's aims as El Hassan.''

"*Was*?" Sverdlov frowned.

"We have received word that he has been captured by elements of the Chaambra in northwest Algeria who are largely opposed to El Hassan." The KGB offical shrugged. "Possibly he is still alive, though I doubt it.''

The espionage head took up another sheet. "Bey-ag-Akhamouk, the only real African close to El Hassan. Born a Tuareg, he was taken to America as a child and educated there and took his degree in political science. We have no record of where he stands politically but Comrade Baker and Anton rated him an outstanding intuitive soldier. A veritable genius in combat. It would seem he's had military experience somewhere, but we have no record of it.''

"Intuitive soldier?" the colonel said, and his tone indicated —more mysticism?

Menzhinsky chuckled sourly and said, "Do not forget such men as Trotsky, Mao, Tito, Castro, none of whom had much, if any, military training, except Tito who was a sergeant in the First World War.''

He sorted out still another sheet. "Kenneth Ballalou, born in northern Louisiana, educated in Chicago. Another young man but evidently as capable and devoted to Crawford as the others. So far as we know, he holds no political stand whatsoever."

He went over to the bar and brought back the bottle of vodka and poured them both another drink. When it was down, he went on. "Which brings us to Isobel Cunningham. Born in New York or New Jersey, master's degree in journalism. Comrade Baker recruited her into the Party while he too was a student. On graduation, she went to work with the Africa for Africans Association with two colleagues, Jacob Armstrong and Clifford Jackson. All three became early followers of El Hassan. Indeed, the more elderly Jacob Armstrong is now supposedly El Hassan's Minister of State and Ambassador to the Reunited Nations in New York. Clifford Jackson we have little information on, beyond the fact that he is an American black and probably from California." Menzhinsky looked up. "There you have it."

Serge Sverdlov ran his right hand down over his cheek, thinking about it.

His superior said, "I see that you are disguised as a Negro. How will you maintain the dyeing in the desert?"

The colonel grunted deprecation. "It's not a dye matter. The pigmentation of my skin has been altered. I've also been circumcised. They're thorough in Moscow."

Menzhinsky laughed gruffly. "Wait until your girl friend back in Moscow sees you!"

Sverdlov laughed too. "It's reversible," he said. "The change in pigmentation, at least. Are there any new instructions, beyond those I received from the Minister? That is, I am to find El Hassan, join him as Anton did, try to rise in his organization, do all that I can in his attempt to come to power and to amalgamate and forward the progress of North Africa until it is advanced sufficiently to be fruitful ground for Party activity.''

The other shook his head. ''That's about it. It's an assignment, Comrade, that could take the better part of the rest of your life—if you are successful.''

The KGB agent nodded wearily to that. ''So it would seem. Do you know where El Hassan was last heard from?''

''Tamanrasset, right in the middle of the Ahaggar, the most desolate area of the Sahara. There is just one thing.''

The colonel looked at him.

Kirill Menzhinsky said slowly, thoughtfully, ''As I told you, one of his closest aides has been captured by Abd-el-Kader, who is the chief of the Ouled Touameur clan of the Chaambra nomads. He is also of Shorfu blood, a direct descendent of Mohammed, through his daughter Fatima. Our information is that he has called for a *jedah,* a holy war, against El Hassan. Since he holds, or has already killed, Elmer Allen, he has put El Hassan in a double spot. If Homer Crawford doesn't react, he's going to lose a great deal of face among the desert men. It's possible that, even now, he's heading for Chaambra country.''

''I see.'' Sverdlov thought about it. ''Where can I get detailed information about the Chaambra, the areas they control, what towns, where they rendezvous, that sort of thing?''

His superior said, ''The Soviet Complex Embassy has an extensive library. It is open to the public. You need not even reveal your true identity, which might be best, since your assignment is most hush-hush. It would never do that it get out that the Soviet Complex is aiding El Hassan even against such socialist countries as Algeria.''

X

PAUL KOSLOFF

PAUL KOSLOFF TOOK the supersonic to London and from there a jet to Gibraltar and from there a ferry plane to Tangier. The faint scars from the plastic surgery he had gone through were all healed. He had spent the time that took poring over material on North Africa and what little material they had on El Hassan in the State Department files.

He hadn't liked what he found about El Hassan. The man was obviously an anti-Marxist and had no intention of being swayed by the Soviet Complex. Kosloff had spent his life fighting Marxism and was now being sent out against another who felt the same way he did.

His was a one-man expedition. So hush-hush was it that only the commissioner who had given him his instructions knew that Kosloff was on his way to forestall El Hassan. It was absolutely imperative that the world never learn that the United States was involved in frustrating a revolution against Marxist regimes. No, he didn't like it but

Paul Kosloff was a dedicated member of the Western team and it wasn't up to him to formulate policy. He fully realized that on occasion the freest of governments must resort to devious ways, to compromise, to outright Machiavellianism, if it wished to survive. He didn't like it, but Paul Kosloff wasn't starry-eyed.

There wasn't a great deal of traffic between Gibraltar and Tangier. There were only two other passengers, both of them, by their looks, North Africans.

At the Tangier airport, he followed the other two to the administration buildings. He'd never been in this city before, and they seemingly knew their way around. They entered through a metal detection booth. Paul Kosloff wasn't worried. The only metal he carried was a wristwatch, a small pocketknife and some coins. They passed him through and he went on to the customs counters.

His bags were already there and the raggedly uniformed officials were going through them with minute care. They found nothing that mattered. Paul Kosloff wasn't silly enough to pass over a border carrying anything suspicious.

Next was the immigration desk and the unshaven official there looked at the passport Paul Kosloff presented, then up into the other's face.

"Why do you come to Morocco, Mr. Smithson?"

Paul Kosloff, alias Kenneth Smithson, said easily, "Vacation. I'm an amateur historian and I want to check out the theory that the Phoenicians first settled Tangier. I'll do other sightseeing too, but that's by big interest."

The other grunted, stared at him some more, but then took up a rubber stamp and stamped the document and handed it over. "Welcome to the Kingdom of Morocco," he said.

There were a couple of battered-looking Chico hovercabs in front of the airport. With a raga-muffin carrying his bags, Kosloff approached one. He had his luggage put in the back and sat up next to the driver.

He said, in French, "Take me to the Hotel Keb-ruk."

The driver said, "*Oui*," dropped the lift lever of the hovercab and they took off.

He had been in North African and Near Eastern towns before and thus was neither surprised nor impressed by the appearance of Tangier. If any-thing, the city was getting a bit shabbier than usual. Some decades past it had been in the hands of France and what semimodern architecture existed obviously went back to that time. Most of this seemed concentrated in the town's center, along with governmental office buildings.

But first they had entered through a native dis-trict where vehicular traffic was at a minimum; pedestrian, swarming. The sidewalks were jammed and the crowds overflowing into the streets. Some rode or led burdened donkeys and he even spotted two or three camels in the *souk* area on the outskirts. He reminded himself not to bother going into the *souk*. He had seen North African markets before and they stank.

All in all, Paul Kosloff decided, a pretty crumby-looking bunch. Even the commies, in the Soviet Complex, were far in advance of this feudalistic, absolute monarchy. How could the advent of an El Hassan make it any the worse?

Eventually, they pulled up before a large hotel that had obviously once been luxurious. It was on the weather-beaten side now. There was a large black in front in what was probably meant to be the costume of the sultan's guard, or some such. He had a monstrous but phony-looking scimitar in his sash.

There didn't seem to be any bellhops so Paul Kosloff got out of the cab and brought his bags from the rear. He took the luggage and approached the door. The black opened it for him but didn't make any motions toward the bags. Who in the hell had decided on this hotel for him? Evidently, somebody who had thought he'd be less conspicuous in such surroundings.

Paul Kosloff approached the reception desk and asked for a small suite. His cover was that he was an American businessman on vacation. He would be expected to be in funds.

His suite, he found, was as run-down as the Hotel Kebruk's lobby. However, there was hot water and he took his time cleaning up and then brought from one of his bags a tourist guide. The guide went back to the days before the Sultan's return and to the regime of the International Zone but he assumed that the map it contained was still valid, though possibly they had changed some of the street names, He looked up the boulevard the hotel was on, then traced with his finger to another location.

Well, there was no use putting it off. He slipped the guide into his pocket, reached down into the bag again to emerge with an impressive looking, king-size camera. He hung it around his neck, tourist fashion, and headed for the door.

The boulevard outside was named Pasteur, and this obviously was the best part of town, if any part of present day Tangier would be thought of as best. The pedestrians were largely Europeans. Paul Kosloff stuck his hands in his pockets and sauntered along, once again, tourist fashion. He peered into shop windows, took occasional snapshots. He was obviously in no hurry whatsoever, and obviously had no particular destination.

He could hardly know it but he was duplicating the motions of Serge Sverdlov, not long before.

He took a full hour to assure himself that he wasn't being followed. He hadn't expected to be, but you never knew in one of these off-beat dictatorial countries.

He drifted down a narrow street that seemed largely devoted to small shops of a type tourists would frequent looking for souvenirs in North Africa, or bargains in the various products manufactured in the Soviet Complex that were sometimes cheaper in the West, including art objects from China.

He entered one establishment, somewhat larger than most of the others and stared at the display of camel saddles, leather dolls, copperwear and babouche slippers. There was one other customer present and the proprietor was showing her about. She didn't seem to be any more avid than Paul Kosloff to actually buy something. Finally, she left.

Paul went over to the shop owner and said, "Battista?"

The other was seemingly a late middle-aged Arab, on the fat side, djellabah clad and sporting a bedraggled, gray streaked beard.

He frowned and said, "My name is Mohammed-ben-Abdallah."

"Your name is Joseph Battista and you're an American Italian. I was instructed to contact you. I'm Paul Kosloff."

"Of course. The commissioner informed me you were on your way on tight-beam. Shall we go into the back room?" He turned his head and called out something in Arabic.

A young man of possibly twenty-five entered from a back door. He looked at Paul Kosloff questioningly. The older man spoke to him again in Arabic and he answered and went over and stood in the doorway to the street, as though awaiting customers.

Paul Kosloff followed Joseph Battista into a back room. As soon as the door was closed behind them, he made a motion with his head. "Who's that?"

"Supposedly my son, actually another of our men."

There was a very low Arabic-type table in the small room's center, with hassocks about it. The two men seated themselves.

Paul Kosloff said, "How good is your cover here?"

"Excellent. I've been a small shopkeeper in Tangier for nearly twenty years."

"Good. Did the commissioner tell you what my assignment is?"

"No, but I can guess."

"Oh, you can, eh? Well, what do you guess?"

"You've come to help El Hassan. Who else would they send but the famous Cold War's Lawrence of Arabia to overthrow the corrupt governments now in North Africa?"

Inwardly, Paul Kosloff winced, but he said, "I'm going to need a .38 Recoilless and a shoulder harness holster, some grenades, a Tracy, an electronic mop and a scrambler. You can provide them?"

"Yes, of course. I have already been instructed."

He got up and went over to a cabinet and brought forth the articles Paul Kosloff had called for. The troubleshooter came to his feet, shrugged out of his jacket and put on the shoulder holster, under his left arm. He put the recoilless, noiseless gun in it, and drew it twice to see if it was riding correctly. Then he got back into his coat. The electronic mop looked like a pen. He clipped it into his breast pocket. He took off his watch and handed it to Battista and took up the Tracy and put it on his wrist. It looked identical to the other watch but wasn't. It was a watch, true enough, but also had other qualities.

Battista said, "Why in the world do they call it a Tracy?" He seated himself again.

Kosloff said, adjusting the metal straps, "I understand that in the old days they had a comic strip detective who used a two-way radio that was strapped to the wrist like a watch. This, of course, is more than that. It operates on a tight-beam and can't be tapped.'' He picked up the scrambler, which looked something like a cigarette case and dropped it into a side pocket.

He sat down again too. ''Now then, brief me a bit on El Hassan. They don't have too much on him in Greater Washington.''

''I don't have much on him either. He keeps on the move, usually accompanied by a half dozen close associates.''

''Where is he now?''

''The last report we had, near Tamanrasset, though there are rumors that he is heading north. You can't depend upon them. All about El Hassan is rumor.''

''So,'' Paul Kosloff mused. ''There are a group of them and usually on the move. How could I get in touch?''

''El Hassan has various followers here in Tangier. I can get in contact with them and possibly arrange a meeting for you. They'll be overjoyed to know that a top operative from Greater Washington is coming to El Hassan's assistance.'' He hesitated before adding, ''Undoubtedly, you are in a position to promise finanical aid. Any revolutionary organization can use money.''

''Okay,'' Paul Kosloff said. ''Locate El Hassan for me. Now one thing. You say he keeps on the move with half a dozen close associates. What would happen to this revolution if El Hassan and these closest colleagues were . . . eliminated?''

''The revolution would collapse,'' Battista said definitely. ''They are its heart and soul and brains.''

"I see," Paul Kosloff said.

"Which brings to mind something I must warn you about," the other said. "Serge Sverdlov is in Tangier. From what I understand, if you're the Cold War's Lawrence of Arabia, he's sort of a Tito, Castro and Ché Guevara rolled into one. By the way, he's disguised as a black, which might indicate he is preparing to go into the interior."

Paul Kosloff's eyes narrowed. "Serge, eh? Yes, I've run into Serge on occasion. I thought he was in Indonesia on some commie cloak and dagger assignment or other."

"Possibly the Kremlin is of the opinion that North Africa takes precedence with this threat of counter-revolution by El Hassan. Most of the police in this part of the world are inexperienced clods. But Serge Sverdlov would have lots of know-how if he devoted himself to reaching El Hassan's team."

"Yes," Paul Kosloff muttered. "If he had to liquidate half of the male population, of the area, Serge would get him. Where's he located?"

"We don't know. We spotted him entering the Soviet Complex library."

Kosloff stood and said, "Okay. You'd better wrap up a couple of souvenirs for me to leave with, so that it'll look as though I bought something here. Contact me at the Hotel El Kebruk, under the name Smithson, as soon as you know where El Hassan is."

Back at the hotel, Kosloff unwrapped the souvenirs Battista had given him and put them on a table in the suite's living room. They'd help give him authenticity as a tourist.

He brought the electronic mop from his breast pocket and began going about the room, pointing it here, there, everywhere and especially at any electrical fixtures. Shortly, it began to go beep, beep, beep and he located what he was looking for. The bug was in the base of the telephone.

He took the mop into the bedroom and then the bath but neither were bugged. He went back to the telephone. The fact that there was an electronic bug in his suite didn't mean that it was being monitored, of course. They probably had a bug in every room in the Hotel El Kebruk, but surely not enough men to monitor them all at once. And from what he had seen thus far of the Moroccan economy he doubted that the bugs would be computerized.

However, he couldn't take the chance. He brought the scrambler the shopkeeper had given him from his pocket, set it on the stand next to the phone and flicked its stud.

He had to work fast now. There was always the chance that the scrambler would be detected and someone on the other end of the bug become suspicious. Then the fat would be in the fire. What American tourist would be equipped with such sophisticated devices?

He took his Tracy from his wrist and propped it up on the room's desk and sat before it. He pressed the tiny stud and said, "Paul calling. Paul calling."

A thin voice came back. It was the commissioner's. He had arranged for Kosloff's Tracy to be tuned into his alone. They were *really* going ape about security on this assignment.

Paul said, "I've arrived and made contact with

Battista. The subject is in the south. Battista thinks he can find out where. He also thinks I'm here to help the subject and evidently approves of that."

The thin voice said, "It is not important what he thinks."

Paul said, "The subject has followers here in Tangier. Battista believes he can make arrangements for a meeting."

"What is your excuse for such a meeting?"

"It will have to be that I'm an agent from the United States coming to offer him assistance. He'll take that bait and reveal where he is—I hope."

"Fine. Get in there and do the job. We'll never get another chance if you fail. He'll be leary of our government. Do this right, and there's a hefty bonus in it for you."

"I don't want a bonus," Paul growled. "I didn't sign up with the Western team for money. And, listen, Serge Sverdlov's here in Tangier."

There was a momentary silence. Then, "Sverdlov's in Indonesia."

"Battista says he's here in Tangier, disguised as a negro. That guy's the sharpest counter-espionage man in the KGB."

The thin voice said, "I know who he is. Well, for once you and he are on the same side."

"Yes, but he doesn't know it. If anything happens to my cover, he'll be on me like a ton of uranium and he undoubtedly has plenty of manpower on tap. Can't you at least send me a couple of heavies from Paris, or wherever, to run interference?"

"Absolutely out of the question. Nobody must know about this but you and me."

"All right," Paul said in resignation.

"Good luck," the thin voice said, before fading. "And reconsider that bonus."

Paul Kosloff said bitterly, after deactivating the Tracy, "Does he think I'd take on a job like this for the sake of a bonus?"

He went over hurriedly to the scrambler and flicked off its stud.

For the next week, Paul Kosloff spent most of his time in the hotel, taking all of his meals there. He trusted the plastic surgery he'd had in Greater Washington but he was taking no chances. Altered facial features alone are insufficient to disguise a man. There's the set of shoulders, the way the head is held, the stride, the shape of hands, and all the rest of it. Serge was up on such things and he had no desire to have the other spot him on the streets of Tangier.

On the third morning, he found an envelope that had been slipped under his door during the night. The note inside was typed.

It read: *Tokugawa is in town. His cover is that he is a member of a Japanese trade mission here. He is staying at the Japanese embassy.*

"It sounds like a convention," Kosloff muttered. "Sverdlov, Tokugawa and myself." He grunted. Battista was a more efficient operative than Paul Kosloff had originally given him credit for being.

There was nothing for it. He was going to have to check out the newcomer. He knew where Sverdlov stood, but not the Japanese. He couldn't afford to begin operations and run the risk of coming up against him. Possibly, it was something entirely divorced from his own mission. Possibly, but he doubted it.

The approach might as well be a direct one. That evening he left the hotel by a side door and got into a cab as soon as possible. He ordered the driver to take him to the Japanese embassy. There was no way he could think of to avoid being seen entering the building, if the place was being observed.

He left the cab half a block from the embassy and walked, wanting the chance to case the place before entering. He couldn't make out any obvious plants, however, nor even a local policeman.

He entered and approched the petite Japanese girl at the reception desk. She was in western garb and the room was furnished western style.

Her French was perfect. "Good morning, sir."

Paul said, "I wish to see Colonel Tokugawa."

Her almond eyes turned wary. "There is no Colonel Tokugawa here, sir."

"Tokugawa Hidetada. Supposedly he's here on a trade mission. Tell him Paul Kosloff wishes to see him."

"I assure you, sir . . ."

Paul Kosloff simply looked at her.

She flicked on a desk communicator and spoke into it in Japanese, then listened. Her eyes widened slightly in surprise. She deactivated the device and looked up at him. "Yes, sir," she said.

A door behind her opened and the top Japanese counter-espionage operative entered. By his appearance, he couldn't have been less offensive, right down to his thick lensed glasses.

"Paul," he said, his hand outstretched. "I didn't recognize you at first. Plastic surgery, of course."

Paul said, "Hidetada," and they shook.

"Please come in here, Paul" the slightly built Japanese said, leading the way back through the door he had just entered from.

Beyond was an office, simply furnished. On the desk were several piles of what were obviously reports, all of them, of course, in Japanese.

"Sit down, Paul. It seems a long time since last we met during the Asian war."

Paul Kosloff took a chair and said, "Yeah. And thanks all over again for taking those two commies off my back. I spent three months in the hospital afterward."

The Japanese bowed his head agreeably in response and said, "It was my duty, Paul. We were on the same side . . . then."

Paul Kosloff looked at him.

Tokugawa Hidetada said gently, "Paul, I am afraid we are not on the same side now."

"Go on."

"Paul, Japan desperately needs the raw materials of North Africa, resources that are largely going to the United States today. It is in our interest that El Hassan not come to power."

"Granting that I know what you're talking about, and I'm not admitting that, *why*?"

"He is a fanatic. From the rumors we have heard, we prefer his lieutenant Bey-ag-Akhamouk. Although Bey-ag-Akhamouk largely supports El Hassan, it is said that he is at the same time the leader of an element in their organization that has differences. Bey-ag-Akhamouk is an anti-American. You know, the American imperialism thing, so rumors tell us, at least. If he came to power, he would switch trade to Japan. However, he is faithful to El Hassan and on his own would never attempt to replace him. But if something happened to El Hassan, then it would be Bey-ag-Akhamouk who came to power.''

''I see. And you think the American State Department wishes to see El Hassan win his revolution?''

The Japanese said gently, ''Of course. He is anti-Marxist.''

Paul thought about it. He said finally, ''To sum it up, then, you wish this revolution to take place but you want Bey-ag-Akhamouk to take over rather than El Hassan.''

''Yes, Paul. And, believe me, in spite of past associations, I cannot let you stand in the way. Japan cannot. We must have the oil, iron, copper, nickel of North Africa, or we die.''

Paul Kosloff came to his feet. He said, ''I'll be seeing you, Hidetada.''

''Paul, I am warning you.''

''Yes, I know. I'll be seeing you, Hidetada. The next time you write, give my regards to your wife. I'll never forget that *tempura* she cooked for us.''

By the time he left the embassy, night was well along. The Hotel El Mekruk wasn't as far as all that. He decided to walk and try to sort things out. It was unlikely that he would be spotted in this darkness.

Things were piling up. The governments of the

Soviet Complex and Japan, not to speak of the United States, wouldn't have their top espionage men in the country unless the revolution some wanted and some didn't was well under way. For that matter, he wondered if Common Europe had some of their aces around.

Something there is in the man of action that must be an instinct, possibly one come down from the caves, from the time of the saber-tooth, from the time of the cave bear. An instinct for danger. Had Paul Kosloff not had it, he would have been dead long years since.

Suddenly, unconsciously, he dropped to one knee and his right hand blurred for his holstered .38 Recoilless. A pencil-thin hiss of light cut a foot above his head. A laser!

The other was only the vaguest of shapes, back a few feet in the alleyway Paul had been passing. His six silent bullets ripped the man through from the crotch almost to the neck line.

Paul Kosloff shot his eyes up and down the street. He could see no one close enough to have observed the split-seconds of action. He moved in quickly, bent over the fallen would-be assassin.

To his relief, the man was a complete stranger. Seemingly, he was a Moor. That, of course, meant little. He could have been a hired killer in the pay of Sverdlov, Tokugawa or, for all he knew, of some other element on the scene with whom Paul Kosloff was not as yet acquainted. Possibly even an adherent of El Hassan.

He frisked the dead man quickly, efficiently, but, as he had suspected, the other bore no identity papers, nor anything else that would give a clue to who he was, who had sent him on his mission of death.

Paul Kosloff had to get out of the vicinity. The other might have an accomplice around, possibly a driver of a get-away car. And, above that, a supposed American tourist should not be found bent over a corpse and in possession of a .38 Recoilless. He reloaded, then hurried to the street, double-checked for anyone in the vicinity, then hurried along back to the hotel, his right hand ready to dart for the gun again at the slightest indication of additional hostility.

Back at the hotel, he made no further attempt to contact Battista but kept even closer to his rooms than he had before. The American agent knew where Paul was and the only reason for their getting together again was when the plans had been completed for his meeting with El Hassan.

At the end of the week, there was a discreet knock at the door. It was the boy who had been at Battista's shop. When Paul Kosloff opened the door, the other side-stepped in. The international troubleshooter led him into the living room and looked at him.

The other was sharp. He pointed at his ear and then around the room, his face questioning. Paul took him to the phone stand and pointed at it. He brought his electronic scrambler from his pocket and activated it momentarily.

He said, "I'm afraid to keep this on for any length of time. Don't say anything you don't want heard." He flicked the device off again.

The younger man nodded and said, "Mr. Smithson, sir, I have made the arrangements for your drive into the countryside."

"Excellent," Paul Kosloff said. "When can we leave?"

"Immediately, sir. The car is outside the hotel. I am to be your chauffeur and guide."

"Wait just a minute. I'll pack a small bag and get my camera."

Paul Kosloff waited until they had got into the countryside on the outskirts of Tangier before saying anything of importance.

He said finally, "All right. What's your name?"

"Nafi-ben-Mohammed."

"What's your real name? You're an American, aren't you?"

"No. I am a national of Morocco. I was educated in the American School of Tangier, before it was closed by the Sultan. However, as you know, I am employed by the American government through Mohammed-ben-Abdallah, supposedly my father."

Kosloff nodded. He said, "Where are we going?"

"Possibly on a wild goose chase. We have been unable to get accurate information on the whereabouts of El Hassan. However, strong rumors are that he is heading for Chaambra country to rescue one of his viziers. Our immediate destination is Ksar-es-Souk on the Moroccan, Algerian border. From there we will have to feel our way eastward, enquiring of news about El Hassan."

"How far is it?"

"Perhaps five hundred kilometers."

"About three hundred miles, eh? Can we make it in one day?"

"The roads are quite good. Built by the French in the old days. We should be able to."

"All right. I assume our power packs are sufficient for the whole trip so we won't have to make any stops except for food. Then there won't be any record of the trip."

"Yes, sir."

Paul Kosloff looked at the younger man from the side of his eyes. He said, "What do you think of El Hassan?"

The other's voice took a different tone. "He is the sole hope of North Africa."

Paul Kosloff thought about that. He said, "Are you armed?"

"Yes. The same as you. With a .38 Recoilless."

"Ever had to use it?"

"Yes, sir. I've been in this service ever since the Sultan took over again here in Morocco. He is at least as bad as the Marxists."

"Dedicated, I see."

The Moslem boy was embarrassed. He said finally, "My two older brothers were killed by the Marxists in Algeria." Then he added: "They aren't really Marxist, of course."

"They aren't? How do you mean?"

"A good many so-called Marxists in all parts of the world, including the Soviet Complex, pay lip service to the name of Marx and his work but their governments have no similarity to what he was talking about. He wanted the State to wither away:

they strengthen it and keep it in their own hands and to their own profit.''

Paul Kosloff looked at him from the side of his eyes again. ''Did you pick that up at the American School?''

The younger man was embarrassed again. ''No, sir. I used to study political economy on my own. That is why I support El Hassan. He wishes to bring both democracy and a modified form of capitalism to North Africa—I think. He realizes that the country is not sufficiently developed to achieve a more advanced society.''

''How do you mean, both democracy and capitalism? And how do you mean, a more advanced society?''

''The words are not synonymous, of course. You can have one without the other, in spite of our western propaganda to the contrary. For instance, we have had democratic societies down through the ages. In your own country, the American Indians were democratic before the coming of the white man, but they were certainly not capitalistic. Nor were the Greeks of the Golden Age. The economic system then was based on slaves, though the government was democratic—among male citizens. Hitler's regime was certainly not democratic, but it was capitalistic. Capitalism is an economic system, democracy a governmental one. Undoubtedly, one day capitalism will become antiquated, as both slavery and feudalism were in their time, but that does not mean that the next socioeconomic system will not be democratic.''

The international troubleshooter changed the

subject and said, "Do you have a map of Morocco and Algeria here in the car?"

"Yes, sir. In the dash compartment there."

Paul Kosloff got it and opened it up. "Okay. Tell me the route you're taking, town by town. I want to know where we're going and how we're going to get back."

"Oh, that won't be necessary. I'll drive both ways, and I know the route quite well."

Paul Kosloff said coldly, "I want to know in case something happens to you and I have to drive back myself."

Damn it. Was he going to have to kill this one too? Thus far, he had liked the boy.

XI

EL HASSAN

HOMER CRAWFORD at the wheel, Bey-ag-Akhamouk, Kenny Ballalou and Cliff Jackson were heading westward from In Salah to Adrar, in one of the two original hoverlorries which Homer's Sahara Division, African Development Project of the Reunited Nations, team had driven through half the Western Sahara. All except Cliff Jackson had been over this route time and time again. Cliff was appalled. He, Isobel and Jake Armstrong had largely worked along the Niger river and had seldom seen the desert proper.

"Jesus," he said. "This is the ass-hole of creation."

"I've often wondered where it was located," Bey murmured.

Kenny laughed and said to Cliff, "Man, you're lucky we didn't take the other route, southwest to Kidal and then north through Bidon Cinq and Poste Weygand. The Tuaghi call the route between Tamanrasset and Kidal the Land of Fear and

Thirst. That's where you get the *simoons*, or perpetual sandstorms, which blow all day, every day. During the day hours, you can't eat. As soon as you open a tin of food, even though you're inside your vehicle, it's smothered in sand. The only possible way you can get something to eat, during the day hours, is to munch on some bits of dried bread, by squeezing your body up against the car on the lee side. Even then, you can feel the sand gritting between your teeth."

They had by-passed In Salah, to keep from being spotted by anyone who might recognize El Hassan and his closest advisers, and shortly passed Hi Tahaidour, going through the famous *Bois* pétrifié, one of the largest petrified forests in the world.

Cliff gaped at the circumference of the boles of trees which had fallen millennia ago.

Bey chopped out a short laugh. "Something, eh? The whole Sahara was once tropical in vegetation. And not so long ago as all that, either. They've got cave and cliff paintings throughout the desert, something like those Cro-Magnon cave paintings in southern France and northern Spain. They portray not only men but such animals as giraffes, mammoths and hippopotami."

Homer Crawford said, "It's something that must give a boost in morale to Ralph Sandell, over there at Bidon Cinq, with his afforestation project. I hope the hell he's all right. Supporting reforestation of the Sahara is going to be one of the biggest feathers in El Hassan's cap, if we can keep it going."

Bey said, "I told Isobel to have Guémama send

one of his first organized *goum* camel patrols with a really *reliable mokkadam* over to guard Sandell's seedlings and transplants. Later, we'll send other *goums* to the rest of the afforestation projects, but Ralph's trees are the most exposed.''

Homer said,''I hope the hell you told Jimmy Peters to issue them ample funds. He don't want any of our people sponging on the project, not to speak of looting or having our camelmen enjoying a quick unwelcome roll in the hay with the local girls—if any hay's available in those parts. Or girls, for that matter.''

''I did.'' Bey nodded.

The sun burned down outside in such wise that it was impossible to look out through the windows without their very dark sun glasses. The white sand reflected the light like mirrors.

There was no road, properly speaking. Roads are impossible in most of the central Sahara. It is seldom that a vehicle spots the tracks of another car or truck before it. The sand has blown over them in less than half an hour. Instead, the French engineers who originally surveyed the routes, placed a steel petroleum barrel approximately every half a kilometer, filled with stones so that they wouldn't blow away. One drives across the Sahara by going from one steel drum to the next. And woebetide the man who gets off the track and becomes lost in the erg or on the reg.

In the old days, when the French controlled the area, they made it a rule that no vehicle could leave one town, or military post, for another without reporting. The officials would then radio ahead that the vehicle was on its way. If they didn't show up on schedule, the French sent out aircraft to search for them. Sometimes they found them.

Out of a clear sky, Kenny said, "Where're we going to have our capital city? We've got to have some seat of government, where we can have embassies, welcome trade missions, that sort of thing."

They all thought about it.

Bey said, "I'm in favor of keeping on the move, the way we did when we were infesting Tamanrasset. That way, no potential enemy ever knows where El Hassan might be. A tent city. Oh, house trailers and that sort of thing too, for outsiders who couldn't exist without airconditioning, refrigerators, and all that. But something that could be moved every week or so, or even more often."

Homer shook his head. "You can't run a viable government, in this age, on the move. In no time flat, we're going to be so deep in paperwork and all the secretaries and clerks and what not that goes with it, that we couldn't possibly haul them all around. Personally, I'm in favor of Tamanrasset."

Cliff looked over at him and said, "Why that hole? We're going to be getting into IBM machines and everything else before we're through. Why not, say, Dakar? It's a relatively modern city." He smacked his lips. "Restaurants, nightclubs and all."

Homer shook his head. "Tamanrasset is centrally located, so far as we're concerned. And it's remote. Hard to get at, isolated in the middle of the Sahara. Timbuktu, or even Lhasa, Tibet, wouldn't be much more inaccessible to those we'd rather not see. Including the armed forces of enemies."

Bey said, in rebuttal, "A division of paratroopers could be vomited down on Tamanrasset a couple of hours after they left whatever base they started from. We're figuring on a permanent force of some one thousand men, as the core of our army—if that's what you could call it. They wouldn't last minutes before a division of paratroopers. Hell, these days an airborne division even carries along heavy tanks and artillery."

Homer accepted that, but said, "Our thousand men wouldn't wait. We'd all melt into the erg. You saw what happened at Fort Laperrine to Colonel Ibrahim's motorized regiment, and they were desert-trained troops. How would you like the logistics problems of supplying a full division of paratroopers in the Ahaggar Sahara? They need seas of oil, endless supplies, food being only one. A division soaks up water like a sponge. Where would it come from? The few wells and springs about Tamanrasset? Or would they have to fly it in? Can you imagine flying in enough water for twenty thousand men? You'd have your work cut out flying enough tankers to give your soldiers water to brush their teeth with. And meanwhile, the moment that first parachute blossomed out, we'd be on our way to some other town a few hundred miles off."

He looked over at Cliff. All four of them were sitting in the spacious front seat of the hoverlorry.

"Dakar? Now there we'd be sitting ducks, right on the sea. They could drop elements to block the railroads and the paved highways in Senegal, and we'd never get our people out. Besides that, even if we weren't attacked, we'd be bedeviled by multitudes of newsmen and foreign delegations until they ran out of our ears, and one of our deals is to keep El Hassan and his government mystery figures. We wouldn't remain mysteries overnight, in a big center such as Dakar, Algiers, Casablanca, or wherever—if and when we take them, and thus far we haven't as yet taken a single major city."

Pools, lakes, oceans of mirage shimmered and danced before them continually. The sun reflected off the dancing mirages and shot through their eyes, in spite of the sun glasses. At times, the landscape ahead was so covered with mirage that they had the impression of driving across a gigantic beach toward a surf which retreated endlessly with the outgoing tide—a tide which moved faster than one could drive.

"What're we going to do once we get up into Chaambra country?" Cliff said, his voice sour. "I'm beginning to think Bey was right. We should have brought along at least a couple of hundred of our best Tuaghi in some of those captured Arab Union trucks."

Homer shook his head. "With that many men, we'd wind up in a pitched battle with Abd-el-Kader's clan and all the rest of the Chaambra to boot. We'll play it by ear. Question around until we find where his encampment is, then decide what to do. It might entail nothing more than snaking into his camp early some morning and rescuing Elmer and getting the hell out without a shot being fired."

Bey chuckled quietly at that.

After a drawn-out silence, Kenny said, "What was this bit about the Swedes advancing us ten million in gold-backed kronor? I didn't even know the Swedes were on the gold standard.''

Homer laughed lowly and said, ''They're not, and tried to give us an argument. But we held fast. Ifriqiyah is going to accept no paper money, as such. There hasn't been a really stable paper money since the Second World War. The United States got going early in the trend. Following the war, they had most of the gold in the world buried at Fort Knox. Against it, they started printing billions of dollars in paper money, supposedly backed by the gold. They'd soon printed several times as much paper as they had gold. With it, they bought up most of what was valuable in Canada and one hell of a lot of Europe. The gold in Fort Knox began to melt away, as some foreign countries demanded it for the paper they had accumulated. Nothing was backing fifty dollars or so in paper money but the word of Uncle Sam, and after awhile they reneged on that and refused to cover their paper with any gold at all. Obviously, inflation then set in with a vengeance. Everybody seemed surprised that the dollar would buy only a fraction of what it used to. The other countries got wise after a time and began doing the same thing; that is, printing paper money to pay off their debts. So the inflation became world wide. *No* currency was backed by anything more than the smell of stale urine.''

Kenny said, ''What's all that got to do with the Swedish kronor?''

Homer said, ''Like I said, Ifriqiyah isn't going to accept paper for its raw materials. It might not necessarily be backed by gold; alternative valid commodities are acceptable, such as silver, platinum, uranium and other precious metals. We'd even accept one of the strangest backings of currency I've ever heard of. The Bulgarians are the biggest producers of attar of roses in the world. Invaluable as a base for perfumes, of course. They stash large amounts of it in bank vaults and buy commodities abroad backed by the attar."

Cliff said worriedly, "Trouble is, Homer, we'd soon have on hand all the gold, silver, and platinum in the world. These industrialized nations *have* to have copper, iron, bauxite, lead, zinc, just as badly as they have to have oil."

And Homer said, "Don't worry. We'll be spending it as fast as we get it. We'll maintain a balanced budget. We'll expend each year on imports all that we take in on exports. We want no aid, particularly no military aid, and we want no long term credits. We'll pay our way as we go. We'll have temporary credits, working both ways, of course, since it would be difficult to handle international business otherwise."

Bey said, "The way those trade delegations were beginning to swarm into the vicinity of Tamanrasset, even before we'd taken the town, we're going to have to spend like crazy to keep up with them. What'll we be buying?"

"One hell of a lot of things," Homer told him, statisfaction in his voice. "Road making equipment, oil drilling and refining machinery, mining equipment from prospecting instruments to the most modern mining machinery."

Kenny growled, "Why don't we make our own?"

"Because the highly developed industrial nations can do it better and cheaper, they have the technology and the highly skilled engineers, technicians and workers. Later, as we get more settled in, we'll import refining plants, smelting plants, so that instead of exporting crude oil, we'll export gasoline and petrochemical products, and ingots of iron and aluminum, rather than iron ore and bauxite.''

Kenny was still in argument. ''Why not put up plants to process the aluminum ingots? We could manufacture the products from it that are now being made in Common Europe, Japan and America.''

''Same answer,'' Homer said. ''Because they're too far ahead of us already and there's more than enough manufacturing capacity in the world; in fact, too much.''

Cliff said, ''Once we get going, how about aid from us to the other developing countries?''

Homer said slowly, ''I'd say, let's see about that when the time comes but my first reaction is to hang back. Except in extreme cases, such as famine, I don't believe in it. It doesn't work, certainly not to the profit of the country getting the aid. The best example is the race between India and China. India, which hadn't even been devastated by war, the way China was, got its independence about the same time China threw out Chiang Kai-Chek. India received billions from a dozen countries, particularly the United States and the Soviet Complex, in everything from outright grants to long term loans. At the end of thirty years, she was worse off than when she started and up to her ass in debt. China received practically no aid, except a little from Russia in the early years before she split with them. Instead, she put her people to work and at the end of thirty years China was a respected world power. She was no longer threatened with famine and flood. There was a network of railroads, roads and airlines linking the country. The warlords were a thing of the past and China was a single entity for the first time since Kubla Khan and the Mongols. No, I'm inclined to think that every time a developed country offers so-called aid to a developing one, they have some ulterior motive in the background. Backward countries need 'aid' from the rapacious advanced ones like they need an extra hole in the head.''

Bey said, ''You know, talking about gold, it occurs to me that there's possibly quite a bit of it in the realm-to-be of El Hassan. Since Carthaginian days the caravans from Timbuktu carried gold across the Sahara. Where did it come from? Where were the mines that the ancients drew their gold from in North Africa? Look at all the gold the Pharaohs had. Where'd it come from?''

Kenny said, ''When we get back, we'll send Cliff looking for it. He's Vizier of the Treasury.''

Cliff ignored him and said to Homer, ''We've been talking pretty fast and free about all these raw materials we are going to sell. But how about the companies that currently own them?''

Homer shook his head. ''They've long since been nationalized, Cliff. When these pseudo-socialist governments took over, or the military dictatorships, the first thing they did was to confiscate national resources. When our people take over, in turn, from them, they remain the property of the state. And at this stage of the game, at least, we're the state.''

A few miles to the west of Crawford and his hoverlorry a small convoy was approaching. It consisted of a hoverjeep and two desert lorries, with their outsized wheels, suitable for travel over the roughest reg and to some extent through the erg.

Sean Ryan and his company of mercenaries had picked the vehicles up in Adrar, one of the last oases of any size, as they headed down into the complete wastes. Uniforms and weapons, carefully hidden away, with the vehicles, in a small native warehouse, had also awaited them. The uniforms for the three officers were quite acceptable and typical of desert wear. Those of the men differed radically, and no two were exactly alike. For instance, pants ranged from the short-shorts affected by Israeli troops, to the below-knee length type the British customarily utilized in hot climates, to full length khaki or denim trousers usually seen on Americans. It was all part of the cover. They were supposedly a more or less unorganized group of mercenaries who had banded together to offer themselves as bodyguards to El Hassan.

Captain Raul Bazaine had supervised equipping the trucks and jeep. There were to be jerricans of petrol sufficient to take them half again as far as was necessary to get to the next point where fuel was available. There were jerricans of water sufficient for at least four gallons per person, each jerrican to be refilled every time water was available along the route. There were some ten shovels. There were tools and spare parts for each of the vehicles, from spare springs to spare carburetors. There were sufficient spare tires, mounted on wheels and attached to the sides of each vehicle, to have put an entire new set on each truck. On the roofs of the trucks were carried three types of sand mats to be put under the wheels, if a vehicle became stuck. One type was that most commonly used by desert trucks and were old sections of steel landing-strips, left over from the days of Rommel, Montgomery and Patton. There were also wire mats about twenty inches wide and fifteen or twenty feet long, and these could be rolled up and put on the luggage carriers. Finally, they had steel ladders, just long enough to fit between the front and rear wheels. When the back wheels climbed up on these, the driver was usually out of trouble. They also, of course, had a considerable supply of canned and dehydrated food, rations for at least a month.

The three vehicles, when underway, looked like a gypsy caravan, with pots, pans, jerricans, tires, tents and a multitude of other necessities bound everywhere there was an empty space. The jeep was monopolized by the officers and Meg, and ten of the mercenaries occupied each of the trucks. There was ample room; the vehicles were large as desert trucks went.

Sean, Bryan and Raul Bazaine had immediately contacted the two pilots awaiting them as soon as the group had gotten in from Algiers. They were French and Raul knew them both. Sean and Bryan instantly accepted them for what they were, pilot mercenaries. In fact, later, over wine in one of the canteens, they found that they knew a good many colleagues in common. It was a time for reminiscences and a time for the last drinks that Sean's expedition would probably enjoy for quite a while. South of Adrar, there were precious few Europeans or other whites, and the Moslem doesn't drink alcohol.

The hoverjet, carefully placed under canvas in an improvised hangar on the edge of the airfield, had proven satisfactory. It would most surely carry the full twenty-five of them if too much equipment wasn't taken along. And they didn't figure on carrying much equipment, save weapons, once the job was done. All else would be abandoned.

They headed southeast toward In Salah. The pilots reassured them about one thing they'd had in mind. It would hardly do for a convoy such as their own, twenty-five persons, all armed to the teeth, save Megan, all looking the tough customers they were, to be intercepted by the local military. But there evidently *was* no local military. The whole area was in a state of chaos. The Algerian government, in at least temporary confusion, was pulling its small outposts back further north. Too many had already defected to El Hassan. And although there were bands of El Hassan adherents here and there and the other place, they had not as yet coalesced to the point of taking over the few centers. No, twenty-four well-armed veterans had little to fear. Nevertheless, they kept on the alert.

Sergeant Lonzo Charles, now wearing a well-worn green beret, to the amusement of the others, drove. Megan McDaid, attired in a chic denim desert travel outfit from an Algiers shop, sat beside him. Sean Ryan and Bryan O'Casey were in the rear, their automatic rifles with their thirty round clips, handy. Raul Bazaine, who had taken on plenty of cognac the night before, was in the second truck, stretched out on several blankets and groaning his regrets. A hangover, Sean and Bryan had inwardly decided, must be something in this broiling sun. They felt virtuous, having stuck to the excellent Algerian wine the night before.

Lon Charles said over his shoulder, "Dust up ahead. Not much. Must be a single vehicle."

It was the first traffic that they had thus far run into, though they had been some hours on the road.

Both Sean and Bryan quietly took up their weapons, checked them, threw cartridges into the firing chambers, and set the safeties, then put the guns down again.

Bryan said to the driver, "Remember what Captain Bazaine said. When you meet another vehicle in the desert, you always stop and exchange greetings, ask if they're having any difficulties, and swap information on the road ahead."

"Yes, sir," Lon said.

The approaching vehicle turned out to be a moderate sized desert hoverlorry, containing four blacks, all dressed in khaki desert uniform rather than in native attire.

The small convoy dragged to a halt when it came abreast of the other vehicle and so did the hoverlorry.

A door in the lorry opened and a smiling head

protruded from the driver's side. It was a handsome negro, by the looks of him, somewhere in his
early thirties. He said something in a language
none of those in the jeep understood.

Lon Charles shook his head but grinned back in
friendly fashion.

All four of the blacks in the lorry were in the
wide front seat. One of them leaned over the driver
a little and called out in French.

The three whites had that language, but Sean
whispered, "Hold it. I'd like to know if they speak
English."

So Lon Charles called out, "Man, don't you talk
no English?"

All four of the hoverlorry occupants got out,
stretching, and approached the jeep, smiling.

One of them said, "I speak English. How's it
going with yawl? Everything okay?"

"Sure," Lon said. "We just come through
Adrar this morning. Everything's fine. You got lots
of gas and water?"

"Yeah, thanks," the other told him. "We're having no trouble at all. And you folks'll find the
road fine between here and In Salah."

Sean said, in a whisper, "Ask him the whereabouts of El Hassan."

So Lon said, "Man, you wouldn't know the
whereabouts of El Hassan, would you?"

The other's face went blank and he said, "Why
would you enquire about El Hassan? May his life
be as long and flowing as the tail of the horse of the
prophet."

"Oh, oh," Bryan murmured. "El Hassan
men."

Lon said cheerfully, "We're looking for to join up with him."

The faces of the four blacks were empty, though not unfriendly. The speaker said, "But three of you, including the *Sitt* are white. And the others, back in the trucks?"

Lon said, "They're white too. But we figure, before it's all over, El Hassan is going to need all sorts."

The other shook his head in disbelief but said, "The last we heard about El Hassan, he was in Tamanrasset, his new capital. It's about a thousand kilometers and a spell from here but you can pick up any supplies you need in In Salah."

The four returned to the hoverlorry and got back in and, after a friendly wave from the driver, the desert vehicle took off.

Before they started up again themselves, Sean said thoughtfully, "None of those four were Africans."

Meg looked around at him. "How do you mean? They were all as black as Lon, here."

Sean grunted acceptance of that but said, "Lon isn't an African either. He's an American. That chap who was speaking English had an American Southern accent you could hang your hat on."

Bryan said, his head cocked questioningly, "And how about the others?"

Sean shook his head. "They all projected an—how would you put it?—an educated, sophisticated air." He hesitated before adding, "And I'm after wondering if we just ran into El Hassan and some of his intimates."

Bryan snorted. "Unescorted, out here in the wilds?"

Sean shrugged and said to Lon Charles, "Let's get going, man dear."

Further up the trail, Bey was saying to Homer Crawford, "What do you think?"

"Damned if I know. That black driver spoke with a New York or New Jersey accent. There must have been twenty-five or so of them altogether."

"And from what I could make out of those in the trucks behind, as we passed, as tough a bunch as I've ever seen in Africa." Kenny muttered. It had been he who had spoken to Lon Charles.

"Hell, it's not important," Cliff said. "Isobel and Guémama can handle them. There's only twenty-five. They might have a couple of machine guns in those trucks, but certainly nothing heavier than that. One of our armored cars could do the lot in."

XII

ISOBEL CUNNINGHAM

ISOBEL CUNNINGHAM LOOKED up from the mountain of paperwork on her desk. The French and English was easily enough handled but although her Arabic was fluent, spoken, she had her work cut out writing in the language. She had taken over one of the larger offices in Fort Laperrine's administration building, since Homer and the three of the El Hassan inner circle had headed north. She had two male secretaries, newly recruited from the former Africa For Africans Association, the teams of which had all come over to the El Hassan movement when the New York headquarters had joined lock, stock and barrel. They were trickling in daily, along with elements of Homer's former Reunited Nations project and even Doctor Smythe's American Medical Relief organization. Not to speak of units from the French African Affairs sector and the British African Department. All of these, educated blacks, born, raised and schooled in lands beyond Africa.

Rex Donaldson, El Hassan's Minister Without Portfolion, as he had named himself, in dismay at the work piling up, had headed south for Dagon country where he had operated before, on the excuse that the tribes there weren't coming over to El Hassan fast enough.

Isobel had found it necessary to take over command. Jimmy Peters was a workhorse but hadn't the capability to make firm decisions, and Doctor Smythe was fully occupied with his medical problems.

No, it was a matter of Isobel, as the secretary of the supposedly temporarily withdrawn El Hassan, to assume direction. It was piling up so fast that she couldn't even remember the names of these two young men who were now looking at her, waiting to be told what to do. One was Donald something or other; but the other?

She had turned over the greeting of the flood of newcomers to Jimmy Peters and he was assigning them as rapidly as possible to tasks within whatever abilities they laid claim to. Most likely, upon Homer's return—knock on wood—there'd be a lot of switching around, but meanwhile they were doing their best.

The foreign delegations and newsmen, including Tri-Di TV cameramen, were temporarily at loose ends. She refused to make decisions involving them until El Hassan's return from his alleged seclusion with his viziers.

But now, there was commotion out on the parade ground. She came to her feet wearily and said to her two aides, both of whom were manfully trying, with little success thus far, to figure out just what it was they were supposedly doing, "Carry on, fellas. I'll check out what's cooking."

She left by the door that led onto the parade ground and put a hand over her eyes to shield them from the glare of the mid-day sun, after the comparative dimness of the office.

Approximately fifty of Guémama's camel corps and two of the weapon carriers, liberated from the Arab Union, had filed in through the gates, accompanying a jeep and two desert lorries. In the jeep were seated four whites, including a woman, and a black driver who wore, of all things, a bedraggled green beret.

Isobel walked out aways and waited for them.

The stranger vehicles came to a halt and some twenty men issued forth from them. They were in a wide variety of desert uniform and half carried advance model rifles, and the other half submachine guns.

The occupants of the jeep also climbed from their vehicle and the green bereted black one barked commands. The soldiers lined up, in two lines of ten men apiece, those with rifles in the front, those with submachine guns to the rear. They were efficiently snappy in their drill. The black stood to one side of them and snapped another command and they all came to salute.

Guémama's camelmen had formed a semi-circle behind the newcomers and now the young Tuareg chieftain came up to Isobel on his white *hejin* camel, struck in smartly with his *mish-ab* stick, struck it smartly again and barked the usual *Adar-ya-yan*. The camel was not quite to the ground before he nimbly jumped off and saluted the American girl.

"*Aselamu, Aleikum, Sitt* Izubahil," he said.

Isobel knew that Homer's chosen leader of the Tuaghi forces wasn't quite sure just where she stood with El Hassan. Whether she was his wife, or concubine, or simply one of his most intimate associates. Vizier, certainly she could not be. As all men knew, never had there been a woman vizier. Yet, before his leaving, El Hassan himself had made it clear to Guémama that until his return, the *Sitt* Isubahil's word was as his own as she was to be obeyed by all followers.

Isobel nodded to him and said, "*Salaam Aleikum,* O Guémama, *mokkadam* of El Hassan's most faithful. And what transpires?"

The three white men from the jeep had taken their place before the two lines of soldiers. One, in advance of the other two, bore a swagger stick, nothing more. The others had side arms, the holsters buttoned. The young woman stood a bit to one side of them. The men were at attention.

Guémama said in Tamaheg, "Verily, it is strange. One of my *goum* patrols of twenty came upon them as they advanced down the way from In Salah. They offered no resistance and allowed themselves to be captured."

"*Wallahi!*" Isobel said. "And what do they will, O Guémama?"

The Tuareg warrior shrugged hugely. "They do not speak Tamaheq, O *Sitt* Izubahil. Few of the Roumi do, as each man knows."

Isobel nodded and looked at the lead stranger.

Guémama stepped one yard to the left and rear of her.

Sean Ryan marched forward, came to a halt before her, tucked his swagger stick under his left armpit and saluted, British style.

He said, "*Parlez-vous Francais, Mademoiselle?*"

She took him in for a long moment and finally said, "Yes, however, you may speak English, if you would rather. Your Irish accent is somewhat overpowering.

She was by far the most attractive woman that he had seen thus far in North Africa. He grinned in self-deprecation, saluted again and said, "Major Sean Ryan. At your service, Miss . . ."

"Cunningham. Isobel Cunningham. And your companions?"

Sean half turned and looked at Raul, Bryan and Meg. They came forward, the two officers marching perfectly. They stopped a few yards off and came to attention again.

Sean said, "Doctor Megan McDaid, Captain Bryan O'Casey, Captain Raul Bazaine. I introduce you to Miss Isobel Cunningham." He raised his eyebrows at Isobel. "Of El Hassan's staff?"

"That is correct," Isobel said, without even a nod at the introduction. She looked cooly at Sean Ryan. "And why do you come to the headquarters of El Hassan, fully armed?"

"To offer our services."

She took him in, her eyes narrow. Finally, she said, "This sun is unbearable. We'll discuss it inside. Meanwhile, your men cannot bear arms in

Fort Laperrine, nor in the vicinity of Tamanras-set.''

Raul Bazaine made an about face and called, in French, which was the language most common to the mercenary company, "Ground arms!"

Isobel turned to Guémama and clipped out a few words in Tamaheq.

He said, *"Bilhana!"* and turned and called an order to the suspicious camelmen who had watched all this, weapons in hand.

A score of them dismounted and began disarming the mercenaries, who stood, empty-faced, and offered no resistance.

Guémama himself went forward and relieved the two captains of their sidearms.

Sean said, with all courtesy, "Is there some place my men can be sheltered? As you say, the sun . . .''

Isobel frowned. She said, "Tamanrasset is not a large settlement. Hundreds of premature newsmen, trade delegations, diplomats and recruits to El Hassan's banners have been descending upon us. All facilities in Tamanrasset are filled to capacity. Many are living in tents, or in the vehicles, some of which are trailers or campers, in which they arrived. It is quite chaotic. The fort, here, is reserved to the officials and forces of El Hassan. However, for the time, I suggest that your men and their vehicles retire to the shade of the former non-commissioned officer's mess, over there.'' She pointed. "They will be guarded but otherwise free to bring forth their cooking equipment and prepare food. I assume you are short of fresh provisions. You may have delegated two of your men to go into Tamanrasset and to the *souk* to purchase food—under guard.''

She turned to Guémama and gave instructions and then turned back to them. ''And now will you follow me?''

Bryan O'Casey went over quickly to Lon Charles and spoke to him briefly, then turned and hurried after the others who were heading for the administration building. The two camelmen at the portals saluted as Isobel and the four strangers passed into the interior. Guémama brought up the rear and, as he passed, took the submachine gun from the hands of one of the guards.

Isobel led to the way to the once-staff room, with its long, heavy table and its ample complement of chairs. She took the larger seat at the table's head, once the prerogative of the *commandant* of the fort and motioned them to chairs.

She looked at Megan and said, ''Would you like to freshen up a bit, Doctor?''

Meg said, ''Thank you, but I can wait.''

Isobel turned her eyes to Guémama, who had stationed himself to one side of the door and said in his own language, ''Please order mint tea for the strangers, O Guémama. Let all men know that El Hassan is aware of the hospitality due . . . strangers.''

''*Bilhana*,'' the Tuareg said, but didn't himself leave on the errand. He opened the door and spoke to one of his two camelmen who were stationed there, then turned back and resumed his stance.

The three mercenaries had noted that not only

was his sub-machine gun cocked but the safety was off.

Isobel looked at them, one by one. "Very well," she clipped. "The purpose of your intrusion into the realm of El Hassan?"

Sean said, with all the gentle tone of the Irish, "Intrusion is not quite the term, my dear Miss Cunningham. And would it be possible to present our petition to El Hassan himself?"

"Not at this tine. El Hassan has withdrawn into seclusion with his closest viziers to lay further plans for his uniting of all Ifriqiyah. He is not available."

Bryan looked over at Sean, remembering what the other had said about the possibility of the four men they had passed on the other side of In Salah being El Hassan and some of his confederates. Sean realized what was behind the glance, but ignored it.

He said, "Could you tell us when he will be available for an audience?"

They were interrupted by the advent of the tea, and waited until all had been served.

Then Isobel said, "I truly cannot say. He is in *ekhwan*, in great council, with his viziers and it might go on for days . . . or even longer." Isobel looked at him flatly. "However, I am El Hassan's secretary and presently detailed to make minor decisions until the problems he works upon are resolved."

Captain Raul Bazaine said gallantly, "You seem young, as well as supremely attractive to hold such an arduous post, Madamoiselle."

She looked at him bleakly but didn't deign to answer. She returned her level eyes to Sean Ryan.

The Irishman cleared his throat and went into his pitch. "Our group is composed of soldiers of fortune, Miss Cunningham. For the present, at least, there are few openings for our profession in the world. When word of El Hassan's, ah, movement began to filter out we came to the conclusion that perhaps here was employment. We banded together, pooled our resources to buy our vehicles and other equipment, and headed south to offer our services."

"And why do you think your services are required?" Isobel said. "Every day individuals, small groups and large contingents of Sahara tribesmen come in to volunteer. So many that we must turn away all but the most experienced warriors and most, even, of them. The Sahara does not have the resources of Common Europe, the Soviet Complex or America, to maintain large standing armies. On top of which, we of Ifriqiyah consider ourselves a peaceful nation, not a militaristic one. We seek no war, only the unification of all North Africa. We rally to us blacks, berbers, rifs, the Hamitic tribes, even such Arabs as have resided for centuries in Africa, largely on the Mediterranean coast. You are whites."

Sean accepted that and nodded and gave her the story which was their cover, though they didn't truly expect it to be acceptable. He said, "You have heard of the Janissaries of Turkey, the Mamelukes of Egypt?"

Isobel said, "Of course. We of El Hassan's staff are not uneducated, Major Ryan."

"Of course not. The Turkish Janissaries were the most trusted troops of the sultans and usually composed his bodyguard. They were more fully trusted than even his fellow Turks because they could only be without political ambition. They were Christians who had been captured while infants, circumcised and raised as Moslems. But they were still whites, still Europeans by birth, and had no possibility of rising to the throne. Had they attempted to seize power, the Turkish people as a whole would have risen and overthrown them, and all were aware of this. So they made an ideal elite to act as the sultan's bodyguard and as his most trusted soldiers in combat."

Isobel said skeptically, "Go on."

"This is what we offer El Hassan. We are admitted mercenaries, who offer our experienced services as bodyguards or in any other capacity. All of us have led native troops. We are sophisticated veterans, knowledgeable about the latest weapons and tactics. I myself, in my time, have been commander in chief of the armed forces of one—undeveloped—nation. Obviously, we could have no ambitions in the direction of a *coup d'état*. Like the janissaries before us, we would be rejected by the people of North Africa, since we are white. Our only allegiance would be to El Hassan, who would be responsible for our pay."

Isobel's voice was cold. "You are of the opinion that our *native troops*, as you put it, are in need of being led by you and your men?"

He looked at her for a long moment before saying, "Beggin' your pardon, Miss Cunningham, but we are some of the most highly trained veterans to be found in the world today. Not only the veterans of one or two wars or military revolts but of literally dozens and on every level from guerrilla affairs to the most sophisticated. We could drill your most awkward recruits to a hair. We can crew any tank, armored car, weapon carrier, or service any piece of artillery you might have on hand or acquire. And we can also *repair* such equipment. How many of your bedouin can do the same? I strongly suspect that if a minor screw on one of your simplest machine guns becomes loosened to the point where the weapon is inoperative, the machine gun is abandoned by its helpless gunner.''

Instinctively, Isobel didn't like him. She didn't know why. What this major of mercenaries was saying made considerable sense. Face it. They had a few in the service of El Hassan who had served under the French, British or Spanish in the old colonial days. But largely these were older men and had usually been utilized as infantry or in the Méharistes, French Camel Corps. They were ignorant of mechanics.

She looked over at Megan McDaid, who had her underlip in her teeth and, for reasons unknown to Isobel, was frowning. The Irish girl, doctor or no, Isobel thought, was handsome, obviously intelligent, and didn't seem the type inclined to an intricate intrigue.

She looked back at Major Sean Ryan. ''I could possibly make a decision and send you packing, under an escort of our men, but I would rather not. Very well, Doctor McDaid will move into my quarters. You and your men can set up your tents, where your vehicles are now. You will be allowed to remain there until El Hassan's return and with him the Field Marshal, his Vizier of Defense. They will decide.''

Captain Bryan O'Casey spoke up for the first time since they had taken their places at the table. He said, looking doubtfully at Megan, ''We would prefer to stick together.''

Isobel's eyes were again cold. She said, ''This fort was originally one of the largest of the French occupation of Southern Algeria. However, the facilities are quite primitive. You three officers may occupy what quarters you can find in the former non-commissioned officer's billets. However, you will discover the sanitary facilities inadequate. I do not know if there is even running water. My quarters are those of the former chief of staff of the French *commandant*. They are adequately furnished and there is even a bathroom. The Doctor will stay with me.''

She came to her feet, in dismissal.

Bryan shot a glance at Meg and shrugged in resignation. But she looked about and saw that no one else was observing her and stuck out her tongue at him, as though pleased with her fortune as compared with his.

XIII

EL HASSAN

AFTER HOMER CRAWFORD, Bey, Cliff and Kenny had bypassed Colum-Béchar, the largest town in the northern Sahara and the furtherest south the French had pushed their Trans-Saharan narrow gauge railroad, a century earlier, they headed eastward toward Figuig, the Mountains des Ksour—and Chaambra country. And now they dropped their attempts to keep secret their presence. It was necessary that they learn the whereabouts of Abd-el-Kader and of Elmer Allen, if he still survived.

There was no way to accomplish this without asking questions of every traveler they met, of every sedentary *zenata* working the date palms and gardens of the few and far between oases. They didn't reveal their identity, but, on the other hand, there was no manner in which they could keep the locals from jumping to conclusions. They were going to have to move fast or the suspicions of their identity were going to filter through to

Abd-el-Kader and his Chaambra and the four of them were in no position to meet head on, the full forces of the Ouled Touameur clan, not to speak of whatever other Chaambra elements he had already recruited to his horsetail banner and to the green pennant of the Moslem in *jehad*.

What they learned, bit by bit, was disconcerting.

Elmer Allen was indeed still alive, or, at least, had been so until quite recently. Abd-el-Keder had imprisoned him in a round iron birdcage-like affair in which it was impossible to either stand up, stretch out, or even sit. He was given a minimum of garbage in the way of food and enough dirty water to sustain life. The cage was portable and Elmer Allen was being hauled from town to town, from nomad encampment to oasis, and displayed to all as an example of the power of Abd-el-Kader, the newly proclaimed mahdi, and the weakness of the upstart, El Hassan. For here was his closest vizier, powerless before the strength of Abd-el-Kader.

Elmer, from the talks of those who had seen him thus displayed was philosophically enduring the camel dung, stones and mud thrown at him, along with the jeers and laughter at each stop. But Homer and his three companions all knew, inwardly, that it was only a matter of time. A man could not long survive out in the open sun in this climate without shade or headdress. Could not keep from coming down with *hemma,* one of the endemic fevers of the area, drinking such water and living in his own filth, since the cage, it was told, was never cleaned. Nor, for that matter, was it impossible that some enraged tribesman, perhaps seeking to gain merit in the eyes of the mahdi, might rush in near enough to the cage to spear or knife the prisoner, or even to crush in his head with a stone larger than those ordinarily thrown.

There was other news. The claim of Abd-el-Kader to be the newly arisen mahdi had spread over the northern Sahara and the African lands bordering the Mediterranean. And now to Chaambra country were pouring marabouts and khatibs, muezzins and ulemas, muftis and dervishes, imams, hezzabs and even some green turbaned ones of Shorfu blood, descendents of Hasan, son of Fatima, daughter of Mohammed. For while it is true that there is no equivalent to priests and clergymen in Islam, that is not to say there are no religious officials and holy men of every strata.

It was said to be the greatest *djemaa el kebar* ever known to man, nor was it only the usual council of elders and chiefs of the Chaambra but one which would be attended by all nomad leaders yearning to drink the milk of war against the false El Hassan, who, as all men knew, was a tool of the hated Roumi whites who would destroy the old ways of the desert.

At the last news, Homer looked thoughtful as they drove along.

He said, ''I think I know where this *djemaa el Kebar* of Abd-el-Kader will be held. There's a traditional oasis where the Chaambra tribes, the Mouadhi, Bou Rouba, Berazga and Ouled Fredj, meet every few years for a conference. It's where we first came in contact with our boy, Adb-el-

Kader. Not too long ago, at that. He was all hot to form raiding parties against the new dams, the afforestation preserves, the irrigation projects, roads and so forth. I was able to fox him with a bit of karate and haul him off to the slammer but we were hardly out of sight before the corrupt bastards in Colum-Béchar let him loose again."

"Yeah," Kenny said, "Bey and I were around, and Elmer and Abe Baker, for that matter. You think they'll hold this new gathering there?"

"Almost sure to."

"Now, wait a minute," Bey said. "You're not figuring on inviting yourself to that hoedown are you?"

Homer looked over at him. "That's where Elmer'd be, cage and all."

"Sure," Bey said in disgust. "And every Moslem religious fanatic from Egypt to Morocco. They'd tear us apart. They know damn well that El Hassan, though giving lip service to Islam, is their kiss of death, if he ever comes to power."

Homer said, without denial, "Our ultimate rejection of Mohammedism is a basic of the El Hassan movement. But at this stage we can't do it openly. Actually, it will wither away eventually of its own accord. It's already doing so. Among the educated elements in Tangier, Casablanca, Algiers, Cairo and the other centers they pretend to follow Islam but actually are no more Orthodox Moslems than the average educated American is a fundamentalist Christian. Who in America today believes literally in the books of Genesis? Only the most ignorant, largely located in the benighted Bible Belt of the South. And the Q'ran is even more nonsensical than the early chapters of the Bible. Let me see if I can quote that *sutra* describing Paradise, the Garden of Allah.

He narrowed his eyes and recited. " . . . *the water of the brooks is never bad; the rivers of milk are always fresh; the rivers of wine are a delight; the rivers of honey are pure, the faithful lie on carpets of brocaded richness, and they are shaded by trees which let down their fruits of themselves. The just shall be served in silver goblets and served by boys eternally young; at their feet will run streams of limpid water; they will have as wives dedicated virgins with round breasts, big black eyes, and complexions like ostrich eggs hidden with care in the sand; and concubines specially created for them, having been touched by neither man nor genie.*"

"Jesus," Cliff muttered, "What does an ostrich egg hidden in the sand look like?"

Homer said, "Or that bit from Mohammed about women. *God has created two things for the pleasure of man: woman and perfumes. Your women are your field. Go to your field and plough it as often as you like. How can one attribute to God, as his offspring, woman who, because of her lack of reason, is always ready to quarrel without motive?*"

He snorted. "Now consider that crap. Obviously, the Islamic position on women, the fact that they have no souls, not having been created by Allah, and will hence not go to Paradise, but will be replaced there by *houris,* especially created for the men, is ridiculous. The Islamic position on women can't endure in an advanced society. Women's lib, in its time, will come to Islam as it did the West. And take that description of Paradise. It makes about as much sense as the Biblical one. Heaven with its streets of gold. Maybe that Paradise makes sense to an uneducated nomad, but to his city living, educated, sons and daughters?''

''All right, all right, so you've wooed us away from Islam, get back to the point,'' Bey said. ''We can't go busting into that nest of fanatics, all *four* of us, and come out as anything more than chunks of meat to be eaten with the couscous.''

Homer said, ''We have one advantage. El Aicha, the elder of the Ouled Fredj tribe, and, as such, the senior member of the *djemaa el kebar*, has no particular admiration for our boy Abd. He's old enough to remember the French occupation and, seemingly, instinctively knows that the old days will never return. Remember, he sided with me, when I had my run-in with Abd-el-Kader, even lending me his sword? He'll hold off the hotheads and crackpot religious leaders long enough for us to have our say.''

''Yeah,'' Kenny said gloomily. ''And *then* they'll slit our throats. Or maybe not bother. Just hand us over to the womenfolk for the usual castration and related bits of torture, desert style.''

Homer said, ''I've got the germ of an idea. Listen. . . .''

Homer Crawford had been correct. The *djemaa el Kebar* was being held in the traditional location. But this one differed greatly from the one Crawford's team had come up against the first time. It must have been three times the size, and it was obvious that at least half of the assembled tribesmen were other than Chaambra. Their tents spread out from the small oasis far into the desert and hammada, the rocky uplands between the mountains.

There were religious speakers everywhere, with varying sized crowds of listeners, the numbers seemingly dependent upon just how hysterical the marabout or muezzin might be. Those who frothed at the mouth, rolled their bloodshot eyes up to the point of disappearance and jerked uncontrollably, were highest in demand. As the Americans drove on, their windows rolled up to make identification more difficult, they even passed dancing, spinning and whirling dervishes, going through their ecstatic, violent dancing and pirouetting, together with howling dervishes with their vociferous chanting and shouting.

"Beats a state fair all hollow," Cliff muttered unhappily. "Why the hell didn't I become a garbage man like my sainted mother wanted? Do you know what a garbage man makes in San Francisco these days?"

Nobody bothered to answer him. Bey and Kenny looked as glum as he did. Homer was inwardly rehearsing his speech to come.

The *djemaa el kebar* pavilion, a large, ornate awning strung on a dozen sturdy posts, was located on the far side of the oasis, at a point where the craggy, black hammada came down to its edge. Heavy rugs covered the sands beneath it and leather hassocks, in yellow, green and red, those thick, heavy cushions preferred to chairs in desert lands, provided seating for the chiefs and other assembled dignitaries. Amidst the hassocks were scattered *narghileh* water pipes and brass dishes of dried dates for refreshment.

Obviously, the *djemaa el kebar* was already in session.

A considerable number of other vehicles were in the encampment, including desert trucks and buses, which had evidently brought in pilgrims and the curious from considerable distances, so the new vehicle was not as out of the way as all that, despite the fact that it was the only hoverlorry represented. The native-owned transportation was aged, rusted, weathered and battered.

Homer Crawford was able to drive up to the entry of the open pavilion, to stop there, drop the lift lever of the vehicle and let it flatten to the sand. The four of them got out, their Tommy-Noiseless, .10 caliber submachine guns, with their clips of two hundred rounds of high-velocity explosive shells, slung over their shoulders.

The entry was guarded by two Chaambra tribesmen. One bore a World War Two .30 caliber carbine. The other had an anachronistic muzzle loading musket with its six foot long barrel, made a century and more before to be especially adapted to firing from camel back. It would have brought several hundred dollars from any collector in Common Europe or America, enough to have bought the bearer a few of the latest model automatic rifles.

To the right of the entry, about ten yards, was the iron bird-cage the four newcomers had heard about. It was hanging from a wooden tripod of stakes dug into the sand, and in it was Elmer Allen. He was nude and filthy beyond description.

His head was bare to the Sahara sun and his cracked lips were thick with sun sores. His eyes were bleary with exhaustion but he was able to look up and mutter, "It's about time you chaps got here."

Homer Crawford could feel a well of nausea inside but he played the role of El Hassan and looked straight ahead. Bey gave Elmer a quick nod and Kenny gave him a wink which he probably couldn't see, but no one spoke to him.

The two guards looked hesitant and confused at the determined march of the four and did nothing to halt them. Already a crowd was gathering behind, most of them armed warriors of the Chaambra. Within moments, there would be thousands. The murmur was going through them, *El Hassan . . . El Hassan . . . El Hassan . . .*

The chiefs and headmen of the *djemaa el kebar,* in session, were seated in a half circle. All of them were elderly, save one, all dressed in ceremonial desert garb. In the center position sat El Aicha. As a chief of Maraboutic ancestry and hence a holy man as well as the elder of the Ouled Fredj tribe of the Chaambra, he presided. So old as to look senile—he wasn't, as Homer well knew.

But to his dismay, Homer Crawford recognized Abd-el-Kader seated in the place of honor next to El Aicha. This could only mean that his claim to being the mahdi was being recognized, or was about to be. The young warrior chieftain was attempting to suppress his satisfaction at seeing El Hassan and three of his closest adherents in this spider's web. Abd-el-Kader was a perfect figure of desert man. His eyes were those of the Sahara hawk, piercing and aggressive. His posture was straight and strong. From his turban, white as the snows of the Atlas, to his yellow leather boots, he wore the traditional clothing of the Chaambra and wore them with pride. Beneath his white burnoose he wore a gandoura of lightweight woolen cloth and beneath that a longish undershirt of white cotton, similar to that of the Tuareg but with shorter and less voluminous sleeves.

Bey, Kenny and Cliff came to a respectful halt but Homer Crawford took another two steps forward. He touched forehead, lips and heart in the graceful gesture of greeting and said, *"Aselamu, Alekum, O El Aicha,* May your life be as long and lustrous as the beard of the Prophet." He then turned to the chieftains to the left and right of the aged desert leaders and saluted them as well. *"Ssalam-o 'alaykoom."*

El Aicha hesitated but then made standard greeting in reply. "Salaam Aleikum, O El Hassan, and what will you here at the great *ekhwan* of your . . . enemies.?"

Homer looked at him evenly and said, "O El Aicha, as each man knows, there are no enemies of El Hassan amongst the true dwellers of the Sahara. Only a few false pretenders who stand in the way of the great movement to bind together all Ifriqiyah. And it is to confront such pretenders and great liars that El Hassan and his three most trusted viziers have come."

Abd-el-Kader had had enough. His face suffused with anger now, he came to his feet. He said, snarl in his voice, "Verily, he who names himself El Hassan is audacious. *Wallahi!* But as all men can see, he has placed himself at the mercy of the Chaambra and who among us can feel mercy for this Son of Shaitan?''

Homer Crawford didn't deign to look at him. Instead, his eyes were level on those of El Aicha. He said, ''As before, O El Aicha, we demand the right of strangers in your camp to a trial by combat to determine who are false, El Hassan and his followers, or the self-proclaimed mahdi, who opposes the uniting of all the lands and the bringing of the blessings of Allah to all the people.''

Abd-el-Kader was furious. He well remembered his defeat at the hands of Crawford, his being humbled before his tribesmen of the Ouled Touameur clan.

''With what weapons?'' he snapped.

Homer looked at him for the first time. ''Verily, that is a problem. The last time we fought, it was with swords, a weapon of the past with which you are acquainted, as all men know, but with which I am but passingly familiar. But, to the other extreme, are my own weapons, which are the product of the new ways. *Bismillah*, thus be it. Verily, it is as unreasonable for you to attempt to fight with our weapons as it is for us to fight with yours. Observe, O chieftains of the desert.''

He stepped quickly to one side of the pavilion which faced upon the hammada. A hundred feet into the rocky area stood a lone gnarled *baobab* tree. Homer unslung the Tommy-Noiseless, switched it to full automatic, and cut loose. He was well aware that Abd-el-Kader and some of his warriors were equipped with automatic weapons, usually such as Sten guns and other left-overs from the wars of yesteryear. But they were unacquainted with such as the Tommy-Noiseless.

He fired a full hundred rounds of the tiny, explosive .10 caliber loads, in a *Gotterdammerung* of sound that had even those veteran tribesmen, veterans of a hundred desert raids, wincing. And the hardwood tree, almost impossible to cut down with ordinary bedouin tools, became a heap of splinters and sawdust.

Homer reslung his gun, turned and shrugged hugely. "*Bismillah*," he said. "A single such weapon could wipe away a whole *harka* of warriors. Verily, it would be unfair to use the weapons of El Hassan—with which all of his followers are rapidly being armed—as it would be to utilize the sword."

El Aicha fingered his thin white beard, thus allowing himself to hide his amusement.

"Then what is the alternative, O El Hassan, provided that the *djemaa el kebar* agrees to your challenge?"

"That the contestants strip to the waist and unarmed enter the hammada. There they will meet in man to man combat and who issues forth is found the victor."

Abd-el-Kader was no coward but he had witnessed before the abilities of this El Hassan to fight with hand and foot and wanted no more of it.

He said, contemptuously, "The mahdi does not descend to common brawl with every verminous black come out of the southern erg. I refuse to enter the hammada, stripped like an Ouled Nail prostitute. Instead, I shall summon my guards and we will dispose of these upstarts."

A murmur went through the assembled chiefs and headmen and largely it was derogatory but none spoke up. The followers of Abd-el-Kader were on hand in their thousands.

It was Bey who stepped forward, his face expressing surprise, and saying, one hand lifted. "Verily, the, ah, mahdi, if mahdi he be, has misunderstood El Hassan and his challenge. El Hassan does not suggest that he meet the, ah, mahdi, in single combat. But that he and his viziers retire to the hammada and that the whole of the Ouled Touameur clan, which Abd-el-Kader leads, follow after them. And they who emerge will have triumphed, as will be obvious to all men."

Silence fell like a curtain as the assembled *djemaa el kebar,* including El Aicha and Abd-el-Kadar, bug-eyed the four khaki clad black Americans.

XIV

EL HASSAN

EL AICHA MANAGED to get out finally, "Verily, you speak nonsense. The Ouled Touameur clan numbers fully a thousand warriors."

Homer Crawford rubbed his mouth thoughtfully, as though thinking that obvious truth over. Abd-el-Kader's face was too livid with fury for him to be able to speak.

Homer nodded his head and said, "You speak even the truth in your wisdom, O El Aicha. If a thousand warriors were sent in after us at once, then all would be as confused as the lost souls in *Gehennum*. So I suggest that we proceed as follows. I and two of my viziers will proceed to go into the hammada and await. The, ah, mahdi, will dispatch three of his champions after us. If none emerge victorious within the counting slowly of five hundred, then three more will enter the hammada to seek us out. And after another counting of five hundred, three more."

He let his eyes run coldly over the assembled

chiefs, his overpowering personality clutching them. "Until we have been defeated—or all one thousand of the Ouled Touameur warriors have gone down to black death for opposing the will of El Hassan. And then . . ." Homer turned and directly faced Abd-el-Kader. " . . . and then, our brave, self-proclaimed mahdi, can enter behind his fallen warriors and come face to face with El Hassan whom he dares brand an upstart."

Abd-el-Kader, his face suffused in his rage, screamed, "He plans to call upon the *djinn* and *efrit* of the wastelands to aid him!"

Kenny Ballalou spoke up for the first time since entering the pavilion. In amusement he said, "He calls himself the mahdi and he is afraid of *djinn* and the *efrit*. As all men know, the true mahdi, when he returns, will control the *djinn* and *efrit,* for he will hold power second only to Allah. If there is danger in the hammada from *djinn,* it will be to El Hassan and his viziers, not to the followers of the mahdi—*if* mahdi he be."

The desert warrior chieftain came to sudden decision and strode to the entry to the pavilion. He shouted out instructions to a score of his men, who threw themselves atop their desert horses and rode at breakneck speed into the wastes behind the pavilion tent. Obviously, Abd-el-Kader was checking out the area to be sure that El Hassan had set no traps, that the hammada was empty.

The members of the *djemaa el kebar* were still stricken speechless. Their eyes went from Homer to the Chaambra champion and back again. This was madness, as each man knew. Three against a thousand!

El Hassan turned to Kenny Ballalou and said, "It is my will that you remain here to see that all transpires as agreed. But three of our enemies will enter behind us at one time, and three more, and so on, only after the slow counting of five hundred."

"But, great El Hassan, I would fight beside thee!" Kenny protested. He was by far the smallest of the four.

"It is my will," El Hassan said, command ringing in his voice.

"*Bismillah*, thus it be," Kenny said in dejection. "For thou art El Hassan."

There were thousands now before the pavillion. Indeed, the whole encampment had gathered there. Somehow the word had already spread. The silence was unbelievable, considering the magnitude of the swarm of Bedouin and sedentary elements from the desert towns.

Homer, Bey and Cliff stripped to their waists and headed for the entry to the hammada, a narrow path.

Bey-ag-Akhamouk was as beautiful a physical specimen as the Tuareg had possibly ever produced, undoubtedly augmented by American diet and medical care as compared to that of Sahara nomads. He was lean, wiry and obviously strong. No unworthy foe of any Chaambra. But El Hassan, ah, that was another thing, and all took deep breath. Had these desert people known it, Homer Crawford's physique resembled that of Sugar Ray Robinson, the American pugilist of half a century and more ago. He walked with the grace of a black panther. Ah, but the other vizier of El Hassan! It was from him that no man could tear his eyes. For if Crawford resembled Sugar Ray, then Cliff Jackson could only be compared to the Joe Louis of the early years. His step, too, was catlike, but that of a Bengal tiger, rather than the smaller, more lithe panther.

Abd-el-Kader's horsemen had galloped back to report the hammada empty. Their leader, still stewing in anger, and obviously suspicious, went through the ranks of his men, pointing out those of the outstanding physical dimensions.

Meanwhile, El Hassan, flanked by his two viziers, stood at the pavillion entrance, their arms folded dramatically, waiting.

Cliff Jackson smiled at the guard next to him, the one who carried the old fashioned muzzle loader. He held out a hand politely, in an obvious request to examine the weapon. The Chaambra guard frowned a little worriedly but handed it over. He was proud of the silver embossing on the stock.

Cliff took the six foot barrel, one hand near the muzzle, one near the short stock and hunched his shoulders. Slowly, slowly, the barrel bent. The guard looked at him in shocked horror.

A deep sigh of disbelief went through the multitude. Cold sweat blisters broke on the American black's forehead but he bent the barrel almost double, then twisted the muzzle end under, came up with it on the other side, bent it back through the loop again so that now the barrel of the gun resembled a pretzel. He smiled apologetically and handed the weapon back to its owner, who could only stare at it, his face blank.

Cliff smiled his charm once more and held out his hand for the short barrel carbine of the other guard who quickly jerked it away, in alarm, and hurried off into the crowd.

Bey said, out of the side of his mouth, "Okay, wise guy, where'd you learn *that* party trick?"

El Hassan ignored the whole incident, as though it was a common thing among his people.

Cliff hid his grin but whispered back. "Trick is right. I used to mess around with weight lifting back in college days. Most of these strong man acts you see in circuses or carnivals are largely tricks. It's a matter of knowing how to do them. That old musket, with its long barrel was made of thin gauge iron, not even real steel. You probably could have bent it yourself, if you'd put it over your knee. Now that British carbine with its heavy steel barrel was another thing. If the second guard would have handed it over to me, I couldn't have bent it in a million years. But, of course, he wasn't about to give me a chance."

"All right, all right, you jokers," Homer said softly, "Here come our first three boys. Let's get going." For the first time, he looked up at Elmer Allen, in his cage. He could make out on the distressed man's hand where his severed finger had once been. He nodded and Elmer made a very faint movement of his head in reply.

The three marched toward the jagged, rocky wasteland of the hammada, abreast. When they reached the narrow path that wound into it, they had to switch to single file, El Hassan going ahead. The area looked similar to a broken lava field, which perhaps it was.

After a few minutes, Abd-el-Kader made an abrupt motion with his hand and his three chosen men followed after, one of them looking quickly at the twisted gun muzzle still in the hands of the bewildered guard, as they passed.

El Aicha, who, with the rest of the *djemaa el kebar,* had come to his feet and approached the side of the pavilion, stopping just short of emerging into the sun, pointed a finger at a tribal scribe who began counting in Arabic.

When he had reached five hundred, all present stared at the path. No one materialized.

Kenny Ballalou said dryly to Abd-el-Kader, "Three more."

The warrior chieftain didn't look at him. Instead, he jabbed out his finger, once, twice, thrice, at his followers and the three chosen stripped down to the waist and headed for the path. The scribe began counting again.

Toward the end of the allotted time, Kenny yawned and looked at Abd-el-Kader, but didn't bother to say anything.

Three more of the alleged mahdi's followers headed for the path into the hammada. They walked somewhat less briskly than had their comrades before them.

The scribe began the new count-down.

Kenny faded into the background a little and brought his wrist up to his mouth. The device on it looked like a watch, and was, but it was more. He said into it, "How's it going?"

Homer Crawford's voice came back thinly and there was even a dry humorous quality. "As to be expected. Here comes the next batch of poor bastards."

Kenny returned to the foreground, in time to see

still another trio of the Ouled Touameur clan, these wan of face, stripping preparatory for heading toward what they obviously believed to be their doom.

When they were gone, Kenny looked at his watch and said, "The day is half through. Perhaps we should hasten this matter. After all, the, uh, mahdi's men number a thousand."

El Aicha looked at him and said, "What do you suggest, O Vizier of El Hassan?"

"That the scribe count to but four hundred, or perhaps three hundred, before sending in more of the unfortunate followers of the, uh, mahdi."

But the aged chieftain of the Chaambra shook his head. "No, the agreement made with El Hassan was the count of five hundred."

Kenny muttered, "He doesn't need that much time, as all can see. We shall be here throughout the night and well into the day beyond. Never in all his life has El Hassan met defeat. He is the chosen of Allah."

Abd-el-Kader was breathing deeply and unbelievingly. The count had come to only four hundred, but he pointed out three more of his men to begin stripping. There were murmurs and dark looks from others in the ranks of his formerly jubilant and laughing clansmen. None pushed forward to volunteer.

The crowd behind them were muttering. Individual words and phrases could be heard. *"El Hassan . . ."* *". . . the supposed mahdi . . ."* *". . . Verily, El Hassan and his viziers are as the first followers of the Prophet who issued forth with scimitar and spear from the deserts of far Arabia to conquer the world." ". . . and why does not the brave mahdi enter the wastes to confront El Hassan?"*

Abd-el-Kader heard that last and spun and glared out in the direction from whence it had come. But the crowd stared back at him, unrepentant and undisclosing of the whereabouts of he who had been so bold.

Elmer, up in his cage, began laughing uncontrollably, in spite of his physical condition.

All eyes went to him. Verily, the man was mad and a madman is the afflicted of Allah, and blessed. And El Hassan alone, save for three followers, had come to his rescue, though all men knew that the Sahara swarmed with his followers and he could have brought a *harka* of a size never before seen.

Seven trios of the Ouled Touameur clan, twenty-one men in all, had filed up the path into the hammada before the rest of the followers of Abd-el-Kader called it quits, turned their backs on the once adored leader and walked off, their faces dark with more anger than shame.

It was not that the warriors of the Ouled Touameur were not brave men. They had proven themselves a hundredfold over to be as valiant as any tribesmen in the Sahara. But this was a combination of superstition, fear of the unknown, and disgust with their leader, who was once always in the forefront and was now holding back to send them to their doom. And, yes, a desert warrior's respect for El Hassan and his two viziers who were willing to stand alone against a thousand.

Abd-el-Kader, breathing deeply, his face

empty, though still in despair, stared his incomprehension. Two hours past, before the appearance of the hated El Hassan, he had been the strongest man in North Africa, already being proclaimed the mahdi.

Those nearest him, edged away, leaving him staring at the path up which a score of his bravest had walked—not to return. His hand went to his sword and, for a moment, it looked as though he was about to dash into the hammada seeking revenge against his destroyer. But he could not bring himself to move, in the face of all the disaster that had flooded over him.

And from the multitude a shrill laugh was heard. And then there was a brief moment of hesitation at the audacity. And then two or three more laughs, less hesitant now. And then the teeming hundreds and thousands who had come to celebrate the newly proclaimed mahdi, dissolved into uncontrollable laughter, hoots of derision and even screams of curses.

Abd-el-Kader suddenly dashed forward, flung himself on his famed white Arabian steed and dashed for the crowd which, in its hilarity, hardly had time to make way. He rode on through, at breakneck speed, and into the desert beyond, and never looking back.

El Aicha, his years-aged face empty of expression, turned to Kenny Ballalou and said, ''And will you, then, O Vizier of El Hassan, go and inform him that no others of his foes dare confront him?''

Wordlessly, the American black headed for the path.

He hadn't gone far into into the stark wasteland

before he made out Bey who was leaning against a jagged rock.

Kenny said, "Hi, nigger."

Bey snorted. "Look who's calling who a nigger. Why you're so black, each time you go out into the sun I expect you to fade."

Kenny said, "Where the hell's Homer and Cliff?"

Bey made a motion of his head as he came over. "Up ahead. I'm a decoy. I'd let the boys spot me and then I'd head off down this gully, with them after me at full speed. They'd have to go single file because it's so narrow."

He led the way, continuing, "There's this kind of a little clearing up ahead. Homer would be standing to one side, Cliff to the other. As you know, Homer used to teach a karate class for the Marines. Cliff was a heavyweight runner-up in the Golden Gloves. I'd stand to one side and wince at the slaughter. These poor bastards have never fought with their hands in their lives. Most of our time was taken up tearing strips of cloth out of their fancy bloomer pants and tying them up and stashing them to one side. There might be a couple of busted jaws and a broken arm or so, but otherwise they're mostly okay. Some are still unconscious, of course. What happened down below?"

They had entered the small clearing of which he had spoken. It was sand floored, as though an arena, which in some ways it resembled. Homer and Cliff leaned against the walls, to each side, breathing deeply.

Kenny looked at them in pretended disgust. "A couple of musclebound clods," He said. "Down below, the crowd is laughing itself silly. First the remainder of his clan and then Abd-el-Kader himself, took off. I wouldn't swear to it, but I have a sneaking suspicion that even those whirling dervishes out there are now devoted adherents of El Hassan. Why don't the three of you go out and do kind of a soft shoe dance, and then Cliff can climax the act with bending more rifle barrels. It'll wow 'em.''

Cliff looked down at his right hand and said, ''I hope the hell I didn't bust a knuckle on that last one. He had a head like a cement block.''

And Homer said, ''Well, we couldn't have kept up the pace much longer. Not in this sun. They didn't put up much of a fight, but you can't last forever. Let's go down and get Elmer out of stir.''

''To hear is to obey, O El Hassan,'' Cliff grinned. ''My descendants will never believe this. What did you do in the big war against the Chaambra A-rabs, granddaddy. . . ?''

XV

EL HASSAN

THEIR FIRST INSTINCT was to get away soonest and back into the desert, not exposing El Hassan to the limelight, maintaining his mystique. But it wasn't in the cards. For one thing, Elmer Allen was in no condition to travel, not immediately. For another, the convening of the *djemaa el kebar* of the Chaambra confederation, not to speak of the chiefs present from other tribes, was too good an opportunity for conversion to the El Hassan movement to be missed. They were going to have to strike while the iron was as white hot as at present.

But it wouldn't do for El Hassan and his viziers to be seen erecting their tents and utilizing their mundane camping equipment as other men would do.

The problem was solved by El Aicha appropriating for them the quarters of the headman of the small mud-brick settlement of the oasis on which the gathering was taking place. Squalid though it might be, windowless and practically without furniture, it was the best the tiny village provided. There was a smell of mildew, airlessness, sickness and dirty clothes. Strips of old carpet hung from the walls. Some filthy rags had been thrown into corners, here and there, obviously to be used as beds. The owner wasn't overly put out. In fact his *Keif halak*, 'all in my house is yours,' was effusive. For the rest of his life he could relate that El Hassan himself had once dwelt in his humble home.

They refused the offer of servants and even armed guards, and although El Hassan himself remained aloof, his three viziers busied themselves in hauling into the interior of the hut various items of folding furniture, cooking equipment and supplies.

Elmer Allen had quickly been rescued and a folding, heavy khaki camp-bathtub used several times over to clean him up. He was too shaky to handle a razor himself and Kenny took over in that department. They had also brought clothing his size. Bey assumed the role of doctor and went over him with what skill he possessed. There was little that could be done until they reached a doctor: the root of the severed finger had festered and this was cleaned, sulfa applied and he was given a double shot of antibiotics along with vitamin and mineral shots.

At first he spoke little, though they gathered about him. When he did, there was a stammer, a stutter in his voice.

In the medical footlocker was a bottle of excellent French cognac, which Kenny opened. He poured a couple of ounces into a tin cup and proffered it, but the hand that Elmer extended shook so that Kenny himself held the cup to the other's sun blistered lips.

Cliff had been working over the camp stove and now brought over a heavy ceramic mug of steaming broth.

Elmer took several mouthfuls but then snarled, "Fer . . . fer . . . crissakes, give a . . . a . chap something to sink . . sink his teeth into. I've been . . . been eating camel dung, or what . . . whatever it was, for donkey's years."

The others laughed and Cliff went back to his stove.

Elmer looked over at one of the army cots which had been set up and got out, "I say. I . . . haven't really slept since they . . . they put me in that portable med . . . medieval torture chamber."

Cliff said, "Get this stew down and we'll tuck you into beddy-by."

Elmer snarled at him and then looked accusingly at Homer Crawford. He said, "What . . . what in the hell took you so long to clobber those blokes?"

Homer said, humorously placating, "There were twenty-one of them altogether and we didn't want to hurt our fists."

Later, when Elmer was snoring in complete exhaustion on the army cot tucked away in one corner of the not overly large hut, Homer, Bey, Kenny and Cliff sat around the folding camp table, finishing their own meal.

Kenny said, "What now?"

And Homer said slowly, poking at his stew with his fork, "We'll address the *djemaa de kebar* tomorrow. Present a program for their spreading the word of El Hassan in this area, then make with a quick inspirational, slogan-shouting, address to the assembled multitude, and take off south.''

Bey made a motion of his head toward Elmer. "How about him?"

"We'll rig up a bed in the back of the lorry. If it looks too tough for him, we'll camp out in the boondocks somewhere until he's more nearly recovered."

Cliff said, "Why not take Elmer to Colum-Béchar and get him into a hospital? One of us could stay to watch over him and the rest could go on."

Homer thought about it but shook his head. "No. Double reason. Colum-Béchar isn't in our hands yet. There might be elements that would shoot their way into the hospital and finish you both off—not necessarily local people. The whole damn Reunited Nations has taken a preliminary stand against us, not to speak of the Arab Union. And not to speak of any remnant followers of our chum the mahdi—if any. Besides, it wouldn't do for word to go out that one of El Hassan's viziers was in hospital. El Hassan's viziers are too tough to ever have to go to a hospital."

Bey looked over at the door, which consisted of a soiled piece of homespun hanging like a curtain. He said, "We'd better take turns as guards tonight. It seems a remote chance, under the prevailing circumstances, but it's possible that Abd-el-Kader, or some of his lads, might come a-calling. I'll stand first watch for three hours."

"Sounds like a good idea," Homer said. "I'll stand second watch."

Bey shook his head. "Nope, not you. No one should see you doing guard duty. You're El Hassan. I'll wake Cliff in three hours."

Cliff said, "Dammit, when we started this outfit why didn't we pick me as El Hassan, instead of Homer? Hell, I'm bigger than he is."

Bey snorted and picked up his Tommy-Noiseless and turned toward the door.

Kenny swatted at his arm and snarled, "A mosquito. How in the devil do mosquitos get onto these oases, five hundred miles into the desert?"

Cliff said, "They carry canteens." He looked about the hut. "This is going to be some night. Sandflies, ticks, fleas, scorpions . . ."

"Scorpions!" Kenny protested. "I'm allergic to scorpions. Even the little ones make me break out in hives."

"Well, start breaking then," Cliff said sourly. "Didn't you see those Saharan chickens running around the settlement? They keep them to scratch up and eat the sand scorpions. Otherwise these damn oases would be unliveable."

"You mean they're liveable now?" Kenny growled. "Hell, I'd rather live in Hoboken."

Homer, Cliff and Kenny were just beginning to slip from their shoes, preparatory to knocking off, when Bey stuck his head through the door's curtain and said, ironically, "Visitor." He added in a lower voice, "He speaks Esperanto, the legal language of El Hassan's domains." He stuck a hand through the curtain and tossed a pistol onto the camp table. It had an oversized clip.

Homer looked down at it. "A Tokarev. Polish model," he said. He looked up at Bey. "Wait a minute, then show him in. This is interesting."

Homer, Cliff and Kenny shuffled back into their shoes and sat behind the camp table, Homer in the middle.

Bey held the curtain aside and a stranger entered. The three took him in.

The newcomer wore the Libyan *tarboosh* on his head and the white toga-like *barracan*, of that country, the ends of which were thrown over the left shoulder, toga-style.

He made the standard Arabic obeisance and said, in halting Esperanto, "I am Hassan el Akhdar of Tripoli and seek audience and to offer my services to El Hassan."

The three looked at him for a long moment.

Finally, Kenny, to Homer's left, said, also in Esperanto, "If it would suit you, make you more at your ease, you may address El Hassan in Russian."

The other couldn't help stare at him. "Russian!"

Kenny sighed and said, "You say you are from Tripoli but you wear the *barracan* prevalent in the Wadi Rumia of the Gebel country of the Fezzan. On top of which, you speak Esperanto, although admittedly, haltingly, as though you have been given a crash course. There are no scholars in the Gebel. In fact, I doubt if there's anybody who can read in the Gebel. As one who has in his time studied anthropology, I would say that in spite of your complexion, which resembles that of an Ethiopian Hamitic tribesman, your skull shape leads me to suggest that you are either of Russian or Finnish ancestry. I can think of no reasons why the Finns would be interested in El Hassan."

Colonel Serge Sverdlov took a deep breath, even as he inwardly cursed the inefficiency of the KGB department in charge of his cover. They should have come up with something else, obviously knowing practically nothing about the interior of North Africa.

However, his expression didn't change. He said, in Russian, "Then El Hassan speaks Russian? I am admittedly surprised."

Cliff Jackson said, off hand. "El Hassan speaks every language on Earth—of course."

The colonel stared at him. Was the man a clown, to expect him to believe that?

But it was then that Homer Crawford spoke up for the first time. He said mildly, in Russian, "I note that you have the Leningrad accent. Please forgive me if I am hesitant in your idiom which is quite picturesque."

Indeed, Homer Crawford was quite a linguist; aside from an imposing selection of Sahara tongues, including various lingua franca such as Swahili, Wolof of Senegal and Songhoi of the Niger bend, he also had excellent French and Spanish and a smattering of German. But, as a coincidence in this meeting, Russian—as Cliff knew—had especially intrigued him in college and he had taken four years of it. One of his favorite instructors had been from Leningrad.

The other was obviously taken aback.

Homer said politely, "Please draw up the other camp chair, there, and tell us that which you desire. We have had various other representatives from the Soviet Complex attend on us, but, admittedly, none so interestingly attired and disguised.''

Still cursing inwardly, Serge Sverdlov drew up the indicated folding chair. He'd probably be roasted for this fiasco, back in Moscow, but what had the fools expected, from Minister Kliment Blagonravov right on down? And especially Menzhinsky, in Tangier, who was supposedly an expert on North Africa. Though, admittedly, how in the name of Lenin could he be expected to know how they dressed in the Wadi Rumia of the Gebel country of the Fezzan, such information as was seemingly held in detail by El Hassan's immediate group?

His cover was obviously already blown to the skies. All he could do was improvise.

He looked at Cliff and Kenny, ''Am I to assume that these gentlemen are Clifford Jackson and Kenneth Ballalou, and that your guard is the Tuareg-American Bey-ag-Akhamouk?''

Homer eyed him for a moment, then nodded. ''You may.''

''Then I suggest that we speak English, since I assume that all here are not as conversant with Russian as you prove yourself to be.''

''Very well,'' Homer said in English. ''And now, to the point. What is it that you desire of El Hassan?''

Sverdlov said, ''To serve him. To join his followers and do all in my power, and I have considerable resources at my command, to further his aims.''

Homer eyed him for another long unspeaking moment, and finally said, ''Our aims are not only the assimilation of such presently reactionarily ruled lands as Morocco with its feudalistic, absolute monarchy, but also the Marxist Algeria and Libya, among others.''

The Russian nodded. ''We know. And also the assimilation of the dozen and one military dictatorships thoughout North and Central Africa.''

Kenny said evenly, ''You don't deny that you are from the KGB?''

''No. I have been sent from Moscow to forward the program of El Hassan. We are interested in progress, particularly industrial progress, throughout the world. We feel that El Hassan will accomplish this more quickly than the pseudo-socialistic regimes in such countries as Algeria.''

Homer nodded wearily, ''Your late colleagues, Abe Baker and Anton, put over the same general idea. But your eventual goal, your long view, involves, of course, your attempting to direct Ifriqiyah, as we call it, to the Communist camp.''

Serge Sverdlov hesitated before meeting that full on, but he realized that this was no time, nor these the men, for ambiguity. He nodded agreement. ''But that is far in the future and the future will take care of itself. Meanwhile, we support the program of El Hassan.''

Cliff snorted.

But Homer said, ''Just what form could this offered support take?''

The Russian bent forward. ''We could supply you with the most modern arms, arms that would enable you to overrun such nations as Morocco, Algeria, Libya, Tunisia, Senegal, at will. We could come to your assistance with our intelligence services, disclosing to you the attempts being planned by your enemies."

Homer Crawford said, "We don't need arms."

The colonel's eyes narrowed. "You expect to get them from the Americans, then?"

"Nor from them, either. If we are to succeed it will be because the people themselves arise and overthrow their corrupt and inefficient present governments, not because El Hassan shoots his way to power. This so-called arms aid of the great powers is one of the greatest blots of modern history. In the name of aid, the great powers subvert and impoverish half the undeveloped nations of the world. As far back as the nineteen-seventies, the United States was selling twenty billions of dollars a year in armaments to such countries as Israel and the Arab nations who opposed her, to India and Pakistan, to Turkey and Greece. When these nations fought, both sides were armed by America. She sold billions and billions in weapons to impoverished South America, where there hadn't been a real war in a century and where there was little chance of one developing. The arms there could only be meant for internal difficulties, in short, for the ruling class to keep down the people. El Hassan does not have to defend himself against his people." He snorted and added, "Nor were you Soviets far behind. You too sold to anyone who would buy."

Homer grunted contempt. "There are various facets to this so-called arms aid. Suppose we accepted from you a hundred of your most modern tanks, supposedly given free. What would happen when we ran out of the ammunition they utilized, and when we needed spare parts? Where else could we turn but to you, since such spare parts and ammunition are manufactured only in the Soviet Complex? We would be at your mercy when our new mechanized army began to deteriorate.''

He shook his head. ''No thank you. And so far as your intelligence is concerned, you see how incompetent you have proven in Ifriqiyah. You Europeans and Americans stand out like sore thumbs in the Sahara. I assume you are a trained KGB agent, but the moment you stepped through that door, in spite of your disguise, we knew that you were no African.''

He shook his head again. ''No, we do not welcome your assistance, sir.''

Colonel Serge Sverdlov came to his feet, knowing defeat. ''Very well,'' he said. ''However, we shall continue to assist in your program to the point we can, in spite of your rejection.''

Cliff picked up the other's pistol, drew the clip and emptied it of its cartridges, then with the heel of his right hand rammed it back into the butt. He handed the gun back to the Russian. ''Nice knowing you,'' he said.

The colonel took the gun and turned and left the tent.

Paul Kosloff and Nafi-ben-Mohammed had pulled into the small oasis settlement an hour or so before sunset and after most of the excitement had died down. They had avoided the pavilion and the multitude of natives about it and had gone into the small village proper. Kosloff was reminded somewhat of the adobe pueblos of the American south-west. There were swarms of children, swarms of flies, a sufficiency of mangy dogs too listless to bark even at strangers, and filth in plenitude.

Leaving Kosloff in the car, in a narrow, dirty alley, Nafi had gone off to discover the where-abouts of El Hassan, always assuming he was in the vicinity, and the rumors that he was had be-come thicker as they approached the site of the *djemaa el kebar*.

By the time he returned, darkness was descend-ing as it can descend only in such areas of the world as the Sahara. One moment, it is bright daylight, a few minutes later, completely dark, save for the moon and stars.

The Moroccan boy started up the car again and drove to the other end of the settlement and parked, once more, in as isolated a spot as he could find.

He said, "El Hassan and his viziers are quar-tered in that larger hut, there before us."

Paul Kosloff said, "We'll wait for a short time, until the town settles down a bit more." Their car didn't seem to be overly conspicuous. The swarm of North Africans that had descended upon the oasis had brought in a considerable number of its own vehicles, as Crawford and his group had found earlier.

They witnessed Bey-ag-Akhamouk emerging and assuming the post of guard and, shortly after-ward, the appearance of Serge Sverdlov, in his na-tive costume and in his disguise as a black. He disappeared inside and remained there for possi-bly fifteen minutes, while Paul Kosloff ran in irritation a thumbnail back and forth over his upper lip. There seemed to be something in the other's stance, the manner in which he held his body, that the American agent recognized but couldn't put his finger upon.

When Sverdlov had left, Paul Kosloff slipped out of his light jacket and then removed his shoulder harness with its gun and handed it over to Nafi.

"I won't be needing this in the presence of El Hassan," he said. "Keep it."

"Of course," the Moroccan youth said, as Kosloff slipped back into the jacket and got out of the car.

Paul Kosloff walked up the street to Bey-ag-Akhamouk and said, "I'd like to see El Hassan."

Bey looked at him quizzically. "White man, eh? And English speaking."

"American," Paul said.

"Long way from home," Bey said. He leaned his Tommy-Noiseless against the mud wall and thoroughly frisked the newcomer. Then he stuck his head around the curtain and said, "This is getting to be like a convention. Another visitor. American this time. He's clean."

Somebody inside said something and Bey held the curtain to one side and grinned at Kosloff and said, "Enter into the presence of El Hassan."

Paul Kosloff went on through and found himself in a small room, furnished only with camping equipment. Aside from a man on an army cot, snoring slightly as he slept, there were three men present, behind a folding camp table. All were blacks, and all dressed in military khakis.

The one in the middle gestured to an empty

folding chair across from him.

Paul said, "Professor Crawford? I am Paul Kosloff, presently, in a roundabout way, of the American State Department, and assigned to open preliminary negotiations with you."

Homer Crawford nodded and said, "And these are my aides, Kenneth Ballalou and Clifford Jackson."

Kenny said musingly, "Paul Kosloff, Paul Kosloff. I've read a bit about you. The so-called Cold War's Lawrence of Arabia."

Paul looked at him and said, "In the kind of work I am usually assigned, we seldom welcome publicity."

He looked back at El Hassan. He had to play this right. It couldn't be too obvious, or he'd never get his opening. He had to look authentic. These three were no fools.

He said, in answer to Homer Crawford's questioning look, "Frankly, El Hassan, my superiors have doubts about some elements of your program and would like them resolved before they grant you the all-out support the State Department will possibly provide."

The big black's smile was wry. "We have just had—and refused—another offer of support, Mr. Kosloff. But please proceed."

Paul Kosloff said earnestly, "Of prime importance is your proposal to double or more the price of the raw materials we are at present buying in Morocco, Algeria and other areas you plan to take over. Can we assume this is but a campaign promise, as our politicians call them in the States? That is, you don't really plan to go through with it?"

El Hassan shook his head. "No. It is no empty promise, Mr. Kosloff."

"But if the other underdeveloped nations go along with you, it could eventually mean the collapse of the economies of the West."

El Hassan nodded his head this time. "Yes, the collapse of the economies of the West, as we know them today."

Paul Kosloff stared at him.

Kenny Ballalou spoke up. "You see, Mr. Kosloff, the economies of the West and of Japan are destroying our world with their ever expanding production. Within decades, there will literally be no more raw materials. Our oil, our minerals, our forests, will have disappeared. The economies of the West, including the United States, must be forced to face reality and readjust. Yours is a waste economy. Let us use a few examples of planned obsolescence in your country. You make lead batteries for your cars that are deliberately designed to wear out after a year and a half, when it is possible to build them to last practically the life of the car. And lead is growing scarce. You make electric light bulbs that burn out in one thousand hours, when they could be manufactured to last for practically the life of the house. The houses you build are slum houses in less than twenty years, though your grandparents could build them to last a century or more. All this, of course, to increase sales, to increase profits. Your socioeconomic system is one based on production for profit, not for use. It is a mad system and we of the more backward countries must do something to force you to change, or when you go down to economic chaos you will drag us with you.''

Paul Kosloff was scowling. He said, ''But we've got to have your raw materials if we're to keep going. We no longer have our own. And you've got to have the money we pay you for them, if you're ever to become developed.''

El Hassan said softly, ''That is the point, Mr. Kosloff. We are never going to become developed. Nor are any of the other underdeveloped nations. For one thing, there isn't enough copper, lead, zinc and other basic necessities of industry to allow the backward countries to ever catch up with you, you've so wasted these irreplacable gifts of nature in your mad scramble for increased national product.''

Paul Kosloff said, ''Then you are deliberately planning to wreck the economies of the West?''

''Not wreck them. Force them to change. If you are made to pay triple for your copper, I doubt if you will continue to make such items as ladies' lipstick containers out of it. If you pay triple for your chrome, you will think twice before continuing to make your cars garish with it. Somehow, we of the backward countries and you of the advanced, must amalgamate in such a way that we can improve our living standards without industrialization but only by judicious exploitation of our raw materials and agriculture.''

Paul Kosloff pretended to think about it. He came to his feet and said, ''Just a moment, I wish to return to my vehicle and get a device there with which I can communicate by tight-beam to Greater Washington. What you have said is most interesting. We weren't aware of your motivation.''

"Of course," El Hassan nodded.

As Paul Kosloff left, he said to Bey, as he went by, "I'll be back in a minute."

He returned to the car in which he had left Nafi and said to the young agent, "Give me my gun." At the same time he reached into the back of the vehicle and secured a small package there.

The boy frowned at him.

Kosloff said impatiently, "They want to see an example of the type of weapons we can supply for their revolution."

The other handed the gun over and Paul Kosloff put it into his belt, under his coat. He turned and left the car again and headed back toward El Hassan's hut, emptying the package as he went. It contained two small but ultra-powerful demolition grenades which he put into his side pockets. It was completely dark now with no one at all on the streets.

He squared his shoulders, albeit somewhat unhappily, as he walked. It was simplicity itself. All he had to do was walk up to the guard, who would never suspect that he wasn't still unarmed, and shoot him down and toss the two grenades into the hut. He'd then stand aside, in the unlikely chance that one or more of those in the interior would survive and emerge, and finish him, or them, too. He doubted that they were suspicious, that they were very old hands at intrigue. They were obviously too idealistic, too honest.

A slightly accented voice from behind him said, "Very well, Paul Kosloff. Put your hands behind your neck."

He did as he was told and a hand came around

from behind him and plucked the .38 Recoilless from his belt.

The voice said, "Turn now."

Paul Kosloff turned and said, "Hello, Sverdlov. I thought I recognized you earlier. You're making a mistake, this time."

The Russian KGB man was slightly smaller than Kosloff but perhaps more lithe. His teeth were white and his smile good, but there was something about his eyes.

"Ah?" he said. "Please elucidate, Kosloff."

"This time, I have the same assignment you have. We're on the same side."

"I doubt it."

"I've been sent here to eliminate El Hassan and his lieutenants. My government wishes to see the regimes in Algeria, Libya and so forth continue."

"Ah, but mine doesn't," the other said evenly, softly.

Paul Kosloff gaped at him.

The Russian agent chuckled. "You see, Kosloff, in spite of the fact that our countries have reached detente, the battle for men's minds goes on and will not end until one of our sides prevails. We wish to see El Hassan's program succeed for various reasons. If it does, his regime will be the first major element to collapse your economy. We have not been able to control the governments of Algeria, Libya and the others, in spite of the fact that they call themselves Marxist, but we won't have to control El Hassan. He wants to do exactly what we would like him to do. We of the Soviet Complex have within our borders all the raw materials we need. You don't."

Paul Kosloff looked at him for a long empty moment. He said, "You mean that I, an agent of the West, have been sent to rescue Marxist regimes, and you, an agent of the Soviet Complex, have been sent to insure El Hassan's take-over in these countries?"

Serge Sverdlov chuckled again. "Quite a contradiction, eh?" His finger began to tighten on the trigger of the heavy pistol he carried.

A voice clipped from the darkness of a narrow alleyway between the mud huts. "In the name of El Hassan, that will be all!"

Serge Sverdlov spun and, simultaneously, from the doorway of a hut across the street a laser beam hissed out. Paul Kosloff took no time to discover who was the target of the deadly ray gun. He fell to the ground and rolled desperately.

The Russian was also on the ground but apparently not out of action. Footsteps came pounding down the street from the direction of the car.

Paul Kosloff recognized the voice that had interrupted Serge Sverdlov as that of Homer Crawford. It would seem that the four revolutionists hadn't been as naive as he had thought. They had followed him to check what he was doing.

Several figures emerged from the narrow alleyway and spread out, seeking shadows. They carried what seemed to be submachine guns. Serge Sverdlov, from his prone position, began to bring up his gun toward Paul Kosloff.

Nafi-ben-Mohammed, his own gun at the ready, came dashing up. He took in the figures on the ground. Paul Kosloff was still trying to roll to some sort of cover.

The Russian's pistol barked at the same time that the laser beam hissed from the doorway across the street again. Tokugawa Hidetada stumbled forth from the mud hut, reeling, his pistol dropping from his hand.

Nafi's gun came up, the .38 Noiseless went *ping, ping, ping,* and two of the three slugs thunked into the prone Russian agent.

From the shadows into which the figures from the narrow alley had faded came the voice of El Hassan again. "Drop that gun, boy, or you die."

Nafi obeyed orders, then quickly leaned down over Paul Kosloff. "You are unhurt?"

Kosloff, in disgust, came to his feet. Now he could make out the crumpled body in the narrow alleyway from which El Hassan had first called.

"What is this, a damn massacre?" he growled.

He went over to Tokugawa Hidetada. His once Japanese colleague was going out fast. Paul Kosloff knelt beside him and said urgently, "Is there anything I can do?"

The small man attempted a rueful chuckle. "In the crisis, I attempted to come to your succor, friend Paul. I am not very clear on just what has happened. Whom did I shoot?"

Paul Kosloff took a deep breath. "One of El Hassan's men, Hidetada."

"It would be my fate for it to be Bey-ag-Akhamouk," the Japanese groaned. His eyes closed in pain and he never opened them again.

Paul Kosloff stood and looked back at Sverdlov.

The Russian was also dead.

El Hassan and Cliff Jackson emerged from the shadows, their guns still at the ready. El Hassan's eyes took in the two fallen agents, then went back to his own valued follower, who was now being helped from the alley by Kenny Ballalou.

"How bad?" Homer Crawford said.

Bey muttered, "Just a crease, but, Jesus, those laser beams hurt."

"Get him back to the hut, Kenny," El Hassan ordered and then returned to Kosloff. He indicated the Japanese, "Who is this man?"

"Tokugawa Hidetada. His government wanted to see the regimes in Algeria and the other so-called socialist nations of North Africa overthrown, but Field Marshal Bey-ag-Akhamouk come to power rather than you."

Homer snorted at the idea that Bey might be a potential rival, but pointed to the Russian and said, "And this one? We have met him, but who was he really?"

"Sverdlov. Serge Sverdlov, of the KGB. His government wanted to see your revolution a success so that the United States and the West would be economically devastated."

"I see." El Hassan looked at Paul Kosloff and Nafi for a long thoughtful moment. He said, "I heard enough of your conversation with the Russian to realize that you are not truly interested in supporting my cause. Perhaps I should kill you, Mr. Kosloff, but I do not kill unarmed men. Please leave. And so far as your nations are concerned, the United States of the Americas, the Soviet Complex, and Japan, all I can do is paraphrase the

Engish poet. A curse on all your houses."

Nafi blurted, "But, El Hassan, we came to assist you."

"It seems unlikely, boy. Now leave."

Paul Kosloff and the Moroccan youth returned to their car. In silence they got into it and started back for Tangier.

After a time, Paul Kosloff put his Tracy to his mouth and said, "Paul calling. Paul calling."

The commissioner's thin voice came through shortly, "Yes, I receive you. What is happening?"

Paul said flatly, "Everything and its cousin has gone to pot. Sverdlov's dead. Tokugawa Hidetada, of Japan, is dead. I'm not but probably should be. Your strategy laid an egg. El Hassan will undoubtedly take over here."

"You fouled this up, Kosloff!"

"It's according to how you look at it. It was fouled before it started," Paul Kosloff said wearily. "Oh, yes, and one more thing. I'm tired of being the Cold War's Lawrence of Arabia. It's getting too complicated for me. I'm resigning."

XVI

ISOBEL CUNNINGHAM

ISOBEL CUNNINGHAM WAS less than happy. Matters were getting out of hand by the hour. She desperately needed the presence of the team and especially Homer Crawford.

It was unbelievable how rapidly things were progressing. Whole tribes that she had never even heard of were coming over to El Hassan en masse. Nations which she knew little more about than their names, were overthrowing their military dictatorships, or their pseudo-socialistic regimes and declaring for El Hassan. And Tamanrasset was the center to which all delegations streamed. She and Jimmy Peters and Doctor Smythe were working like Trojans and none slept for more than a few hours at a time, but seemingly they made little more than a dent on the required work.

The elderly Doctor Smythe put them both to shame. Already matters medical had gotten beyond the point where he, himself, had time to treat patients. Half of Fort Laperrine was already a hospital, staffed almost exclusively with blacks who had taken their medical educations in lands beyond Africa. Smythe now devoted his full energies to administration. When new medical groups centered in on Tamanrasset, seeking instructions from El Hassan, he sent them to other areas to establish hospitals and clinics. To Timbuktu, to Mopti, to Niamey in Niger, to N'Djamena on the shores of Lake Chad. Planes were coming in almost daily with medical and other supplies through the efforts of such pro-El Hassan organizations as the Africa For Africans Association.

Isobel had taken a walk, in an effort to achieve a bit of relaxation, through Tamanrasset, the day before. To her astonishment, she had run into an improvised hospital going up on the edge of the *souk*. She had never even heard of it. She had approached a white smocked negro doctor, who, in the open, was treating a child that had been bitten by a sand scorpion. The five year old's fingers were swollen and stiff. Red streaks were visible all the way to its shoulder.

Isobel said, "Who are you?"

And the doctor had replied impatiently, without looking up, "I'm busy."

Isobel, miffed, had said, "I'm El Hassan's secretary."

"I don't care if you're the Virgin Mary." The other came erect and glowered at her. He was a nice looking young man, very sincere. "If there's anybody in charge around this madhouse get them to requisition some sort of insecticide spray, in the DDT tradition. There're enough poisonous insects in this damned town to kill off half the human race." He turned back to his diminutive patient, who was whimpering.

"I'll see what I can do," Isobel said, and left.

But in spite of the administrative load on her shoulders she had found time to wonder about Major Ryan and his contingent of mercenaries. Possibly it was woman's intuition that caused her to feel a twinge of apprehension about the twenty-four whites and one green bereted black who had come out of the desert supposedly seeking employment as bodyguards.

This morning she had arisen at dawn and checked over some odds and ends before the others of the rapidly growing administrative staff had turned up.

When she returned to her quarters, it was to find Megan McDaid, in negligee, at the table in the dining room, enjoying coffee and the local native sweet bread. Isobel wondered wearily how long it had been since she, herself, had been robed in a negligee. She couldn't remember.

Meg smiled as she looked up at her. "Good morning," she said. "As a doctor, I prescribe that you get some rest."

Isobel looked rueful and got a cup and saucer from the side board. She sat down opposite the Irish girl and poured some of the thick coffee for herself, adding sugar liberally in the North African tradition.

She said, "I can see *myself* in this part of the world, Doctor . . ."

"Meg," the other said.

"All right. I'm Isobel. I can see myself here but I

wonder why you would ever leave green Ireland for the end of the Earth.''

Meg made a face and said, ''Women aren't popular in the medical field on the Emerald Isle. Bryan and I were hoping to accumulate enough of a nest egg to immigrate to Canada or the United States, where women aren't ashamed to take off their brassières in front of another woman, or a man doesn't give a damn who removes his appendix, just so it's removed.''

Isobel laughed sympathetically.

Meg said, out of a clear sky, ''Isobel, you're obviously opposed to our coming. Why?'' Even as she spoke, inwardly she disliked herself for the position she occupied. But she had already rationalized and now felt she might pick up something, informally, that might be of use to Bryan and Sean, to be used against this brute El Hassan, when he finally appeared on the scene.

Isobel sipped her coffee and looked at the other young woman over the top of her cup. ''You're white and have no place in the new Ifriqiyah,'' she said.

Meg frowned. ''But there are thousands of whites helping develop North Africa. Mining engineers, oil technicians . . .''

Isobel was nodding. ''But they have no place in North Africa, really, beyond a temporary one. In fact, they all hate it. I wonder if you have ever seen one of these oil camps. They consist of rows of boxlike houses, each with its air-conditioning unit, toilet, shower, bed, armchair, and desk. European food is provided in the mess hall. European newspapers, paperback books and magazines are flown in by the company aircraft. European music and shows are on the radio and TV sets. The only luxuries missing are European women. A week's vacation every month takes care of that. They are flown back to the Mediterranean cities, or even as far as Paris, and taken to luxury hotels which cater almost exclusively to them. They are engaged, these engineers, mechanics, clerks, administrators and executives, in making their living. They're not living in the desert from religious, idealistic, or patriotic motives. Isolated within their air-conditioned huts, waiting for the company plane with their fresh supply of orange juice and canned beer, they have no more feeling for the desert around them than the submariner has for the ocean outside the hull of his craft. They can't wait to get back to their homes, families, and to *their* civilization. They have no interest in bringing civilization to Ifriqiyah.''

Meg frowned at her thoughtfully.

Isobel shrugged and said, ''It's not the only unloved place to which the white man goes in search of his god, money. The same applies to the far north. The area around Point Barrow, in most northern Alaska, is similar. It is Esquimo country, and the Esquimo would live nowhere else happily. The white man's camps there are the equivalent of those in the Sahara with cold and snow rather than heat and sand. And none can wait to leave the north behind and return with his fantastically high pay to his own land.''

Meg shook her head, trying to assimilate it. ''But how long do you intend to remain . . . Isobel?

226

You yourself are an American, aren't you? And used to the comforts of . . . civilization.''

Isobel sighed, finished her coffee and readied herself to come to her feet. She said, ''I imagine I'll be here for the rest of my life. The job is a big one. I was born in America, but racially I am an African. I have the El Hassan dream, to bring my people out of the Dark Ages. We can't expect others to do it. The white man comes to North Africa solely to exploit it, in one way or the other.''

She stood and looked down at the attractive Irish girl and wound it up by saying, ''I understand that Ireland, in her day, also had to fight to gain her independence.''

Meg looked at her emptily. Both of her grand-fathers had died in the Black and Tan fighting with the British.

For some reason, unbeknownst even to herself, Isobel had forbidden the white soldiers of fortune to leave the limits of Fort Laperrine but had given Lon Charles freedom to go where he would in Tamanrasset. Her excuse was that he was a black and in no danger, but that she was unable to guarantee the safety of whites. Which wasn't true. There were quite a number of European and American journalists, diplomatic representatives, and trade delegations in the area now and more coming in weekly. Most of these refrained from going into the the native areas and remained in their little ghetto on the outskirts of town of west-ern tents, trailers and campers, contemptuous of what they considered the filth of the Saharan cen-ter. But the brave, usually accompanied by some of Guémama's men as guards, occasionally roamed the streets, bringing no more reaction than curiosity and not much of that since whites, including traders, missionaries and even tourists had still sometimes come to Tamanrasset even after the evacuation of the French.

Now, on her way back from town to check out a matter with one of the local bashaws, she ran into the green bereted American. He had obviously been in one of the two or three cafes Tamanrasset supported and where beer and even the atrocious tasting date wine was available. Alcoholic drink was forbidden the good Moslem, but all Moslems are not good ones, and, besides, in this part of the Sahara, all did not follow Islam. Some tribesmen were pagans, and a few even Christians, converted by the missionaries who had plowed millions of dollars, francs and pounds into this area, for the sake of a handful of converts.

The call on the pasha had been routine. Word had come to her that he was shaking down the peddlers of *kif* in the souk. While she, as well as Homer and the others of the inner El Hassan group, had no brief for what the Americans called marijuana; they took no stand against it. Cannabis sativa had been used as an escape from reality since it had wended its way to this part of the world from far China, so remote in history as to be unrecorded.

The bashaw had been aghast. He assured the *Sitt* Izubahil that for as long as the memory of man his family had leveled a tax on all local sale of *kif*.

No more, she had told him coldly and hoped that it would not be necessary to bring the matter to the attention of El Hassan whose love for the people was such that he could not condone their being exploited.

Sooner or later, she thought sourly, as she left him, they would have to have a showdown with these racketeers. It should add immeasurably to the prestige of El Hassan in the eyes of the people, their victims.

Lon Charles had removed his beret and said, "Top of the afternoon, Miss Cunningham." He looked back over his shoulder at the town and grinned. "It's a long way from Newark."

She laughed and said, "How did you know? But it was Teaneck, not Newark."

He grinned again and put his battered beret back on his head, in protection from the sun. She herself wore a sun helmet.

"Jersey is Jersey," he said. "You can tell."

She said, "Are you heading back for the fort? Why don't you walk along with me?"

He fell into step beside her.

She said, "You're as far away from home as I am. Have you ever returned . . ." she indicated his green beret ". . . since Vietnam?"

He shook his head. "No. No, there's nothing for an uneducated black in the States." He thought about it. "And nowhere else for that matter. I was seventeen when I took up soldiering, and I'm still at it."

She said, "It's possible for even a black to get an education, Lon. You've got an inferiority complex."

He chuckled and said, "It's not an inferiority complex. I *am* inferior. Look at that Megan McDaid. She's not half my age and she's a doctor."

Isobel shot a look at him from the side of her eyes as they walked along. She said, "So is Jimmy Peters and so is Doctor Smythe. For that matter, so is El Hassan. I've got a master's degree. The fact that you're black hasn't anything to do with your intelligence."

He shook his head again. "You're only partly right. Sure *some* of us can fight our way up to where we've got as good an education as whitey. But, face it, on an average the black can't compete with a white, or even a Jap or Chink, for that matter."

She scoffed. "Lon, you're believing the other guy's propaganda. When our Nordic friends and other whites were running around in animal skins and squatting round campfires gnawing on half cooked bones, civilization was beginning here in Africa. Most of the fundamentals originated right here on this continent."

He stared at her. "Man, you have flipped. Civilization started in Babylonia, in Greece, and later Rome."

It was her turn to shake her head. "Have you ever heard of Egypt? The ancient Egyptians came down the Nile from Nubia, from Ethiopia. They were blacks. Whitey's been trying to explain it away ever since; he simply can't bear the idea. The Greeks were johnnies-come-lately, not to speak of the Romans, and they inherited most of their civilization from the Egyptians. The sciences, the arts, engineering, mathematics, astronomy, so forth and so on, all went through their infancy in Egypt. Even the Tigris-Euphrates civilizations were later. Practically all of the big break-throughs in man's development were made either in Africa or in Asia. From all the anthropologists can tell us, man himself originated somewhere to the southeast of here."

Lon Charles was scowling. "The Egyptians weren't blacks," he said.

"No? What were they, then? Where did they come from? The very first signs of their culture were found in the upper reaches of the Nile. Take a look at their statues, with their thick lips, their flattish noses. They were blacks then and are still predominately blacks in spite of all the whites that have mixed with them after the various conquests. Their civilization lasted for thousands of years before it fell to white armies. Admittedly, the white race has produced the best soldiers, the greatest inventors of new weapons, up to and including nuclear ones. The Egyptians were never much for the military. But it wasn't just Egypt. During the Dark Ages of Europe, Timbuktu, only a few hundred miles from here, surpassed the Rome, London or Paris of the time. Its universities and libraries were preserving the classics of Greece and Rome while the religious fanatics of Europe were erasing such works so they could use the parchment for inscribing crackpot supposedly holy books."

"I never looked at it that way," Lon said grudgingly.

"That's what El Hassan is all about," ˙nbel told him. "We're trying to bring the black˙ ᴜ˙ their rightful place in the world, a place the oth ˙ races have usurped from us. We weren't born to be the slaves of others, they shot us into that position with their superior weapons and their dedication to conquest.''

The sergeant said slowly, ''They kind of like this El Hassan cat around here, don't they?''

Isobel said, ''Yes. The El Hassan movement is the dream.''

They had reached the fort.

Lon said, ''I'd like to talk to you some more about this some time, Miss Cunningham.''

She grinned at him. ''Isobel,'' she said. ''We Jerseyites have to stick together, Lon.'' Then she looked at him and said, ''You're not as uneducated as you put on. How did you have any ideas on the origins of civilization? Whether or not I agree with them.''

''You get a lot of time to read, layin' around in hospitals, or prison camps, or even barracks, between scraps,'' he told her.

They separated at the gate and Isobel headed for the administration building, dreading whatever new crises might have accumulated in the hour she had been away.

She wished, all over again, that Homer, Kenny, Bey and Cliff would get back—and Elmer Allen with them. They'd been gone a couple of weeks now. As prearranged, there had been no communication. They were equipped with fairly efficient transceivers, but in the world of espionage-counter-espionage that prevailed today, you could never know whether or not your messages were being intercepted. And Homer wanted no word to go ahead that he was on his way to Elmer's rescue. Surprise meant everything. North Africa was awash these days with rumors about El Hassan and all that pertained to him but in the last forty-eight hours in Tamanrasset they had received some broadcasts that they'd had difficulty in interpreting. The religious movement of the mahdi had been in the ascendency only a few days ago, now it seemed to be in collapse. Why?

A voice said, ''Ah, good afternoon, Mademoiselle Cunningham.''

She turned to find Captain Raul Bazaine. He smiled his gallant Frenchman's smile and touched the duckbill of his desert cap in an easy salute, making a slight bow.

''Good afternoon, Captain,'' Isobel said, turning and continuing on her way toward the administration building, knowing that he would fall in step beside her.

When he did, she said, ''Are your quarters adequate—considering the circumstances?''

He smiled ruefully. ''I am a soldier, Mademoiselle. Even a roof is sometimes a luxury.''

Isobel said, ''If you would rather, we can speak French.''

''Ah, no. I consider English a most beautiful language.''

In spite of his tendency toward what Meg McDaid would probably call blarney, Isobel didn't mind the other's company. It was something of a relief to speak to an educated person outside the El Hassan circle, for a change.

She said, in an easy mockery, ''I thought that you French considered your language the only cultivated and beautiful one extant.''

He held his right hand over his heart as though in

dismay. "Oh, no . . . Isobel. English had the most beautiful phrase any language in the world."

She looked at him. "It has? What?"

"Cellar door."

She laughed and said, "You fool."

He laughed too and said, "How long do you think it will be before it will be possible to have an audience with El Hassan?"

She shook her head and made a moue. "We have no idea of just when he might return."

He eyed her and cocked his head a little. "Return? Then he is away?"

She covered quickly, and perhaps too quickly, since there was a questioning look in his eye. "As I've already told you, El Hassan has withdrawn into the erg to a secluded spot where he and his closest aides can confer without hindrance."

He dropped the subject and looked about the enclosed parade ground and the building which surrounded it. "It must be a dreary place for such a beautiful, vivacious young lady. What do you do for entertainment?"

"Work," she said. "When you are involved in an inspirational program such as that of El Hassan, work becomes recreation."

They had arrived at her destination and come to a halt.

"Ah," he said, smiling his charm again. "But isn't there an American saying beginning *all work and no play . . .*"

And she smiled at him again, mockingly. "Yes, but this particular work is far from dull. Good afternoon, Captain."

He made a face of great sadness. "But nevertheless, Madamoiselle, if you find yourself in need of a bit of relaxation—I am most available.''

He touched his finger to his cap again in salute, and turned and headed back for where the soldiers of fortune had pitched their tents.

She looked after him in deprecation. ''I'll just bet you're available,'' she murmured under her breath.

XVII

MEGAN MCDAID

WHEN MEGAN McDAID was admitted to Doctor
Warren Harding Smythe's office the following day,
it was to find that both Isobel Cunningham and
Jimmy Peters were also present. James Peters,
whom she found a small, chunky, rather colorless,
though energetic man, had been introduced to her
as El Hassan's Vizier of Education, though evidently he was not important enough in the hierar-
chy to be attending this mysterious inner conference that his leader was holding somewhere.
However, from what little Meg had seen, the
duties of El Hassan's people seemed somewhat
elastic. Isobel Cunningham, supposedly his secretary, was making important decisions that would
ordinarily pertain to press secretary, through
minister of war, to commissioner of foreign affairs.
Meg wondered how many of the black girl's decisions would be backed by the ruthless El Hassan
when he did reappear.

They went through the standard amenities and

then Doctor Smythe said, "Please have a chair, Doctor. What can I do for you?"

Meg sat and said, "It occurs to me that I might put my time to some use while my group is waiting. From what little I have seen, you can utilize anyone with medical background, though I am taken aback by some of the outdated equipment and treatments you are at present utilizing."

Jimmy Peters said impatiently, even as he pushed his old fashioned spectacles back on the bridge of his nose, "That will soon be remedied. Admittedly, we are stretching out impossibly now, but large quantities of the most recent equipment are on their way." His small smile was deprecating. "You see, every pharmaceutical house, every medical and dental supply house in America, Common Europe, the Soviet Complex and Japan are urging their credit upon us."

Meg couldn't help but frown puzzlement. "Well, why?"

Isobel laughed softly "Because they can see what a potential market we will become and each wants to corner it."

"It would involve millions to make a dent upon your requirements," Meg said. "Through the two thousand or so miles we drove to arrive here, I saw the state of medical needs throughout North Africa."

Jimmy Peters nodded. "Millions is stating it mildly, Doctor McDaid. However, *one* financial offer we received yesterday involved a half billion dollars, American, for a monopoly to exploit the oil and natural gas resources of Senegal alone."

"Half a billion dollars!" Meg protested. "But

are you even in control of Senegal?''

"Practically all of it save Dakar," Isobel said, "and that city should come over to us before the week is out. However, I doubt if El Hassan is interested in the offer.'' She paused a moment before adding, ''Or any other that involves foreign exploitation of Ifriqiyah's raw materials.''

Doctor Smythe came back to Meg's suggestion. "Needless to say, Doctor, your services are welcome. Are you a specialist?''

She shook her head. ''A general practitioner. Place me at any task you wish.'' Her eyes went to Isobel. ''At one time you say you are against the West and the civilization of the whites, but here you are, making every effort to bring it to North Africa.''

Isobel smiled at that and said, ''Not exactly. Possibly it's according to what you mean by civilization. Modern medicine, obviously, we want, along with agricultural techniques, irrigation, afforestation methods, and many other modern developments. But we can do without such things as, say, American-type television, which exists primarily for profit reasons, any entertainment or educational value being incidental.''

"Above all," Jimmy Peters said, "we don't wish to bring to Ifriqiyah the suicidal waste of your so-called civilization. Just take one example. Every year your Detroit spends hundreds of millions in re-tooling to turn out automobiles that *look* somewhat different. The height, the length, the color, the shape of fenders, the upholstery, the number of lights. It's largely for something the advertising men can spend additional hundreds of millions upon, touting the product."

Isobel said, "The one I like is the electric Martini-stirrer. It took a sharp idea man to conceive of it. Skilled engineers to design it. Competent technicians to tool up for it. Trained workers to operate the factory in which it was built. Highly paid publicity and advertising personnel to bring it before the eyes of the public. Probably millions were involved before it was through. All for what? What in the world good is an electric Martini-stirrer save for humor, or as a status symbol? Of course, it most likely made a profit, and that's all that counts in your so-called Western civilization."

Meg had to laugh. "All right," she said. "I'll have to believe you, I shouldn't doubt. You want the blessings of civilization . . ."

"Modern technology," Jimmy Peters corrected lowly.

". . . without its curses." She looked at Doctor Smythe again. "I'm ready to go to work at any post you assign me."

Later that evening, just before sunset, Meg, Sean Ryan, Bryan O'Casey, Paul Bazaine and Lon Charles met in the mess tent of the mercenaries. Half a dozen of their men were nonchalantly lolling around outside, covering the tent from each direction. They were guards, albeit unarmed, and stationed to give warning should any outsiders approach.

The five sat at two of the folding tables, on camp chairs. Lon Charles, in his wanderings about the *souk* and cafes in Tamanrasset, had located, of all things, a bottle of cognac, which had probably been in the town since French occupation days. They had split the astronomical cost of the bottle five ways and now sat around it with tin cups.

Bryan had in hand his Peterson shell briar and had just filled it from the leather pouch he had carried since his first mercenary job in Angola, many years before. In actuality, it wasn't leather, it was human skin and he would never have let Meg know the fact. One of the boys under his command had carefully cured it, had his wife sew it, and had presented it to a then horrified Bryan as a gift. It was a perverse fascination that caused him to continue using it, down through the years.

Sean opened the discussion by saying, "Does anyone have any reason to believe that this tent might be bugged?"

They thought about it.

Paul Bazaine said, "I doubt it. In all my years in North Africa, I have never heard of an electronic bug. They might have them in Algiers, or Casablanca or Dakar, but it seems unlikely out here. If El Hassan's ambitious gang actually did come to power, in a year or so they might introduce such niceties. But now? It's unlikely that such equipment was in Tamanrasset before they took over and doubly unlikely that Reunited Nations teams would have been carrying them; Besides, such devices need trained technicians to install and operate. No, this tent is not bugged."

"I think you're right." Sean said. "Let's get down to our council of war. This not being able to contact El Hassan or find out where he is has its ramifications. Suppose that his adherents overrun

Adrar before we can pull off the job? What happens to our getaway aircraft and pilots in that case?"

"There's nothing we can do about it," Bryan growled unhappily, tamping down the tobacco in his shell briar.

Sean said, "I got a tightbeam from Saul Saidi this morning. He's gnawing his nails about our holdup. It seems that El Hassan's movement is spreading like a brush fire. If he manages to consolidate all of what they call Ifriqiyah before we do him in, then it might be too late. He might become a martyr and elements among his followers take over." He dwelt upon it inwardly. "As a matter of fact, these charismatic leaders are sometimes better off dead, after a certain point. If they lived, possibly their followers would begin to detect feet of clay. But dead, nobody can say a word against them."

"Examples?" Bryan growled.

"There's lots of them" Sean told him. "Take Jesus. Suppose that he had lived on, instead of being crucified as a young man, so that Paul and others could defy him and knock together a viable program. Jesus, himself, never had one, or, if he did, it was evidently edited out of the gospels."

"Why, Sean," Meg said, twisting her mouth. "You're absolutely blasphemous."

Major Ryan ignored her and said, "Lenin's another example. Suppose he had lived? Stalin and the boys must have blessed their lucky stars when he kicked off. If he hadn't, when he did, they probably would have had to take steps to accomplish it."

"Very well," Raul Bazaine said impatiently. "And where do we stand now? Have we any information all aren't acquainted with?"

Sean looked at Lon Charles. "You've been given the run of Tamanrasset. Have you learned anything?"

The black sergeant shook his head. "I don't speak any of their languages, or even French. The only thing I've noticed that kind of set me back, is that they all seem caught up in this El Hassan idea. I've been in a lot of backward countries, in my time, and I found out they got one thing in common, a dislike of work."

Meg said, "People ridden with everything from pellagra to hookworm haven't got much energy or ambition."

Lon looked over at her. "You're the doc. But somehow these people are different. They're all working like bastards. Uh, sorry . . ."

Meg snorted at the apology.

Sean turned his eyes to Raul Bazaine. "I noted you talking to El Hassan's secretary. Did you pick up anything?"

The Frenchman snorted. "The little *cocotte* is tight-mouthed. However, perhaps she let a little something drop."

Meg said, "That's hardly the term to describe Miss Cunningham. I found her a cultivated, sincere and idealistic woman."

The four men took her in, empty-faced.

But Sean said to Bazaine, "Dropped what?"

"Possibly she let slip that El Hassan and his closest aides are not in the vicinity of Tamanrasset at all but have gone off somewhere. This so-called *ekhwan,* the great council, they are supposedly holding, doesn't ring true, at any rate, *n'est-ce pas?* How could but four men take this long to talk things over?"

Sean pursed his lips and looked unseeingly out of the side of his eyes toward the tent opening. He poured himself another slug of the cognac—which he knew he shouldn't do—and then one each for the others.

Then he said, "I'll be thinking that possibly fits in with something Saul Saidi told me this morning. Remember the rumors we heard in the north about some Algerian tribesman proclaiming he was a second coming of some Moslem religious figure and was being taken up by all the marabouts and so forth? His program was anti-El Hassan; in fact he was proclaiming a *jehad* holy war against him and had captured one of El Hassan's closest followers."

"That's right," Bryan said. "He was a Chaambra, wasn't he? And his name was Abd, something or other."

"Abd-el-Kader," Bazaine said. "He's been a minor celebrity among the Arabs and other nomads in the northwestern Sahara for some time. A real bandit before he got this religious, ah, kick as the Americans say."

"At any rate," Sean said. "Somehow this vizier of El Hassan has been rescued and the light of the self-proclaimed religious leader has gone out like a skyrocket."

They all looked at him.

Sean said, "My guess is that was El Hassan and his men we passed near In Salah and that they were on their way north to confront this upstart. If so, they succeeded and it's to be assumed that they're on their way back."

Bryan relit his pipe thoughtfuly and said, "If this was anything more than a guess, the thing for us to do would be to head north—there's only one road, or what passes for a road—and intercept him somewhere along the way. In that manner we'd be up against only the four of them, not the whole of Tamanrasset and Fort Laperrine. That rescue aircraft of ours can sit down just as easily anywhere along the route as it can in this vicinity."

"That's the trouble," Sean growled, wanting another drink and steeling himself against taking it. He had ruled himself onto the waterwagon as long as this assignment was underway and this was his first deviation. "It's only an educated guess, and we can't spare the time to drive all the way up that god-forsaken road, and then come back again if he doesn't show. Besides, it would look suspicious to Isobel Cunningham and the rest."

They all mulled that over awhile, without result, and then Sean turned to Megan McDaid. "Did you have any luck getting information when you volunteered your services as a doctor?"

Meg had been unhappy at the proceedings of this whole war council and now she let it come out.

She said, "I found out one thing. When we started down here I was of the opinion that El Hassan and his closest followers were all adventurers. But in talking to Isobel Cunningham, Doctor Smythe and the Vizier of Education, Peters, I reversed my engines. They're idealists."

Sean looked at Bryan O'Casey, holding his own peace.

Bryan stared down into the dottle of his pipe. "It's an elastic word," he said finally. "But they've evidently convinced you. However, in these things it's difficult to tell who is in the right and who the wrong. If either side is right—or wrong. As soldiers of fortune, we are unconcerned with such matters. Let history decide which side was right and which wrong. And even history doesn't do a very good job. If General Washington, Jefferson, Madison and the other so-called revolutionary forefathers of the United States had lost their war and been hanged how do you think history would now read? They would be considered a bunch of rebels who had revolted against their king and had come to their just desserts. We're mercenaries, Meg. We fight for money. We're not basically interested in who is right or who wrong."

She looked into her lover's eyes. "Do you really subscribe to that?"

He knocked the ash out of his pipe, momentarily considered his tobacco pouch but then returned the briar to a pocket of his bush jacket. "It's one of the reasons I retired from the game, mavourneen. But, to raise our nestegg, I returned for one last job—the most lucrative I've ever been offered. And now I've taken his money and owe my allegiance to Saidi. It's the code of the mercenary."

She looked at the four men, one by one. Only Lon Charles avoided her challenging stare. She said, "So, if Hitler had hired you for some similar assignment to this, you would give me the same argument?"

Bryan said patiently, "If I had signed up with Hitler, yes. The thing is, I wouldn't have signed up with him in the first place. Even we mercenaries *do* have a choice."

Sean leaned forward and took over earnestly, "Meg, this El Hassan is a malcontent and an opportunist, no matter what opinions you might have come to to the contrary. He's upsetting this whole part of the world, which was just beginning to show some signs of progress, what with the oil and mineral developments. I, for one, have no compunction against hiring out as a soldier of fortune to his political enemies."

Meg made a rude noise. "I wonder if Saidi actually represents political elements, or profit-conscious corporations who don't like El Hassan's program. We don't even know who he represents. We accept his money and embark upon what amounts to an assassination assignment."

Raul flicked a fingernail along his blonde wisp of French mustache and murmured, "I don't know about this assassination thing. I strongly suspect that before this is all through, we shall see actual combat. He is too well guarded to expect that ordinary assassination would be practical—that is, if we are expectant of making our, ah, getaway."

Sean took it up again. "Meg, so far as assassination is concerned, you mentioned Hitler a moment ago. In July of 1944, a group of German generals attempted, and failed, to assassinate him. Don't you wish they had been successful? Had they been, millions of lives would have been spared. It's according to who is being assassinated, whether or not the act is despicable.''

She came to her feet and let her eyes go over them, one by one, as she breathed deeply. "I'm confused," she admitted. "I don't know what to think.''

Bryan said gently, "Meanwhile, Meg, if you let anything drop about our mission, it will undoubtedly mean the lives of all of us. Men of the El Hassan caliber are noted for their ruthlessness.''

She turned and left the tent. *"Les femmes,"* Raul Bazaine murmured.

Sean Ryan turned his eyes to Lon Charles and said, "You're havin' the run of Tamanrasset. Tomorrow, when you're in town, hire yourself a camel or horse and take a short trip up the road in the direction of In Salah. Find some sort of a clearing, or area, large enough for our aircraft to land in but small enough that our forces can defend it for a maximum time. It must be close enough to this fort and to Tamanrasset that our long distance rifle grenade launchers will reach to the city and fort. Is that possible?''

Lon twisted his face and said, "It should be. Miss Cunningham said I had the freedom of Tamanrasset though she didn't say anything about taking a horse out into the desert. I don't know how to ride a camel and don't expect to start learning now. I don't think I oughta have any trouble.''

Bryan said glumly, "Now we have to keep our fingers crossed that they'll return our weapons when they kick us out.''

XVIII

EL HASSAN

When El Hassan's hoverlorry entered the main gate of Fort Laperrine, it was unescorted. Homer Crawford and his companions had met a *goum* of Guémama's camel corps several kilometers out, but had waved off the desire to accompany their ultimate leader and his viziers.

The vehicle came to a temporary halt immediately inside the entry and the four occupants in the front seat looked out over the parade ground. Less than precision drill was going on. What were obviously older veterans of desert warfare were putting younger tribesmen through European type evolutions.

Bey, who was bandaged at the waist but otherwise didn't look the less for wear, said, "Who in the hell are they?" indicating with a thumb.

They were some twenty white men, dressed in a wide variety of desert uniforms and sitting on the ground before three vehicles and four tents, over against the non-com quarters. On the faces of some were expressions of undisguised contempt of the efforts of the desert men.

"Damned if I know," Homer said. "Let's see what's going on." He drove the hoverlorry toward the administration building.

Isobel came running out anxiously, to be followed at slower pace by Jimmy Peters.

The four emerged from the lorry and grinned at the girl.

She said, looking as though she didn't know which one of them to grab and hug first, "You're all right?" Her eyes went to Bey and they were wide. "You've been wounded. What happened?"

"I should have zigged instead," he told her. "I'm all right."

She grabbed Homer's arms. "Elmer?"

He put his arms around her and bussed her firmly. "He's in the back of the truck. Mostly exhaustion."

Cliff said, "He's eating us out of house and home. Where's the Doc? Hey, how about me? I've known you longer than Homer has."

Jimmy Peters came up with his shy, slow smile. "It's about time you blokes got back. This place has become a bedlam. Elmer's all right, what?"

Isobel said hurriedly, "I'll get Doctor Smythe and a couple of nurses," and started to turn.

But, from the back of the hoverlorry, Elmer said, "The hell with the bloody nurses—unless they're good looking. I can walk."

He had managed to get out of the desert vehicle from the rear. He looked emaciated, the appearance enhanced by the clothes Homer and the others had brought for him. They were several sizes too large and he looked like a black scarecrow.

They hurried toward him, Isobel and Jimmy Peters muttering soothing inanities.

Bey said, "Hey, here I am. I feel worse than he does. All's wrong with him is he's hungry and sleepy."

They ignored him and shortly the whole group moved toward the administration building, Elmer being aided by Jimmy and Isobel.

Elmer grinned at her. "You look even better than I remembered, old girl. You haven't got a friend have you?"

"Yes," she said, "You. Oh, Elmer, you're so thin!"

He grinned again, even as he stumbled along. He still didn't have complete control of his legs, which had been cramped so long. He said mockingly, "Oh, indeed? I saw the way you leeched onto Homer."

They disappeared into the administration building.

Across the square, in the door that led into the non-commissioned officer' billets, Captain Bazaine watched. When they were gone, he turned and sauntered into the non-com mess where Sean Ryan and Bryan O'Casey were slumped in ennui over ageold copies of European magazines, largely French and German.

They looked up at his entry and Sean said, "Something new?"

"I think that El Hassan has appeared on the scene. It's the same hoverlorry we passed on the other side of In Salah. There's five of them now. Two seem wounded."

The other two sat erect.

Sean's eyes went right and then left as he considered it. He said finally, "We can't push them. Tomorrow, we'll check to find if it's really El Hassan. What does he look like?"

Raul sank down into a chair. "I couldn't tell which is which. They don't act as though any single one is especially the leader. Two of them are big brutes. All blacks, of course." There was the faintest of sneers on his Gallic face.

Bryan said, "Let's find Lon and see if he located that spot north of town where we'll make our stand until the plane comes."

Raul nodded and said, "If there's five of them now, most likely they rescued that follower who'd been captured up north. In which case, El Hassan's stock in this part of the world will have zoomed. We had better get about our business before this whole area, including Adrar, with our helio-jet, goes over to him."

Sean said, "Yes, damn it. But I'm thinking that we have to make doubly sure it's really El Hassan, before we can move."

In the morning, Sean Ryan strolled over to the administration building and to Isobel Cunningham's office. He had a minimum of difficulty getting in to see her in spite of the fact that her reception room was packed with both European-suited whites, and native garbed tribesmen.

When her guards had passed him, he found her

at her desk, looking, as usual, harassed with over-work. Her two secretaries didn't even bother to look up at his entry. They were, at long last, beginning to get into routine.

Sean touched the bill of his cap with his swagger stick and told her good morning.

She nodded and said, "What can I do for you, Major?"

"The rumor has it that El Hassan has returned . . . with his viziers."

"That is correct, Major."

"Obviously, he must be up to his eyes in detail that has accumulated."

"Yes. Obviously. Dakar has come over to us, which means all of Senegal. And such major towns as Colum-Béchar, Laghouat, Ouargla and Touggourt. Everywhere, El Hassan's people are triumphant."

Inwardly, Sean Ryan winced. Colum-Béchar was to the north of Adrar and quite considerably. However, he managed to smile and say, "Congratulations, but I am thinking that, if anything, he will more than ever need an adequate bodyguard."

Isobel sighed and looked down at the sheafs of paperwork before her. She said, "He has been informed of your presence and proposition and undoubtedly will interview you within a few days."

"Beggin' your pardon, but . . . no sooner?"

"El Hassan is very busy, Major."

He touched his swagger stick to his cap again, did an about face and left.

That night, the three mercenary officers and Sergeant Lon Charles were able to raise Saul Saidi on their tight-beam radio.

He listened to the news of El Hassan's return and to their fears that their aircraft, their potential escape mechanism, would be overrun at Adrar.

He said impatiently, "Adrar is now in the hands of El Hassan's adherents but we have established a safe cover. All is confusion and the pilots have managed to assure the local El Hassan heads that the helio-jet belongs to their supreme leader and that as soon as they receive word from him they are to fly it down to Tamanrasset."

Sean said, "But the town it was to have taken us to is reported to have been overrun as well."

Saidi said, impatience in his voice, "It is a long distance craft and capable of flying you all the way to Tunis or Tripoli. Get about your task before those cities too fall. The El Hassan movement is flooding north like a tidal wave. His presence is not even needed. The people are acting on their own initiative, in his name."

When the Levantine had finalized his message, Sean flicked the set off and looked at the others. He growled, "I'm wishing the spalpeen himself was down here. It's enough to choke the pooka."

Lon Charles said, "Maybe we ought to call it quits, man. That greaseball don't give a damn if we get out of here or not. Just so we lower the boom on this El Hassan."

Bryan glowered at him. "Two hundred ounces of gold," he said. "And another hundred and fifty for Meg. You know what that comes to in your American dollars? About seventy thousand, I've taken risks before, but never for anything like that much."

Raul Bazaine flicked his cute mustache. "*Oui*," he said.

It was four anxious days later that the mercenary officers were summoned to the presence. A French speaking camelcorps man came to summon them.

They had been ready. In fact, they had been ready since Sean Ryan had seen Isobel Cunningham. They followed the Tuareg tribesman, as militarily spruce as they could make themselves.

As they proceeded over the sandy parade ground in the direction of the administration building, Sean said, out of the side of his mouth, "And where is the sergeant?"

Raul Bazaine said, "Without doubt, in the town, drinking that miserable date wine."

They were led to the conference room where Isobel had originally interviewed them.

Inside the door, to the wall at one side, was Guémama, armed with a Soviet PPPSh submachine gun. As before, it was not only cocked but the safety was off.

At the heavy table were seated five men, all in khaki uniform, and Isobel Cunningham, notepad and ball pens at hand. There was no doubt which of the group was El Hassan. His personality dominated even before he said a word.

They were all seated side by side at the table, Isobel down a bit. One of the five, not El Hassan, motioned them to chairs opposite and they sat themselves. Isobel Cunningham performed introductions.

Homer Crawford looked at them appraisingly

and they could feel the strength of him.

He said finally, "Miss Cunningham has told me of your proposition. I won't waste time. We are not interested. In the first place, it would be a slap in the face of our present loyal bodyguards to hire whites to replace them. And the word would soon spread throughout the Sahara. Secondly, although as bodyguards you might be more experienced in a large city than my tribesmen, I rather doubt that in the erg or on the reg your troopers, inexperienced in desert warfare, would be as efficient as Guémama's Tuaghi. You'd be out of your element." He hesitated, before adding, "But there is a third matter." He turned to Kenny Ballalou. "This is my Vizier of Security."

Kenny took in the three silent soldiers of fortune and said, "The El Hassan movement has differences from other revolutions that have taken place in recent decades in Africa. In a sense, we're an international movement. There are few major cities in the world that do not contain educated blacks who are in sympathy with El Hassan's cause."

The three of them looked at him unblinkingly. Bryan O'Casey wanted to reach for his pipe, but didn't. Sean Ryan wished that he had a drink. Raul Bazaine touched with a forefinger his perfect mustache.

Kenny looked at a paper before him. "Field Marshal Bey-ag-Akhamouk was rather surprised at one aspect of your appearance. You arrived in three vehicles which were in excellent condition. though not quite new. You also arrived well equipped with arms and all other supplies needed to operate in the desert. Your story to Miss Cunningham was that you had pooled your resources to purchase this equipment.''

He looked at them momentarily, then back to his paper. ''It seemed unusual to the Field Marshal for a group of mercenaries to have such resources. Traditionally, they are financially strained and must be equipped by he who hires their services.''

Sean began to say something, but then shook his head and held his peace. There was obviously more to come.

Kenny Ballalou went on. ''So I put out feelers and backtracked, winding up in Algiers, where most of the equipment was purchased. Algiers is currently to North Africa what Lisbon was to Europe during the Second World War, the espionage-counter-espionage center. Needless to say, we have friends and followers there. They were put to work. The name Saul Saidi was come upon. It was he who financed your expedition. His name and reputation are not unknown throughout the Near East and North Africa. It is not a name that inspires confidence. For some time now he has been in the employ of the Arab Union.''

Kenny put his paper down and turned his eyes to Homer Crawford.

Homer looked at Sean Ryan and said, his voice expressionless, ''I suggest that you gather your men, Major, and leave immediately for Algiers. There are a good many journalists and other representatives from various world powers in this vicinity. We do not wish to give them the excuse for reporting sensational news from Tamanrasset, particularly any news involving clashes between my people and Europeans. Your equipment will all be returned to you. My adherents will be notified by radio of your passing through our country, but though they will keep you under observation, you will not be molested, if you do not deviate from the road. That will be all . . . gentlemen.''

The three mercenaries stood, their faces empty and Major Ryan began to say something.

Homer shook his head. ''That will be all.''

Guémama, though he couldn't understand the language, now came even more to the ready, his weapon half raised, his eyes alert.

Just as the three reached the door, Megan McDaid came through it.

She looked at Bryan and said crisply, ''I'm remaining. I've discussed it with Isobel and Doctor Smythe. They need me. They need any doctor who's really sincere about helping North Africa.''

All three of the white mercenaries were staring at her, Bryan obviously completely flabbergasted. ''But . . . but . . .''

She said definitely, ''El Hassan was hesitant, but both Isobel and Dr. Smythe put in their support. I'm staying.''

Her lover put out one hand, as though in supplication, ''But Meg . . . why?''

She looked at him and then the other two, making no effort to keep contempt from her eye. ''Possibly because I have met El Hassan and his colleagues and was impressed by them. Possibly because of a bit Kipling once wrote.''

Bryon O'Casey's stare was blank.

She recited:

> "*Take up the white man's burden,*
> *Send forth the best ye breed.*"

They didn't know what she was talking about.

Meg said bitterly, "Are you three an example of the best my race can breed to send to help North Africa?"

She turned her back to them and marched over to the conference table and stood behind Isobel's chair, her eyes closed.

Homer gestured with his head, and Guémama gestured with the muzzle of his gun.

The three mercenaries went out, Bryan weaving, each of his companions taking him by the arm.

Outside the administration building, Bryan said to Sean desperately, "What can we do?"

But it was Raul Bazaine who answered curtly, "Nothing."

"We can't leave her here," he pled. "With those niggers."

Their twenty men were standing about the tents, waiting.

Bazaine snapped in command, "On the double. Break camp. We're moving out!"

The twenty moved at disciplined speed, no immediate need to have the urgency explained to them.

While Bryan stood there, breathing deeply, completely disorganized, Sean said to one of the hurrying men, "Where in the name of the Holy Mother is the sergeant?"

"He's not around," the man said back, and hurried on.

Sean groaned and turned to Raul Bazaine. "Hustle them up. I'll go to our quarters and get our gear." He left at a trot for the non-com billets.

Bryan grabbed the Frenchman by the arm. "We *can't* leave Meg!"

Bazaine smiled reassuringly and said, "Come along. I've got something to show you." He led the way to the back of one of the desert lorries. "In there," he said, reassuringly again.

Scowling puzzlement, Bryan O'Casey pulled the canvas curtain back and peered into the interior. The Frenchman clipped him neatly on the back of the neck in a practiced karate blow and Bryan crumbled.

Bazaine said in French to two of the men who came up lugging a section of tent, "Put him in the back and tie him securely. Too much sun, without doubt. A touch of *cafard*."

They looked at him questioningly, but obeyed. He went back to supervise the loading of the trucks.

Guémama, accompanied by a double dozen of his men, and looking unhappy at the orders he was fulfilling, came up and turned over the weapons that had been confiscated from the white men when they had first made their appearance. The equipment included the breeches of four machine guns.

Sean returned from the billets, carrying three

duffle bags. "Where in the hell's that damned sergeant?"

"Probably in town, drunk," Bazaine said. "We can't take the chance of sending looking for him. This bunch of wogs would love the opportunity to start shooting."

The men were working with brisk military efficiency.

Sean looked around. "And where's Bryan?"

"All shook up. He's in the back of the second lorry."

"Poor bastard," Sean groaned. Then, "All right, let's get the hell out of here before that son-of-a-bitch El Hassan changes his mind. He's obviously as suspicious as a leprechaun."

The two officers climbed into the jeep, Sean behind the wheel. The men, their camp breaking completed, their guns now in hand, were swarming into the lorries.

The jeep led the way, over the parade ground, out through the large gate. Guémama and his men watched after them, their faces unhappy.

As soon as they were clear of the fort, Sean snapped, "Get on that tight-beam, Raul. Notify those pilots in Adrar to get on down here as quickly as possible. Tell them we'll be approximately two or three kilometers north of Tamanrasset. When we see them, we'll send up a flare."

The Frenchman leaned over the seat to reach into the back. He said, surprise in his voice, "There's four bottles of cognac here. That damned nigger sergeant must have located some more."

Sean rasped, "I'll be having some, wherever it

came from. Hand me a bottle and get on that damned tight-beam."

The Frenchman shrugged and handed over one of the bottles and took up the tight-beam radio phone. He spoke into it in French.

Back in the fort, Homer Crawford looked at Bey and said musingly, "I suppose that was the best thing to do."

His field marshal nodded. "Yes, So far this revolt has been all but bloodless, save for our confrontation with the Arab Union. It wouldn't do for some garbled accounts of a massacre of whites—mercenaries or not—to filter back to the media in Europe and America. Sorry you returned their weapons, though."

Cliff said, "What in the hell did they really want?"

Meg, invitation obviously not necessary, had slumped into one of the chairs vacated by Sean Ryan and his two captains. She said flatly, "They wanted to assassinate the lot of you."

Homer nodded. "That seems to fit in. Though they would have had their work cut out." He looked at Megan McDaid. "You made a noble gesture. I understand that Captain O'Casey was your fiance. Isobel and Doctor Smythe are correct. Advanced medicine today is in the hands of the developed countries. I suggest that, as a white, you be attached to the doctor's staff as a laison officer in our negotiations with medical bodies of other nations."

A knock came at the door.

Homer frowned and made a motion to the returned Guémama who opened up.

It was Lon Charles, bearing a military gray cannister, and, of all things, looking on the sheepish side.

Bey scowled and said, "Why in the devil aren't you with the others? They must be ready to take off."

"Man, they're gone," Lon told him. "This cat's defected. I like the looks of things around here and thought I'd enlist with El Hassan. Miss Isobel, maybe she wasn't trying to, but she kind of talked me into it."

"Welcome to the club," Cliff said. "You must have holes in your head—like the rest of us."

Homer said, "Sit down, Sergeant. I understand that was your rank with the mercenaries. Tell me, how did they expect to get away with it, this far into El Hassan's territory? If they tried to gun us down, they would have had to run all the way to the Mediterranean. And some of the El Hassan followers are on the fanatical side."

Lon put his cannister down on the table gingerly and sat himself. He said, "We had a helio-jet coming in to pick us up."

Kenny said, "That makes sense. But it doesn't make sense to think that they'd get a crack at us at all. Isobel even had their guns taken away from them, as obviously she would."

Lon said gently, "They wasn't gonna use guns."

All eyes were on him and Lon Charles was a simple enough soul to enjoy his moment.

Bey rasped suddenly, "What's in that can?"

And Lon said, "Fission grenades. That can's their supply of miniature fission grenades."

XIX

FINALE

"Don't be silly. There is no such thing."

The former Green Beret ignored that and spoke to El Hassan. "There's eight of them in that there can. We was going to lay them down in a pattern. It was gonna cover all of Fort Laperrine and Tamanrasset. Just about everybody'd go. But you and these people here was the ones that counted. Including Miss Isobel. That's what stuck in my throat. I been a mercenary for a long time, and I done some pretty bad things, but they just didn't care who all got it, just so long as you did."

Homer looked at Meg McDaid. "You knew about this?"

Her hand was at her mouth, her eyes wide, as she stared at the negro sergeant. "No. No," she said unbelievingly. "And Bryan's with them. He wouldn't . . . " She came to a pathetic halt and said to Lon, "Do they know you took the grenades, or whatever you called them?"

Lon Charles shook his head. "They were hid in

a special compartment built into the chassis of one of the lorries. They probably still don't know they're gone."

Isobel said to Homer, as though indignant that he had even asked the question, "Of course Meg didn't know about it. If she had, she wouldn't have come over to us. Or, otherwise, would have immediately reported the existence of these fission things. I assume Lon means some kind of miniature atomic bombs."

Homer Crawford took a seemingly regretful breath and said to Isobel, "All right. You're our Vizier of Information. Immediately get in touch with those reporters and TV men, in fact get in touch with all the delegations from the developed countries. We'll have an immediate conference here and expose the whole scheme, with both Doctor McDaid and Sergeant Charles testifying."

"Then what?" Bey said deliberately.

Homer sent his eyes to his military head. "Then we'll take after them, complete with TV and photographer coverage."

Isobel hurried off on her mission.

Bey turned to Guémama and snapped in Tamaheg, "Assemble the Camel Corps!"

Homer held up a hand. "No."

Bey, Cliff, Kenny and Jimmy Peters joined Lon Charles and Meg in staring at him.

"What do you mean?" Kenny demanded. "You said we were going after them."

Homer nodded. "But not with a thousand men. There's only twenty-three of them. Twenty-three of us will go after them. El Hassan and two of his viziers, you Cliff and you Kenny, and Guémama and nineteen of his picked camelmen. It's time we taught a lesson to such elements as these white mercenaries. Armed with superior weapons and advanced vehicles such as armored cars and even aircraft, they've been murdering, looting, raping and butchering up and down Africa for decades, against blacks often armed with no more than spears and bush knives. The message got out that a handful of whites were worth hundreds of blacks. We'll prove otherwise and we'll do it before TV and newsreel cameras."

"Okay," Bey said. "But it'll be El Hassan and three of his viziers and eighteen of the camelmen."

"You're wounded."

"But not so badly that I'll miss this hoedown," Bey said defiantly.

"Seventeen of the camelmen," Lon Charles said. "When this cat defects, he defects all the way. I never did like that bunch of bums." He looked at Meg. "Only Doctor McDaid."

Homer drew over a chart from a pile of papers on the table. "All right. Let's get the preliminary tactics laid out. Sergeant, do you know where they'll wait for this helio-jet?"

"I ought to. I found the place." He came over and pointed it out. "It's a little less than two miles north of town. Good terrain for a stand."

"How are they armed?"

Bey said, "Half automatic rifles, half submachine guns. Four heavy machine guns."

"No mortars?"

"Not that I know of." Bey looked at Lon Charles.

The veteran mercenary shook his head. "No mortars. We considered them but didn't think they'd look right for bodyguards."

Homer nodded at that and said, "That helio-jet. Is it armed?"

"I never seen it," Lon told him. "The officers did, but I didn't. But it's big enough to carry the whole bunch, so it's probably big enough to have a coupla guns."

"Or bombs, for that matter," Bey said, scowling.

"All right," Homer said. "We'll go in similarly armed. We could, of course, stay back and lob mortar shells into them. Or even bring up a couple of the field pieces we captured from the Arab Union. But that wouldn't look so good to the TV cameras."

"For that matter," Cliff said. "We've got some light tanks and armored cars. Now, that's the way I figure wars should be run. You dash around in a tank while the other guy's got nothing but a rifle."

Homer grunted at him. "We'll take our two flac rifles in to counter their machine guns and anything that might be in the aircraft but otherwise we'll be armed the same way they are. Bey, start getting it organized." He looked back to Lon Charles. "How good a man is this Major Sean Ryan?"

"The best," Lon said flatly. "I never fought under him but I know his rep. He's probably had more experience than any fighting man alive. But we got one thing going for us, far as he's concerned."

"What?" Kenny said.

"I left four bottles of cognac in his jeep. He's a rummy."

At that moment, Sean Ryan took another pull at the bottle he held in his hand and eyed the twenty soldiers of fortune gathered before him and Raul Bazaine. "You know most of the story," he said. "But not all. Our employer expected us to carry out this assignment thinking on our feet, pulling it off any way we could."

A big German snarled. "We boshed it. We didn't make our play. We should have rushed that building they were in."

"Without arms?" Bazaine sneered.

"We could have seized arms from the wogs, taken them unawares!"

Sean Ryan held up a hand. "Saul Saidi knew something like this might develop, that we might not get a chance to cut El Hassan and his people down with standard weapons. So he gave us an ace in the hole. Captain, get those rifle grenades."

Raul headed for the nearest truck.

Sean looked about the area they were in. It was almost like an arena, somewhat rectangular in shape. The perimeter was somewhat elevated, the center a depression in which the helio-jet could sink, out of line of fire while landing and taking off.

He said, "All right. Three men each on the machine guns." He indicated: "We'll spot them there, there, there and there, on each point of this rectangle. Dig in but good and keep improving your entrenchments until they come up on us. If this comes to a fire-fight, they might bring in mortars or even artillery. We've got to last until the aircraft gets here. Portion out all of the ammunition between the four guns. We're not going to be able to send runners back to the trucks after the action's been joined.''

He took another heavy slug from his bottle, ignoring the resentful, thirsty, longing looks on the faces of the men.

He said, ''The other eight men will dig in, with their rifles, two to a side. So far as we know, they don't even know we're here. We'll wait until we spot the helio-jet coming. Then we'll use our *secret weapon*.''

''What secret weapon?'' the Frenchman who had confronted Lon Charles back in Algeria said, obviously voicing the unhappy thoughts of them all.

''We have a way of knocking out Fort Laperrine and Tamanrasset, taking El Hassan and his gang with them. Now, get your equipment, including your canteens, and especially your entrenching tools.''

They began moving off, to follow orders, muttering among themselves about the mysterious secret weapon. Sean Ryan returned to the jeep to get a fresh bottle. His instincts told him that this wasn't going right.

Captain Raul Bazaine came up, his handsome face white. ''That goddamned nigger,'' he said. ''That goddamned nigger.''

The mercenaries stopped and turned back to listen. Sean Ryan stopped twisting the top off his new bottle.

''What's the matter?'' he rasped.

"The cannister of mini-fission grenades—it's gone. He's the only one, besides us, who knew where they were, and what they were."

The major closed his eyes in resigned pain. He finished opening the bottle and tilted it up. When he took it away from his mouth, he said, his voice on the slightly blurred side, "Where in the hell's Captain O'Casey?"

"Tied up in the back of that lorry," Bazaine gestured with his hand. "He wouldn't have stood for using the grenades with his damned female pig there in the fort."

"Turn him loose," Ryan said wearily. "We can use every gun."

His eyes went about the men and he said emptily, "The sergeant took the secret weapon. We've come a cropper. It's our lives now. We've got to hold out until the aircraft gets here."

The aggressive German said, "We can surrender."

Bazaine laughed bitterly. "To Tuaghi?" he said. "You don't know these Forgotten of Allah." He turned and headed for the lorry to release Bryan O'Casey.

El Hassan lowered his binoculars and said to Lon Charles sourly, "You certainly know your terrain, sergeant. It looks as though that rectangle was bulldozed out especially for the purpose."

"Sorry," Lon said. "At the time I dint know I was going to be in on the party going up against it."

Homer Crawford turned to the collected photographers. He said, "This should be the best covered action since the Normandy invasion. I hope the hell you're well equipped with long range tele-photo lenses.''

They were with binoculars as well. One American TV man lowered his and said, ''There've probably been some photographic advances since you took your last snapshot, Professor Craw-ford.''

Kenny Ballalou, who had one of the heavy flac rifles over his shoulder and a Tuareg behind him carrying two cannisters of ammo for the deadly weapon said, ''His Excellency is addressed as El Hassan,'' and was ignored.

Homer said, ''At least I hope you're knowl-edgeable enough not to get in the line of fire. I wouldn't want to see any of you take a hit.''

A French still-photographer, two Nikkon-Leicas around his neck, said laconically, ''Some of our best have taken hits before, Professor. How are you going in?'' He looked back over Guémama's camelmen, all now on foot.

Homer said, ''The Field Marshal will give you a rundown. He's the tactician.''

Bey took over, pointing. ''Our big job is to get the flac rifles close enough. We'll work in toward that northern point of the rectangle. That'll mean only one of their machine gun emplacements will have a clear line of fire. That other one on the west will be able to be brought to bear somewhat, but not as efficiently.''

''Suppose that they bring up one or more of their other guns?'' a Britisher from BBC said, not taking his glasses away from his eyes.

''They won't,'' Bey told him, still staring out at the field where they were shortly to commit themselves. "It'll never occur to them that we haven't brought more men to bear than their own number. Major Ryan is an old hand. He'll even suspect our attack is a feint. He's got to keep the whole perimeter covered. Right now, they're sweating blood; afraid of tanks, afraid of artillery, afraid of mortars. Guémama's men will act as skirmishers, fanned out and advancing a few yards at a time, from cover to cover. They'll try and keep the mercenaries pinned down so we can advance the flac rifles the same way. A flac rifle doesn't have the range of those heavy machine guns but once it gets in, it's more destructive. In spite of my protests, El Hassan will participate with one of the flac rifles. Vizier of Security Ballalou will carry the other. You men had better figure out your locations for your cameras, We're moving in immediately."

One of the newsmen said, "Why particularly the northern machine gun emplacement? That southern one looks weaker."

Bey said, "Because their aircraft will probably come in from the north. We want to get at least one of the flac rifles in place to greet it."

Meg came up to Homer Crawford. She and Doctor Smythe had improvised a field hospital including ten cots and an operating table. She said, an element of pathos in her voice, "My . . . fiance is the tall one."

Homer looked at her and said, "Yes, we know, Meg. And assume that he would have taken measures to attempt to prevent them from using the fission weapons."

She turned and went back to Doctor Smythe who stood there at the cots, scowling at the prospect of more bloodshed. He had three teams of stretcher bearers on hand.

Guémama and his Tuaghi started over the rugged reg at a trot, spreading out as they went. Bey followed, half way between the two groups. He was armed solely with a holstered pistol. In his hands he carried a bull-horn.

One of the photographers, gathering up his equipment, said to Homer, "What's that thing for?"

"He'll be able to keep in touch with the riflemen as they advance."

"Anything he says into that will be heard by the other side too."

Homer smiled grimly, "I doubt if any of them speak Tamaheq."

He slung the heavy flac rifle over a shoulder and motioned with his head to his ammunition carrier. Cliff, armed with a sniper's rifle, complete with telescopic sight, took his place about ten meters to one side. He was Homer's immediate cover, as Lon Charles was Kenny's.

A movie photographer with a hand-held camera started after Homer and his two assistants. He was very nattily dressed in sports clothes, a sun helmet on his head.

Homer stopped and said, "Where the hell do you think you're going?"

"With you."

"It's going to be a little hot where I'm going."

The photographer looked him in the face and said, "It's my job, Doctor Crawford. I'm from CBS." He couldn't have been more than in his mid-twenties.

Homer shrugged it off wearily and started ahead. "I hope you're more experienced than you look," he said. "Keep as near to the ground as you can get—whether you're on your feet, running, or on your belly, crawling."

Isobel came running up. She grabbed him quickly, missed his mouth and ran her kiss along his cheek. "Come back, Homer."

He grinned a tense grin at her. "I'll have to," he told her. "I've got some unfinished business. You."

He turned and headed after Bey's men, bent low. Cliff flanked him to the right, running the same way. The posture of combat men running toward fire.

In the distance ahead, a machine gun stuttered. The Tuaghi skirmishers melted into the landscape, behind rock or desert bush, or into gullies.

"They're just finding the range," Homer called over to Cliff.

Fifteen minutes later, the three of them, including Homer's ammunition carrier, were in a small wadi, peering over its rim. The desert seemed empty before them. They could hear Bey's voice boom through the bull-horn. To the far left, a tribesman suddenly broke from his cover, scurried forward a few meters, and flopped behind a large boulder.

They were inching forward, crawling, wriggling on their bellies, making quick dashes. So far, so far as they knew, no casualties had been sustained.

Homer muttered, "That Major Ryan isn't as sharp as the sergeant seemed to think. He shouldn't move any of his heavy guns, but he could bring more of his riflemen over to this end of his entrenchments. At this stage, they'd probably be more effective than the machine guns.''

Cliff said, ''Maybe Lon was right about that cognac. I wish the hell I had a nip of it right now.''

''Come on,'' Homer said. ''Let's make a run for that next depression. We're getting within range now. And by this time they've spotted the fact that we three, and probably Kenny's crew, are carrying something bigger than a rifle. They'll be laying for us.''

They sprinted for the hole he had indicated and barely made it. Slugs whistled above them.

''They're experienced all right,'' Homer muttered. ''And damned good marksmen with that gun.''

To their right, a Tuareg jumped to his feet and made a dash and flopped down on his belly. The enemy gun had chattered again.

''They're not being careful with their ammo,'' Cliff said. ''They must have plenty. Aren't we near enough to take a pot at them with your flac rifle?''

''No,'' Homer said, gauging the distance.

Cliff wriggled a bit higher and peered through his telescope. He adjusted it carefully, threw a cartridge into the breech, took his time aiming and squeezed off a round.

Homer looked over at him.

Cliff grinned and said, ''They're damn well dug in, but I just thought I'd remind them to keep their heads down.''

They could hear Bey's voice booming over the reg again. Far to the left, they saw Kenny, his Tuareg ammunition carrier and Lon Charles, make a dash. They flopped down in a small cloud of dust.

"Jesus," Cliff said in alarm. "Did one of them take a hit?"

Homer brought up his binoculars. "No. But they're getting closer faster than we are. Let's get to that next clump of rocks."

"Wait a minute," a voice from behind them said, short of breath. It was the photographer, who had been squirming along behind, ignored. His sports clothes were a rumpled and torn mess.

Homer and Cliff stared at him.

He said, bringing up his camera, "How about letting me get a few feet of El Hassan and his Vizier of the Treasury in action?"

Cliff closed his eyes and shook his head. He said. "What a way to make a living. Should I say cheese?"

Aftermath

Homer Crawford, his face in exhaustion, stood on the ridge of the rectangle and stared out over it. His flac rifle had fallen to the ground beside him. Cliff sat on the sand and gravel, panting, and wiping sweat from his face and neck with a dirty handkerchief.

Before them was devastation. The burnt-out helio-jet was still smoldering at one end of the entrenchments, so near one of the machine gun nests that it had almost crashed atop it. In the enclosure, one of the lorries was also burning and the jeep was a shot-up wreck.

About a dozen of the mercenaries were gathered together, those still standing, with their hands behind their necks. The others, wounded, sat or were stretched out on the sand. The remaining of Guémama's camelmen, jubilant, were about them, jeering and sometimes mockingly threatening them with their rifles or arm daggers.

Jeeps and trucks from the fort were beginning to arrive, their occupants in high excitement.

Isobel came hurrying up the hill to them. She stopped before Homer, checked quickly with her eyes to see that he was all right and then Cliff. Relief swept over her face.

"What happened?" she gasped.

"They caved in after Kenny hit the rescuing aircraft with a couple of bursts," Homer said. "But it was all over anyway."

Isobel said, in a gush, "Homer, it's the happy ending. The radio says that Casablanca, Rabat, Algiers and even Tunis have all declared for El Hassan."

Homer shook his head wordlessly.

Kenny trekked up the hill from below and stood for a moment, catching his breath. One of his arms was in an improvised sling. Doctor Smythe and Meg McDaid hadn't arrived as yet.

Homer said to him, "How many casualties?"

Kenny Ballalou took a deep breath and got out, "Three of the Tuaghi dead, seven more took hits, most of them not too bad. And . . . Guémama took his final one when he rushed that machine gun with his grenades. But I guess you saw that in your binoculars."

Homer nodded wanly, "How about the others?"

"The French captain was shot by his own men when he tried to keep them from surrendering. Why he tried, we'll never know. They'd already had it, once that helio-jet was shot down. Major Ryan evidently shot himself. Either somebody else helped, or he managed to get through two and a half of those bottles of brandy Lon left him."

"The other one? Meg's man."

"All shot up, but he ought to live."

Jimmy Peters, alone in a jeep, came driving up the hill alone. He jumped from the vehicle and came hurrying through the sand and gravel.

He said urgently, "Homer. On the radio . . ."

Homer Crawford looked at him. "Yes?"

"The Arab Union has declared war. They're coming south through Libya."

El Hassan closed his eyes in still mounting weariness and looked emptily at the woman he loved. He said, "Isobel, in history there is no happy ending. There is no ending at all. You go from one crisis to the next but there is no ending."

THE END

**ALL TWELVE TITLES AVAILABLE FROM ACE
$1.95 EACH**

_____ 11671 CONAN, #1

_____ 11672 CONAN OF CIMMERIA, #2

_____ 11673 CONAN THE FREEBOOTER, #3

_____ 11674 CONAN THE WANDERER, #4

_____ 11675 CONAN THE ADVENTURER, #5

_____ 11676 CONAN THE BUCCANEER, #6

_____ 11677 CONAN THE WARRIOR, #7

_____ 11678 CONAN THE USURPER, #8

_____ 11679 CONAN THE CONQUEROR, #9

_____ 11680 CONAN THE AVENGER, #10

_____ 11682 CONAN OF AQUILONIA, #11

_____ 11681 CONAN OF THE ISLES, #12

**AVAILABLE WHERE PAPERBACKS ARE
SOLD OR USE THIS COUPON**

— — — — — — — — — — — — — — — —

ace books, (Dept. MM) Box 576, Times Square Station
New York, N.Y. 10036

Please send me titles checked above.

I enclose $ _____ Add 35c handling fee per copy.

Name _____

Address _____

City _____ State _____ Zip _____